Praise for the novels of Heather Gudenkauf

"Fully realized, wholly absorbing and almost painfully suspenseful." —*New York Times*

"Masterful, terrible, and absolutely addicting... Tense, taut, and terrifying." —*Kirkus Reviews*

"Heather Gudenkauf [is] the master of the smart, suspenseful small-town thriller."
—**Gilly Macmillan, bestselling author of *The Long Weekend***

"[A] scintillating psychological thriller."
—*Publishers Weekly*, **starred review**

"Eerily page-turning and wonderfully twisty."
—**Kimberly McCreight,** *New York Times* **bestselling author of *Friends Like These***

"A truly original, immersive experience."
—*O, The Oprah Magazine*

"Gudenkauf is one of my favorite new authors... *Not a Sound* is a riveting thriller."
—**Lisa Scottoline,** *New York Times* **bestselling author of *What Happened to the Bennetts***

"A spell-binding thriller." —*Suspense Magazine*

Also by Heather Gudenkauf

THESE THINGS HIDDEN

HEATHER GUDENKAUF

PARK ROW
BOOKS

PARK
ROW
BOOKS™

Recycling programs
for this product may
not exist in your area.

ISBN-13: 978-0-7783-3386-9

These Things Hidden

First published in 2011. This edition published in 2022.

Park Row Books
22 Adelaide St. West, 41st Floor
Toronto, Ontario M5H 4E3, Canada
ParkRowBooks.com
BookClubbish.com

Printed and bound in Barcelona, Spain by CPI Black Print

For Scott

THESE
THINGS
HIDDEN

Allison

I stand when I see Devin Kineally walking toward me, dressed as usual in her lawyer-gray suit, her high heels clicking against the tiled floor. I take a big breath and pick up my small bag filled with my few possessions.

Devin's here to take me to the court-ordered halfway house back in Linden Falls, where I'll be living for at least the next six months. I have to prove that I can take care of myself, hold down a job, stay out of trouble. After five years, I'm free to leave Cravenville. I look hopefully over Devin's shoulder, searching for my parents even though I know they won't be there. "Hello, Allison," Devin says warmly. "You all set to get out of here?"

"Yes, I'm ready," I answer with more confidence than I feel. I'm going to live in a place I've never been before with people I've never met. I have no money, no job, no friends and my family has disowned me, but I'm ready. I have to be.

Devin reaches for my hand, squeezes it gently and looks me directly in the eyes. "It's going to be okay, you know?" I swallow hard and nod. For the first time, since I was sentenced to ten years in Cravenville, I feel tears burning behind my eyes.

"I'm not saying it will be easy," Devin says, reaching up and wrapping an arm around my shoulders. I tower over her. She is petite, soft-spoken, but tough as nails, one of the many things I love about Devin. She has always said she was going to do her best for me and she has. She made it clear all along that even though my mom and dad pay the bills, I'm her client. She's the only person who seems to be able to put my parents in their place. During our second meeting with Devin (the first being when I was in the hospital), the four of us sat around a table in a small conference room at the county jail. My mother tried to take over. She couldn't accept my arrest, thought it was all some huge mistake, wanted me to go to trial, plead not guilty, fight the charges. Clear the Glenn family name.

"Listen," Devin told my mother in a quiet, cold voice. "The evidence against Allison is overwhelming. If we go to trial, chances are she will be sent to jail for a very long time, maybe even forever."

"It couldn't have happened the way they said it did." My mother's coldness matched Devin's. "We need to make this right. Allison is going to come home, graduate and go to college." Her perfectly made-up face trembled with anger and her hands shook.

My father, who had taken a rare afternoon away from his job as a financial adviser, stood suddenly, knocking over a glass of water. "We hired you to get Allison out of here," he shouted. "Do your job!"

I shrank in my seat and expected Devin to do the same.

But she didn't. She calmly set her hands flat on the table, straightened her back, lifted her chin and spoke. "My job is to examine all the information, look at all the options and help Allison choose the best one."

"There is only one option." My father's thick, long finger shot out, stopping inches from Devin's nose. "Allison needs to come home!"

"Richard," my mother said in that unruffled, irritating way she has.

Devin didn't flinch. "If you don't remove that finger from my face, you might not get it back."

My father slowly lowered his hand, his barrel chest rising and falling rapidly.

"My job," she repeated, looking my father dead in the eye, "is to review the evidence and choose the best defense strategy. The prosecutor is planning to move Allison from juvenile to adult court and charge her with first-degree murder. If we go to trial, she will end up in jail for the rest of her life. Guaranteed."

My father lowered his face into his hands and started crying. My mother looked down into her lap, frowning with embarrassment.

When I stood in front of the judge—a man who looked exactly like my physics teacher—even though Devin prepared me for the hearing, told me what to expect, the only words I heard were *ten years.* To me that sounded like a lifetime. I would miss my senior year of high school, miss the volleyball, basketball, swimming and soccer seasons. I would lose my scholarship to the University of Iowa, would never be a lawyer. I remember looking over my shoulder at my parents, tears pouring down my face. My sister hadn't come to the hearing.

"Mom, please," I whimpered as the bailiff began to lead me away. She stared straight ahead, no emotion on her face. My father's eyes were closed tightly. He was taking big breaths, struggling for composure. They couldn't even look at me. I would be twenty-seven years old before I was free again. At the time, I wondered if they would miss me or miss the girl they wanted me to be. Because my case initially began in juvenile court, my name couldn't be released to the press. The same day it was waived into adult court, there was massive flash flooding just to the south of Linden Falls. Hundreds of homes and businesses lost. Four dead. Due to my father's connections and a busy news day, my name never hit the papers. Needless to say, my parents were ecstatic that the good Glenn name wasn't completely tarnished.

I follow Devin as she leads me to her car, and for the first time in five years I feel the full weight of a sun that isn't blocked by a barbwire-topped fence. It is the end of August, and the air is heavy and hot. I breathe in deeply and realize jail air doesn't really smell any different than free air. "What do you want to do first?" Devin asks me. I think carefully before I answer. I don't know what to feel about leaving Cravenville. I've missed being able to drive—I'd had my license for less than a year when I was arrested. Finally, I'll have some privacy. I'll be able to go to the bathroom, take a shower, eat without dozens of people looking at me. And even though I have to stay at a halfway house, for all purposes I'll be free.

It's funny. I've been at Cravenville five years and you'd think I'd be clawing at the door, desperate to get out. But it's not quite like that. I've made no friends here, I have no happy memories, but I do have something that I have never, ever had in my life: peace, which is a rare, precious thing. How I can be at peace for what I've done? I don't know, but I am.

When I was younger, before I was in prison, my mind never stopped racing. It was constantly *go, go, go.* My grades were perfect. I was a five-sport athlete: volleyball, basketball, track, swimming and soccer. My friends thought I was pretty, I was popular and I never got in any trouble. But under the surface, beneath my skin, it was like my blood was boiling. I couldn't sit still, I could never rest. I'd wake up at six every morning to go for a run or lift weights in the school's weight room, then I'd take a quick shower, eat the granola bar and banana I'd shove into my backpack and go to class all day. After school there'd be practice or a game, then home to eat supper with my parents and Brynn, then three or four hours of homework and studying. Finally, finally, at around midnight, I would try to go to sleep. But nighttime was the worst. I would lie in bed and my mind couldn't slow down. I couldn't stop myself from worrying about what my parents thought of me, what others thought of me, about the next test, the next game, college, my future.

I had this thing I did to help calm myself at night. I'd lie on my back, tuck the covers around me just so and imagine that I was in a small boat. I would conjure a lake so big that I couldn't see the shore and the sky would be an overturned bowl above me, black, moonless and full of winking fairy lights for stars. There would be no wind, but my boat would carry me across the smooth, dark waters. The only sound would be the lazy slap of water against the side of the boat. This calmed me somehow and I could close my eyes and rest. Because I was only sixteen when I got to prison, I was separated from the general population until I turned eighteen. After surviving the first terrible weeks, I suddenly realized that I didn't need my boat anymore and I slept just fine.

Devin is looking up at me expectantly, waiting for me to tell her the first thing I want to do now that I'm free. "I want to see my mom and dad and my sister," I tell her, biting back a sob. "I want to go home."

I feel badly for much of what has happened, especially for what my actions have done to my sister. I've tried to apologize, tried to make things right, but it hasn't been enough. Brynn still won't have anything to do with me.

Brynn was fifteen at the time I was arrested and, well, uncomplicated. Or so I thought. Brynn never got mad, ever. It was like she could store her anger in a little box until it got so full it had nowhere to go and it morphed into sadness.

When we were kids, playing with our dolls, I would grab the one with the creamy, unblemished face and the smooth, untangled hair, leaving Brynn with the doll that had a mustache drawn on with a permanent marker, the one with ratty hair that had been cut with dull scissors. Brynn never seemed to mind. I could have swiped the new doll right out of her hands and the expression on her face wouldn't change. She'd just pick up the sad, broken-looking doll and cradle it in her arms like it was her first choice. I used to be able to get Brynn to do anything for me—take out the garbage, vacuum when it was my turn.

Looking back, there were signs, little chinks in Brynn's easygoing personality that were almost impossible to deduce, but when I watched quietly I saw them. And I chose to ignore them.

With her fingers, she would pluck the fine, dark hair from her arms one by one until the skin was red and raw. She would do it absentmindedly, unaware of how odd she looked. Once her arms were hairless, she started in on her eyebrows. Pulling and plucking. To me she seemed to be trying to shed her own skin. Our mother noticed Brynn's eyebrows getting thinner and thinner and she tried everything to get her to stop. Whenever Brynn's hand moved toward her face, our mother's hand would fly out and slap it away. "Do you want to look strange, Brynn?" she would ask. "Is that what you want? For all the other little girls to laugh at you?"

Brynn stopped pulling out her eyebrows, but she found other ways to punish herself. She gnawed her fingernails to the quick, bit the insides of her cheeks, scratched and picked at sores and scabs until they festered.

We are complete opposites. Yin and yang. Where I am tall and solid, Brynn is smaller and delicate. I'm a big sturdy sunflower, always turning my face to the sun, and Brynn is prairie smoke, wispy and indistinct, head down, nodding with the breeze. Though I never told her, I loved her more than anything or anyone else in the world. I took her for granted, assumed she would always be at my beck and call, assumed that she would always look up to me. But I don't seem to exist to her anymore. I can't blame her, really.

Letter after letter I wrote to Brynn, but she never wrote back to me. That has been the worst thing about prison. Now that I'm free, I can go to Brynn, I can make her see me, make her listen to me. That's all I want. Ten minutes with her, then everything will be all right again.

As we get in the car and drive away from Cravenville, my stomach flips with excitement and fear. I see Devin hesitate. "Maybe we should stop somewhere and get something to eat first, then get you settled in at Gertrude House. After that, you can call your parents," Devin says.

I don't want to go to the halfway house. I'll probably be the one convicted of the most heinous crime there—even a heroin-addicted prostitute arrested for armed robbery and murder would get more compassion than I ever will. It makes much more sense for me to stay with my parents, in the home where I grew up, where I have *some* good memories. Even though a terrible thing happened there, it's where I should be, at least for now.

But I can see the answer on Devin's face. My parents don't want to see me, don't want anything to do with me, don't want me to come home.

Brynn

I get Allison's letters. Sometimes I wish that I could write back to her, go see her, act like a sister to her. But something always stops me. Grandma tells me I should talk to Allison, try to forgive her. But I can't. It's like something broke inside me that night five years ago. There was a time I would have given anything to be a real sister to Allison, to be close with her like we were when we were little. In my eyes, she could do anything. I was so proud of her, not jealous like people thought. I never wanted to be Allison; I just wanted to be myself, which no one, especially my parents, could understand.

Allison was the most amazing person I ever knew. She was smart, athletic, popular and beautiful. Everyone loved her, even though she wasn't all that nice. She was never exactly *mean* to anyone, but she didn't have to try to get people to like her. They just did. She moved through life so easily and all I could do was stand by and watch.

Before Allison became Linden Fall's golden girl, before my parents had set all their hopes on her, before she stopped reaching out for my hand to let me know everything was going to be okay, Allison and I were inseparable. We were practically twins, though we didn't look anything alike. Allison was—is—fourteen months older than I am. Tall with long, sleek, white-blond hair. She has silvery-blue eyes that could look right through you or make you feel as if you're the only one who mattered, depending on her mood. I was small and plain, with wild hair the color of a dried-out oak leaf.

But at one time, it was as if we thought with the same mind. When Allison was five and I was four, we begged our parents to let us share a bedroom, even though our house had five bedrooms and we could have taken our pick. But we wanted to be together. When our mother finally said yes, we pushed our matching twin beds together and had our father hang yards of pale pink netting above our beds so we could draw it around us like a tent. Inside, we would spend hours playing cat's cradle or looking at books together.

Our mother's friends would gush over our relationship. "I don't know how you do it," they would say to her. "How did you manage to get your girls to get along so well?"

Our mother would smile proudly. "It's all about teaching respect," she explained in the snobby way she had. "We expect them to treat each other well and they do. And we feel it's important that we spend a lot of time together as a family."

Allison would just roll her eyes when my mother talked like this and I would hide a smile behind my hand. We did spend a lot of time together as a family—

meaning, we were in the same room—but we never really *talked* to one another.

Allison was twelve when she decided to move out of our room into a bedroom of her own. I was devastated. "Why?" I asked. "Why do you want your own room?"

"I just do," Allison said, brushing past me with an armload of clothes.

"You're mad. What did I do?" I asked as I followed her into her new room, which was right next to the one we shared. The one that would be mine alone.

"Nothing, Brynn. You did nothing. I just want some privacy," Allison said as she arranged her clothing in her new closet. "I'm just next door. It's not like you'll never see me again. Jesus, Brynn, you're not going to *cry,* are you?"

"I'm not crying," I answered, blinking back tears.

"Come on, then, help me move my bed," she said, grabbing me by the arm and leading me back to our room. My room. As we pulled and shoved the mattress through the door and into the hallway, I knew that things would never be the same again. I watched as she arranged her school and athletic medals, trophies and ribbons around her new room and realized we were no longer anything alike. Allison was becoming more and more involved with her friends and extracurricular activities. She had been asked to join a very competitive traveling volleyball team. She spent nearly every free minute exercising, studying or reading. And all I wanted to do was be with Allison.

My parents had no sympathy for me. "Brynn," my mother said. "Grow up. Of course Allison wants her own room. It would be strange if she didn't."

I always knew I was a little different from the other

kids, but I never thought I was *strange* until my mother said this. I started looking at myself in the mirror to see if I could see the oddness that others saw in me. My brown curly hair, if not combed into surrender, would spring wildly around my head. What was left of my eyebrows formed short, thin commas above my brown eyes, giving me a constantly surprised expression. My nose was average—not too large, not too small. I knew that someday I would have very nice teeth, but when I was eleven they were imprisoned in braces, being forced into perfect alignment like straight-backed little soldiers lined up for duty. Except for my eyebrows, I didn't think I looked very strange. I decided it must be what was inside of me that was so weird. I vowed to keep that part hidden. I stayed in the shadows, watching, never offering an opinion or an idea. Not that anyone ever asked. It was easy to fade into the background with Allison around.

That first night, sleeping by myself in our room, I cried. The room felt much too large for one person. It looked naked with my one small bookshelf and dresser, a few stuffed animals strewn around. I cried because the sister I loved didn't seem to want me around anymore. She left me behind without a backward glance.

Until she was sixteen and finally needed me again.

I wasn't even supposed to be at home that night. I was going to the movies with friends—until my mother found out that Nathan Canfield would be there, too. She would have none of that. He had gotten caught drinking or something and he wasn't the kind of friend I should be associating with, she said. So I was forbidden to go out that night.

I often wonder how different my life would have

been—*all* our lives would have been—if I had been sitting in some movie theater that night, eating popcorn with Nathan Canfield, instead of at home.

I don't know what Allison looks like now. I imagine that life in prison isn't helpful to keeping one's good looks. Her once-high cheekbones could be hidden by mounds of fat, her long shiny hair could have turned frizzy and been cut short. I wouldn't know. I haven't seen Allison since the police came to take her away.

I miss my sister, the one who held my hand as I cried all the way into the classroom on my first day of kindergarten, the one who would help me study my spelling words until I knew them inside and out, the one who used to try to teach me to kick a soccer ball. I miss *that* Allison. The other one…not at all. I could go the rest of my life not seeing my sister again and I would be just fine with that. I went through hell after she went to jail. Now I finally feel like I have a home at my grandmother's house. I have my friends, my classes, my grandmother, my animals, and that's enough for me.

I'm afraid to find out how five years in prison have changed Allison. She has always been so beautiful and sure of herself. What if she isn't that same girl who could stare down Jimmy Warren, the neighborhood bully? What if she isn't the same girl who could run eight miles and then do one hundred sit-ups without breathing hard?

Or worse yet, what if she is the same? What if she hasn't changed at all?

Allison

I don't even think my sister knows that I'm being released from prison. Two years into my sentence, after she graduated from high school, she left home and moved two and a half hours north of Linden Falls to New Amery, where our dad grew up. She lives with our grandma. Last I heard, she was attending a community college there, studying something called Companion Animal Science. Brynn's always loved animals. I'm glad she chose something that suits her. If my parents had their way, she'd slide into the vacancy I created and be in law school.

Brynn still won't answer my letters or talk to me on the phone when I call her at Grandma's house. I mean, I get it. I understand why she wants nothing to do with me. If I were in her shoes, I probably would have done the same thing. But I don't think I could have stayed away from her this long. For five whole years, she has ignored me. I know I took her for granted, but I was just a kid. For how smart I was, I knew absolutely nothing. I understand the mistakes I made; I just don't know how to bring my sister back to me, how to make her forgive me.

During the drive to Linden Falls, Devin and I don't talk much but that's okay. Devin wasn't all that much older than I was when my parents hired her to represent me. Fresh out of law school, she came to Linden Falls because her college sweetheart grew up there and they were going to get married and open a law practice together. They never ended up getting married. He left, she stayed. If it wasn't for Devin, I could have been in jail for much, much longer. I owe her a lot.

"You have a start at a whole new life, Allison," Devin tells me as she merges onto the highway that crosses the Druid River and leads into Linden Falls. I nod but don't say anything. I want to be excited, but mostly I feel scared. Driving into the town where I was born and grew up makes me feel dizzy, and I clasp my hands together to keep them from shaking. Waves of memories wash over me as we drive past the church we attended every Sunday, past my elementary school and past the high school that I never graduated from. "You okay?" Devin asks me again.

"I don't know," I tell her honestly, and I lean my head against the cool glass of the window. We continue on in silence, past St. Anne's College where I met Christopher for the first time, past the street where we would turn if we were going to the house I grew up in, past the soccer complex where my team won the city championship three years in a row. "Stop," I say suddenly. "Please, pull in here." Devin steers her car into the soccer complex and parks next to a field where a group of young teenage girls are booting a soccer ball around. I climb from the car and watch on the sidelines for a few minutes. The girls are completely engrossed in the game. Their faces are red from the heat and their ponytails are drenched with sweat.

"Can I play?" I say. It comes out softly, shyly. It doesn't sound like me at all. The girls don't even notice me and continue on with their game. "Can I play?" I say again, this time more forcefully, and a short, solid girl with her brown hair pulled back in a headband stops and looks me up and down skeptically. "Just for a minute," I say.

"Sure," she answers, and trots after the ball.

I step cautiously onto the field. The grass is a deep emerald-green and I bend down to touch it. It is soft and wet from the earlier rainstorm. I begin to run, slowly at first, then I pick up the pace. I've tried to stay in shape while in jail, running laps inside the fenced courtyard, doing push-ups and sit-ups in my cell. But the soccer field is at least one hundred yards long and very quickly I become winded and have to stop. I bend over, hands on my knees, my muscles already aching.

The girls head back my way, their skin tan and healthy in comparison to my own white skin that has seen so little of the sun. Someone passes me the ball and everything comes back, the familiar feel of the ball between my feet, the instinct of knowing which way to move. I dart between the girls, dribbling and passing the ball down the field. For a minute I can forget that I'm a twenty-one-year-old ex-con whose life has already passed her by. A girl chips the ball to me and I weave in and out of the crowd of players and break away. With no cleats, I slip slightly in my cheap tennis shoes but quickly regain my balance. The midfield defender is approaching and I feint left, leaving her behind, and send a square pass to the girl with the headband. She launches the ball over the shoulder of the goalie and into the goal, and the girls erupt in celebration. For a minute I can imagine that I'm a thirteen-year-old, playing a pickup game with my friends, and I'm smiling and laughing, wiping the sweat from my forehead.

Then I look over and see Devin waiting patiently for me on the sidelines, an amused expression on her face. I must look silly, a grown woman dressed in khaki pants and polo shirt, playing soccer with a bunch of kids.

"You're a natural," Devin says as we walk back to her car.

"Yeah, a lot of good that does me now," I answer with embarrassment, glad that my face is already red from my workout.

"You never know," Devin responds. "Come on, we have a little bit of time left before they're expecting us at Gertrude House. Let's get something to eat."

As Devin pulls up in front of the halfway house where I will be staying for the next six months, it begins to rain again. It is a huge Victorian, with peeling white paint, black shutters and a porch lined with white spindles. "I didn't think it would be so big," I say, looking up at the house. It would be scary if it weren't for the beautifully landscaped front yard.

"It has six bedrooms, with two or three women to a room," Devin explains. "You'll really like Olene. She started Gertrude House about fifteen years ago. Her own daughter died after getting out of prison. Olene felt that if Trudy had had a place to go to after she was released from jail, a court-mandated place, she would still be alive today. So she opened Gertrude House as a

way to try and educate women on how to live successfully after prison."

"How did she die?" I ask as we get out of the car and
walk to the front door.

"Trudy refused to move back home with her mother.
Instead, she moved in with the boyfriend who'd got her
hooked on drugs in the first place. She overdosed three
days after she got out of jail. Olene found her."

I don't know what to say to that, so we move out of
the rain and onto the porch in silence. Devin knocks
on the front door and a woman of about sixty, wearing a shapeless denim dress, appears. She is slim, with
closely cropped silver hair, and has tanned, leathery
skin. She looks like a withered orange carrot left too
long in the crisper.

"Devin!" she exclaims, wrapping her in a tight hug,
her silver bracelets clinking against one another on her
thin wrists.

"Hi, Olene," Devin says with a laugh. "It's always
good to see you, too."

"You must be Allison." Olene releases Devin and
takes my hand in hers. It is warm and her grip is strong.
"It's so nice to meet you," she says in a low, gravelly
voice. A smoker's voice. "Welcome to Gertrude House."
Her green eyes never leave my face.

"Nice to meet you," I answer, trying to meet her gaze.

"Well, come on in. I'll give you the grand tour." Olene
steps into the foyer. I look at Devin, a flurry of panic
rising in my chest, and she gives me an encouraging nod.

"I've got to get back to my office, Allison. I'll give
you a call tomorrow, okay?" She sees the worry in my
face and leans in to hug me. Even though I keep my
body rigid and tense, I am grateful for the touch. "Bye,

Olene, and thank you," Devin calls. To me, she says, "You hang in there. Everything is going to be okay. Call me if you need anything."

"I'm fine," I say, more to assure myself than Devin. "I'll be fine." I watch as she walks quickly down the porch steps and back to her car, off to live her life. That could have been me, I think. I could be wearing the gray suit, driving clients around in my expensive car. Instead, I'm carrying a backpack filled with everything I own and moving into a house with people who, in my other life, I would never give the time of day. I turn back to Olene. She is examining me carefully, a look of something I can't quite identify on her face. Pity? Sadness? Remembering her daughter? I don't know.

She clears her throat, a raspy, wet sound, and continues the tour. "We currently have ten residents staying here—eleven, now that you've joined us. You'll be sharing a room with Bea. Nice woman. This used to be a library." Olene nods toward a large, square room to the left. "We use it as our meeting room. We gather here every evening at seven. This is the dining room. Dinner's at six sharp. Breakfast and lunch, you're on your own. The kitchen is just through there—I'll take you in when we're done with the tour. Like most homes, the kitchen is the heart of Gertrude House."

Olene is moving more quickly now and I have to focus on keeping up with her instead of stopping and taking in each of the rooms individually. After my plain prison cell, Gertrude House is an overwhelming assault on the senses. There are brightly painted walls, paintings and photos, furniture and knickknacks everywhere. Music is playing in a far-off corner of the house and I think I hear a baby crying. At my questioning look, Olene explains. "Family members can visit. You hear Kasey's baby crying. Kasey is leaving us next week. Going back home to be with her husband and children."

"Why is she here?" I ask as Olene leads me to what appears to be a family room.

"At Gertrude House, we don't focus on one another's crimes. We try to zero in on what we can do to make everyone's lives better and try to help the other residents reach their goals. That said—" Olene acknowledges with a shake of her head "—word travels quickly around here and you'll get to know one another quite well."

I'm suddenly very tired and wonder if Olene will take me to my room soon. I just want to crawl under the covers and sleep. We pass a short, heavy woman with waist-length black hair and several piercings in her nose and lip. "Allison, this is Tabatha. Tabatha, this is Allison Glenn. She's bunking with Bea."

"I know who you are." Tabatha smirks, tossing her hair over her shoulder as she lifts a large bucket filled with cleaning supplies. I never really thought I could keep the reason I was sent to jail a secret, but I would much rather have been known as the girl who stole cars or snorted coke or even been the one to whack her abusive husband than who I really am.

"Nice to meet you," I say, and Tabatha gives a snort so loud I expect the force will cause one of her nose piercings to fly out and hit me on the chest. I think of my friend Katie and almost laugh. When we were fourteen, she got her navel pierced without her parents' knowledge. By the time she showed it to me, it was oozing and infected. I tried to help her, but she was ticklish and started to squirm every time I went near her stomach. Brynn walked in while I was helping her clean it up and we couldn't stop laughing. Every time Brynn and I saw someone with unusual piercings, we'd get the giggles.

I decide to ignore Tabatha and turn to Olene. "Are we allowed to use the phone here? Can I call my sister?"

Brynn

I hear the ring of the phone and my grandma calls, "I've got it!" A minute later she comes into the kitchen, where I'm making a sandwich. I see the look on my grandma's face and I know this has something to do with Allison. "It's your sister," she says. Already I'm shaking my head back and forth. "Brynn, I think you should talk to her."

My grandma is trying to sound stern, but I know she'll never force me to speak to her. "No," I say, and go back to spreading peanut butter on my bread.

"You're going to have to talk to her sooner or later," she says patiently. "I think you'll feel better."

"I don't want to talk to her," I say firmly. I can't get angry with my grandma. I know she's caught in the middle. She wants what's best for the both of us.

"Brynn, if you don't talk to her on the phone, don't answer her letters, Allison is going to find another way."

All of a sudden, it's clear. I see it in her old, kind

blue eyes. *Allison is getting out of jail.* For all I know, she might be out already.

My hands begin to shake and a glob of peanut butter drops from my knife to the floor. I'm afraid she is going to show up here unexpectedly. I'll be in the backyard, training my German shepherd–chow mix, Milo, to walk past a treat without eating it and I'll turn around and there she'll be, looking at me. Waiting for the words that I know won't come. What could I possibly have to say to her? What more could she say to me that she hasn't already said in her letters? How many ways can someone say they're sorry?

I bend down to wipe up the peanut butter with a paper towel, but Milo gets to it before I do. "I can't talk to her."

My grandmother presses her lips together and shakes her head in defeat. "Okay, I'll go tell her. But, Brynn, you're going to have to face her sometime." I don't answer, but follow her into the living room and watch as she picks up the phone.

"Allison?" My grandma's voice trembles with emotion. "Brynn can't come to the phone." There's a pause as she listens. "She's doing great...just great..."

I can't stand it anymore; I hurry back to the kitchen, grab my sandwich and leave out the back door to my car. Animals are so much easier to deal with than people. I learned that a long time ago. My parents never let me have a pet—too furry, too messy, too time-consuming. Every time I brought home strays, I would hope, pray, that they would let me keep them. Just once. I tried to spiff them up—I smoothed their tangled fur with an old comb, spritzed their fur with body spray, scrubbed their teeth with an old toothbrush. Ancient, arthritic mutts...

one-eyed cats with notched ears. I would parade them in front of my parents. See how good he is? See how soft her fur is? See how tame, how sweet, how smart? See how lonely I am? Do you see? But no. No pets allowed. My dad would take me to drop the animal off at the shelter and every time I would cry and hold so tight to the animal that it would claw and scramble to get away from me.

My grandmother lets me have animals in her house, though she has drawn the line at five. We have two cats, a mynah bird, a guinea pig and Milo. Grandma said enough is enough, that she doesn't want to turn into one of those dotty old cat ladies that animal control has to come out and visit.

I'm training Milo to be a therapy dog. He's learning how to sit-stay or down-stay for thirty seconds and to come when he's being called. Grandma is helping me to teach him how to sit quietly by, when two people are arguing. We make up silly fights about whose turn it is to take out the garbage or make dinner. I think Milo knows we're not really serious; he just yawns and lies down and looks back and forth at us until we both start laughing. When we're finished with the training I hope to be able to take Milo into nursing homes and hospitals. It's a proven fact that animals are able to help ease pain and anxiety in the sick and elderly. One day I want to open my own business, training animals for pet therapy. For once in my life I've got a plan. A good one, for that matter. I don't want anyone or anything to distract me from my goal. Not my parents and certainly not my sister.

If only Allison had done what she always did—made the right choice—things could have been so different.

She wouldn't have had to go away. Our parents would have been happy and I could have just faded into the background where I belong. But she didn't. She screwed up royally, and she left me in that house alone with our parents.

I wasn't the perfect girl like she was, and I never will be. Oh, but they tried. All through high school, it was pressure, pressure, pressure. Staying in that house, I couldn't get my thoughts straight, couldn't make a decision, couldn't breathe. I tried to go to St. Anne's College, tried to keep up with my classes, tried to make friends, but whenever I walked into the classroom a wave of panic would come over me. It always started in my ears, a strange buzzing sound that would trickle down my throat and out toward my fingertips, leaving them numb. My chest would tighten; I couldn't catch my breath. The instructors and students would gawk at me and I would stare back until they seemed to melt before my eyes. Their ears would slide down their cheeks, their lips would dribble down their chins, until they were nothing but fleshy puddles.

It wasn't until I swallowed a bottle of sleeping pills that I found in my mother's medicine cabinet that my parents finally decided to leave me alone. They gladly sent me over the river and through the woods to Grandmother's house with a suitcase and a prescription for an antidepressant.

Things feel right here. Grandma got me to go to a doctor; I took my medicine and it got me back on track. I'm doing fine. But I won't talk to Allison. I *can't* talk to her. It's better this way. Better for her and better for me.

For once in her life, Allison got what she deserved.

Allison

I set the receiver back into its cradle, all the while knowing that Olene is watching me carefully with her quick, birdlike eyes. Once I get settled and find a job, one of the first things I'm going to buy is a cell phone so I can have a little privacy when I talk. I'm sure my parents would buy me a phone, but I don't want my first interaction with them to be about money. Besides, I want to show them that I'm going to be okay, that I can take care of myself. I wonder if they are thinking about me right now. Secretly, I had hoped they would have been parked in front of Gertrude House to welcome me when I arrived.

Olene must be psychic, because she says, "Many of the residents have cell phones, but we have guidelines here that phones need to be turned off while doing chores or when we are having group sessions. We want to respect others' need for quiet."

Olene picks up where she left off with the tour. She leads me through the kitchen, where we will take turns making dinner, and to an octagonal room with a ceiling that extends above the second floor. This is where the residents watch television. A gray-haired woman wearing a waitress uniform is dozing on a sofa and a young, petite, dark-skinned woman is holding a toddler on her lap and singing softly to him in Spanish. The television is tuned to a soap opera, the volume muted.

"This is Flora and her son, Manalo," Olene says in a whisper. "And that's Martha." Olene waves a hand toward the slumbering woman. Flora's eyes narrow into suspicious slits and she gathers Manalo more closely to her. The little boy waves a chubby hand at us and grins.

"Nice to meet you," I say.

Flora speaks rapidly to Olene in Spanish, her tone tight and hostile, and Olene responds back in Spanish, as well. I have the feeling that Olene is going to have to do a lot of talking to calm the other residents of Gertrude House when it comes to me.

"Let's go on upstairs and I'll show you your room," Olene says, taking me by the elbow and steering me from the television room to the spiral staircase that leads to the bedrooms. I can feel Flora's eyes on my back as I follow Olene up the steps. I've been here for all of twenty minutes and everyone already seems to know who I am and what I've done. I know I shouldn't let it bother me so much, I had to deal with the same things in jail, but this seems different somehow.

"The expectation is that everyone takes an active role in the upkeep of the house," Olene says, and I can see this is true. There isn't a speck of dust anywhere and the floors gleam. Olene gently knocks on a closed door before opening it to reveal a small room with bunk beds and two small dressers. The beds are made up with blue and white floral comforters and thick, soft pillows. Another rush of exhaustion overtakes me and I want to go lie down. The walls are painted sky-blue and there are crisp, white curtains covering the windows. It's a very peaceful room.

"Your roommate, Bea, is at work right now. She'll be home in a few hours. Why don't you unpack your things, get settled and I'll come back in a little while and we can finish the orientation." I look at the bunk beds and hesitate, wondering which one is mine. "You get the bottom bed," Olene says. "Bea likes to sleep on the top bunk—she says that the bottom bed makes her feel claustrophobic."

Olene pats me on the arm as she moves to leave the room. "Olene," I say. She turns back to me, and I'm stricken by how kind her worn face is. "Thank you."

"You're welcome." She smiles. "Get a little rest and holler if you need anything."

My few belongings fit into one drawer of my bureau with room to spare. In a way, Gertrude House reminds me of the summer camp I attended when I was eleven. I share a room with bunk beds and, from what Olene has said, we follow a very specific schedule that is posted in the main gathering area. From the moment we wake up at five-thirty to lights out at ten-thirty, our day is filled with chores, and group sessions on everything from managing finances to anger management to mastering interview skills.

I sit on the lower bunk and bounce a bit. The springs are firm but giving. This feels like a real bed, not like Cravenville's hard, institutional slab, with rough, scratchy sheets that smelled of bleach. I lift a fluffy pillow and bury my nose in it. It smells of lavender and I feel tears prick at my eyes. Maybe it won't be so bad here. It couldn't be any worse than jail. Maybe the other girls will learn to like me. Maybe my parents will forget about what the neighbors think and welcome me as their daughter again. And maybe, just maybe, Brynn will forgive me.

I inhale deeply one more time and lower the pillow from my face and that's when I see it. Its blank eyes stare up at me and its smudged plastic face is frozen in a half smile. I pick up the baby doll. It's old and battered and looks like it came out of a Dumpster. Across the doll's bare chest is one word, slashed in black permanent marker, a word that I now know will follow me everywhere, no matter where I go. *Killer.*

Claire

Bookends is dim and quiet. A sudden Sunday afternoon rainstorm has driven away the stifling August heat and all of the customers. As Claire Kelby unpacks a box of books, Joshua pokes his head up from behind the counter, his yellow hair standing on end. She tamps down the desire to lick her fingers and smooth the flyaway strands. His dark brown eyes look expectantly up at her.

"Can I help you, young man?" Claire asks her son in mock seriousness.

"I'm bored," Joshua answers dismally, and kicks his sneakered foot against the front of the counter.

"You've read every single book back there?" Claire asks him, and Joshua glances over his shoulder toward the shelves and shelves of books. Looking back at his mother, he nods and tries to bite back a smile.

"Uh-huh," Claire says skeptically. "Where's Truman?"

"Sleeping," Joshua grouches, drawing his eyebrows

together. "Again," he adds about their six-year-old red-brindled English bulldog.

"I don't blame him. It's a rainy day, good napping weather," Claire responds. "Do you want to help me? I've got lots of boxes to open and books to shelve before we close. Or maybe you want to take a nap, too?"

"I'm not tired," Joshua says stubbornly, though his eyes are heavy. "When's Dad going to get here?"

"He'll be here soon," Claire assures her son, and leans over the counter to place a kiss on his blond head. She looks around the bookstore that has been both a refuge and a yoke. Years ago, the store and its responsibilities had kept her sane. The long hours had kept her mind busy, kept her focused, distracting her from the knowledge that her body, which had served her so well over the years, had ultimately betrayed her. Sometimes this realization struck her suddenly, squeezing so tightly she would have to stop whatever she was doing—helping a customer, unpacking books, answering the phone—and deliberately pry away the fingers of anxiety that clutched at her heart until she could breathe again.

Then, inexplicably, Joshua came to them, as miracles often do, on an ordinary day, well after the acceptance that they would never have a child of their own, biological or otherwise, had settled in. More and more, Bookends seems to snatch away all the time she wants, needs, to be with her son. He'll be heading off to kindergarten soon and she guards what's left of her time with him fiercely, even though she knows he'd much rather be playing outside than stay with her in the bookstore.

Claire handled all the business aspects of opening the bookstore nearly twelve years ago. Finding the perfect location on oak-lined Sullivan Street, in the newly revitalized downtown section of Linden Falls, securing the small-business loans, ordering the books and hiring the part-time help. Jonathan, for his part, created the most beautiful bookstore Claire could have ever possibly imagined. The building had originally been a dressmaker's shop, owned by an independent woman who had moved to Linden Falls with her aging father in the mid-1800s. It was lovely, with an intricate tin ceiling and walnut woodwork that Jonathan had uncovered beneath years of old paint, varnish and grime. Rifling through the second floor and the attic, Claire and Jonathan found musty bolts of cloth and bushel-size jars of buttons made of mussel shells, bone and pewter hidden beneath a table. Claire loved to imagine the dresses designed over that table—a christening gown edged with lace, tiny seed pearls sewn to the silk bodice of a wedding dress, a black mourning dress made of cashmere.

Joshua tries to heave himself up on top of the counter, his shoes scrabbling against the front panel. "I'm bored," he repeats as he slides to the floor. "When will he be here?" he asks again.

Claire steps from behind the counter, reaches down, lifts Joshua into her arms and sets him next to the cash register. "He will be here in about—" she looks at her watch "—half an hour to pick you up. What do you want to do?"

"Tell me about my Gotcha Day," he orders. Claire gives him a long, expectant look. "Please," he adds.

"Okay," Claire agrees, swinging him into her arms. As is often the case lately, she is struck at how big he's getting. She can hardly believe that he's five years old. She presses her nose into his neck and breathes in the comforting scent of the Yardley of London soap he bathed with just that morning. Joshua, in a sudden need for privacy, has started ordering her out of the bathroom when he gets ready for his bath.

"Only Truman and Dad can be in here when I take a bath, because we're all boys," he explained.

So Claire, after running the bathwater for him, sits on the floor in the hallway, her back resting against the closed bathroom door, and waits, calling through the door every few minutes, "You okay in there?"

Now she carries Joshua to the plush, comfortable sofa that sits in a corner of the bookstore and they settle in for his favorite story. The story of how Joshua became theirs.

"Before we can talk about Gotcha Day," Claire says, "we have to talk about the first day we met you." Joshua snuggles more deeply against her and, as she has every day for the past five years, Claire marvels at his sweetness. "Five years ago, last July, Dad and I were sitting at the kitchen table trying to figure out what we were going to have for dinner when the phone rang."

"It was Dana," Joshua murmurs as he fingers the milky-colored pearl hanging from her ear.

"It was Dana," Claire agrees. "And she said that there was a beautiful little boy waiting for us at the hospital."

"That was me. That was me waiting at the hospital," Joshua tells Truman, who decides to hobble over to the pair. "And that birth lady couldn't take care of me so she left me at the fire station, and the fireman found me just lying there in a basket."

"Hey, who's telling this story?" Claire asks, and gently pokes him in the ribs.

"You are." Joshua wrinkles his upturned nose and tries to look sorry.

"That's okay, we can tell it together," Claire assures him.

"And all the firemen didn't know what to do!" Joshua exclaims. "They just stood there and looked at me and said, *'It's a baby!'*" Joshua holds his hands out, palms up, a look of animated consternation dancing across his face.

"You were a surprise, that's for sure." Claire nods in agreement. "The firemen called the police, the police called Dana, Dana took you to the hospital, and Dana called us."

"And when you held me in your arms for the first time you cried and cried." Joshua giggles.

"I did," Claire concurs. "I cried like a baby. You were the most beautiful little boy and—" At the same time they hear the bookstore door open and Jonathan enters, his work jeans and T-shirt streaked and dusty from his current renovation.

"Hey, guys," he calls, shaking the rain from his black curls. "What're you doing?"

"Gotcha Day," Claire says, by way of explanation.

"Ahh," Jonathan says, a big grin spreading across his face. "The best day ever."

"Mom cried," Joshua says, hiding his mouth from Claire, as if not seeing his lips meant she couldn't hear him.

"I know," Jonathan whispers back. "I was there."

"Hey, Dad cried, too," Claire protests, looking at her boys with affection. "We took you home and after thirty days the judge said, 'Joshua is now officially a Kelby.'"

"Who was I before?" Joshua asks a bit worriedly.

"You were a badger with three tails," Jonathan teases.

"You were a wish that we made every morning when we woke up and a prayer we said before we went to bed each night," Claire tells him, swallowing back tears the way she always did when she thought about how things could have been very different, if Dana, the social worker, had dialed a phone number that wasn't theirs.

"You were a Kelby the first day we saw you," Jonathan says, sitting down on the couch so that Joshua was squeezed between his parents.

"A Kelby sandwich," Joshua declares, taking up his favorite game. "I'm the peanut butter. You're the bread."

"You're the liverwurst," Jonathan corrects him. "The olive loaf, the fried egg with limburger cheese."

"No." Joshua laughs. "You're a turkey and dressing sandwich."

"Hey, I like turkey and dressing sandwiches," Jonathan protests.

"Blech." Joshua sticks out his tongue.

"Blech," Claire agrees while Jonathan looks at her over Joshua's head and their eyes lock. They both know what it's taken to finally get to this point. The infertility, the wrenching loss of their first foster child. The heartache and the disappointment they have endured. *The past is firmly in the past, where it belongs,* their gazes say. *We have our little boy and that's all that matters.*

Charm

Charm Tullia pushes open the door to Bookends, her textbook list in one hand, her cell phone in the other, in case Gus calls. She wants her stepfather to be able to reach her at anytime. She knows the time will come when she will receive the call that informs her that Gus has fallen, has a fever or worse. The rain has stopped, but she carefully wipes her wet feet on the rug inside the entrance of the bookstore.

Claire greets her warmly, as she has ever since the first time Charm came into Bookends several years ago. Claire always asks how her nursing classes are going and how her stepfather is doing.

"He's not doing very well," Charm tells her. "The home care nurse says we might want to think about getting hospice involved soon."

"I'm so sorry," Claire says with genuine sadness in her voice. Charm lowers her head and begins rummaging through her purse, hiding her eyes that filled with tears at the thought of Gus dying. This is what makes it so hard and so easy for Charm to keep returning to Bookends. Claire Kelby is just so *nice.*

"Is Joshua here today?" Charm asks, looking around for the little boy.

"You just missed him," Claire says apologetically. "Jonathan picked him up and took him home."

"Well, tell him hi for me," Charm says, trying to mask her disappointment, and slides her textbook list across the countertop toward Claire. "I was able to buy most of my books used through the campus store, except for this one, and it is so expensive," Charm explains, pointing to a title written on the paper. "Do you have any ideas?"

"I'll do some checking around," Claire promises her. "When do you graduate? You must be getting close."

"In May. I can't wait," Charm says with a smile.

"I'll give you a call tomorrow to let you know what I can find out about your book. You take care of yourself, okay, Charm? And remember, you call me if you need anything at all."

"Thank you," Charm says again, even though she knows she won't call her for anything beyond finding the book. As much as Charm admires Claire and her family, as much as she enjoys chatting with her, Charm already knows too much about Claire's life. If Claire were ever to find out just how much, Charm thinks, she would never see her in the same way again.

After stopping at the grocery store to pick up a few things, Charm drives over the Druid River and into the countryside between Linden Falls and the small town of Cora to check on Gus. Though she doesn't want to admit it, Gus is getting weaker by the day. As she pulls into the driveway, she examines the small three-bedroom farmhouse she's lived in since she was ten. Gus has always kept the house in perfect condition and she has to look closely to see any signs of wear and tear, but they are there. The paint on the black shutters is beginning to fade and crack and the white siding needs a good power wash. The lawn is neatly trimmed but not mowed the way Gus would do it, if he were healthy. For a while Charm tried to mow the lawn in the diagonal pattern Gus preferred, but though he never said anything, she could tell the imperfect lines frustrated him. Finally, Charm called a fourteen-year-old neighbor who lives a half-mile down the road to take over lawn duty. But Gus won't let anyone touch his flower beds. They are still his domain, although with his illness they have suffered for it.

Charm steps from her car, grabs the bags of groceries and walks around to the side entrance. She sees Gus on his knees, his back to her, head bent, and for a moment she thinks he has collapsed. Dropping the grocery bags, she runs toward him. Gus suddenly turns his head as he hears her approach and slowly gets to his feet, shakily lifting his small, portable oxygen tank. "Charm, where were you?" he croaks. "I was worried." His plaid shirt envelops his thin frame and his khaki pants hang loosely on his hips. He painfully pulls off his gardening gloves and drops them to the ground. He has slicked his thick black hair from his face, and beyond the grayness of his skin and his sunken eyes, Charm can see a glimmer of the handsome man he once was. The man her mother decided to keep around longer than any of her many other boyfriends and actually marry. When Charm was little, she proudly watched the two of them together, her beautiful blonde mother and handsome, funny Gus, the firefighter.

Reanne Tullia was with Gus for four years—a world record for her, Charm thinks. Eventually, her mother got bored playing her part in their happy family, left Gus and then divorced him. Charm was ten when they moved in and fourteen when her mother was ready to move on. Reanne traveled the short distance across the Druid River and went back to live in Linden Falls. Charm went with her for a few weeks, but it was unbearable. In the middle of the night, Charm called Gus and begged him to let her return and he said yes, with no questions. Charm and her brother asked to stay with him and Gus was kind enough to let them.

Now Gus is very sick. Lung cancer, a by-product of his job as a firefighter and years of smoking. Gus took early retirement from the fire department about five years ago, after he got sick. Since his diagnosis, he routinely asks her why she would want to stay with a sick old man. "Because this is my home," she always tells him. "You are my home."

"Hey, Gus." Charm tries to sound casual, not wanting him to know she is worried. "I just went to the bookstore and got some groceries."

Gus holds her gaze for a long moment, then asks, "How's that little boy?"

"He wasn't there, but Claire says he's doing fine. He starts kindergarten next week. Can you believe it?"

Gus shakes his head. "No, I can't. I'm glad he's doing well."

"I brought you *kolache*," Charm says before he can say anything else about Joshua. She hands him the bag of the Czech pastry that he loves so much. "I promise, someday I'll learn how to make them myself," she tells him as he reaches for the bag.

"Nah, this is perfect," he says, though she knows they aren't. Gus used to make delicious authentic *kolache* from his grandmother's recipe. Now, more often than not, he is too weak to stay on his feet for more than ten minutes.

"Your mother called," Gus's voice rasps, making him sound older than his fifty years. It's difficult for Charm to tell whether it's the cancer or whether he is upset about her mother calling.

Charm and her mother rarely speak. Every once in a while, they try to rebuild their relationship but their encounters usually end in bitter tears and angry words.

"What did *she* want?" Charm asks glumly.

They walk into the kitchen through the side door and Charm pulls a chair away from the table, its legs scraping noisily against the faded blue-flowered linoleum. Gus lowers himself slowly into the seat. Gus has been wobbly on his feet and she is constantly worried about him falling. Yesterday he tripped on the ridge where the carpet meets the linoleum and took a tumble. Gus bloodied his knees and bruised his elbows in that fall. Charm had to sit him down like he was a three-year-old and clean his scraped knees, covering them with Band-Aids. She knew then that it was time to have a conversation with Gus about getting someone to stay with him during the day while she was at class or at the hospital.

"She didn't come over, did she?" Charm asks, and her eyes pop open in panic. If her mother has stopped by, she'd have taken one look at Gus and seen how sick he is and, like a vulture, start circling. Gus doesn't have much, but he owns his house and car outright. Reanne always thought she should have gotten the house in the divorce and Charm wouldn't put it past her to try and get her hands on it now.

Gus shakes his head, which looks too big for his body now. He has lost so much weight the past few months. "No, she just wanted to talk." Charm watches as Gus pulls a *kolache* from the bag and takes a small bite. He does this for her benefit; he doesn't want her to call the doctor and tell her he isn't eating. He never eats more than a few nibbles of anything anymore.

"She wanted money, didn't she?" Charm asks, already knowing the answer. So typical of her mother. No phone calls, no birthday cards, nothing. And then out of the blue, *poof!* A phone call. Not to Charm, of course. Reanne knows better than that.

"No, no," Gus says defensively. "She just called to see how we were doing."

"She mentioned me?" Charm asks skeptically.

"Yeah, she did." With a trembling hand, Gus brings the *kolache* slowly back to his lips. His face is pale. He had tried to shave, but missed several stubbly patches on his neck. "She asked how you were, how school was going for you, what was new."

"What did you tell her?" Charm asks almost fearfully. She doesn't like her mother knowing about the details of her life. The less she knew, the less she could use against her.

"I didn't tell her much," Gus says miserably, and Charm knows he still loves her mother. She is very lovable. Until she's not, Charm thinks, and then you just want to slap her away like she's a pesky mosquito. But Gus still hasn't gotten over her, even after all these years. "I told her that you're doing well, that you graduate from nursing school next spring. That you're a nice girl." Then Gus's face darkens, a storm cloud passes over his face. "Of course, she asked about your brother. I told her that I hadn't heard from him in years and haven't missed the son of a bitch one bit."

"I bet she loved that!" Charm smiles. Her brother is her mother's favorite. His father was the only man her mother ever truly loved and, in turn, he wanted nothing to do with her. Smart man, Charm thinks.

Gus sets the *kolache* on the table and looks at Charm, pain ingrained in his tired blue eyes. "She said that he called and left a strange message on her machine."

"Oh," Charm says casually, as if she doesn't care. "What kind of message?"

"She didn't say. Said she wanted to talk to you. She wants you to call her back," Gus says coarsely.

"You look tired," Charm tells him. "Why don't you go and lie down for a while." Gus doesn't argue, which says everything. Slowly, he pushes his chair away from the kitchen table and gets unsteadily to his feet. "Remember, Jane is going to stop over later tonight," she reminds him.

Almost every evening, Jane, a nurse from the Visiting Nurse Association, stops by to check on Gus. She'd arranged for Jane to come when Gus began coughing up blood and was starting to get more and more confused. Jane takes his blood pressure, listens to his lungs and makes sure he is being properly cared for. Gus always takes great pride in the way he looks and tries to straighten up a little more before Jane arrives. He makes sure his shirt is tucked in and his hair is combed. Cancer has given his skin a yellowish tinge and transformed his once-strong arms into twigs, but Gus is still a natural flirt.

"Ah, Jane." Gus smiles. "My favorite nurse."

"Hey," Charm says in mock indignation. "I thought *I* was your favorite nurse."

"You're my favorite soon-to-be nurse," Gus explains. "Jane is my favorite licensed nurse."

"Oh, well. That's okay, then," Charm says, walking right behind Gus in case he falls, like a mother shadowing her wobbly toddler. "Just as long as we're clear on the topic." She makes sure Gus is situated safely in his bed, places a fresh glass of water on the side table and double-checks that his oxygen tank is working.

"Charm," Gus says as he pulls the quilt up beneath his chin. "I talked to someone else today, too." She can tell by the seriousness of his voice that the conversation was important. "I called the people at hospice…"

"Gus," she interrupts. "Don't…" Tears prickle behind her eyes. She's not ready to have this conversation yet.

"I called hospice," he says firmly. "When it's time, I want to be here, in our home. Not at the hospital. Do you understand?"

"It's too early—" Charm begins, but Gus stops her.

"Charm, kiddo. If you're going to be a nurse, you're going to have to learn how to listen to the patient."

"But you're not my patient." She's trying not to cry and begins to lower the shades to block out the early-afternoon sun.

"When the time comes, you call hospice. I left the number by the phone."

"Okay," she agrees, more to please Gus than anything. She's not ready for Gus to die. He's the only real family that she has, that she has ever had. She needs him. Exhaustion and pain pull at his face. "Can I get you anything before I have to go to school?" Charm asks, at once hating to leave and feeling relief.

"No, I just want to close my eyes for a while. I'm okay. You go on," he tells her.

She stands there in the darkened room, next to Gus's bed for a moment, watching the rise and fall of his chest, listening to the mechanical breaths of the oxygen machine.

What am I going to do without him? Where am I going to go?

Claire

Claire and Jonathan don't tell Joshua everything about his Gotcha Day. They don't tell him how Claire watched as Jonathan placed his elbows on the table and rested his head on his hands. How much he hesitated when Dana called about the abandoned infant. How Claire had to tell herself, *Be patient, wait him out.* How finally, when he lifted his head, there were faint red circles dotting his forehead where his fingers had pressed into the skin. How Claire had wanted to go to him, to kiss each red spot gently, tenderly. "Just until they find another foster home for him, Claire," Jonathan said with no conviction. "Do you understand? Nothing long-term. No way. I can't do it." He shook his head as if still bewildered. "I can't do Ella all over again. I can't get attached to a child once more, just to have him taken away in the end. That's the whole point of foster care, to get the kids back to their parents."

"Me, either," Claire had whispered. "I can't do Ella over again, either." But somehow Claire knew this

mother wouldn't be coming back, wouldn't take this
little boy away from them. God couldn't be so cruel,
not after all that has happened.

A year earlier, a dead infant was found in a frozen
cornfield on the other side of the state. After that, the
Iowa state legislature had quickly passed a Safe Haven
law, allowing mothers to drop off their newborns under
two weeks old at hospitals, police or fire stations without fear of prosecution for abandonment. The doctors
figured that this baby was about a month old, and for
one brief moment, Claire worried that the police would
find the mother who had abandoned him. She quickly
brushed away her fears. This little boy, the little boy
they would take home, would be the first baby left at a
Safe Haven site. He would be theirs.

When Dana set Joshua in Claire's arms, it was as if
she was healed. As if all the miscarriages, the surgery,
had never happened. The pain, the loss, became a faint
memory. This was what they had waited for all these
years. This beautiful, perfect little boy.

On the way home from the hospital they stopped
to pick up a few necessities. Diapers, bottles, formula.
As an afterthought, Claire grabbed a book filled with
baby names. Finally, finally, she would be able to name
a child. The book listed each name alphabetically, followed by the name's origin and meaning. This child's
name, Claire decided, needed to have a special meaning.
Since she didn't give him the gift of birth, she would
give him his name and it would mean something.

Claire liked the name Cade, but it meant *round or
lumpy.* Jonathan liked that the name Saul meant *prayed
for.* That was a possibility; they had been praying for
this for years. The name Holmes meant *safe haven,*

but Jonathan thought it sounded kind of stuffy and had images of kids calling him Sherlock. Claire flipped through a few more pages and her eyes fell on the name Joshua. *Saved by God.* "Joshua," she said out loud, weighing the word on her tongue, feeling it on her lips. Claire smiled at Jonathan and turned in her seat to look back at the baby who would become her son. "Joshua," she repeated, a little louder and at that moment, in sleep, he breathed a gentle, whispery sigh. Content. Safe. Saved.

Charm

Ever since she started her nursing practicum hours at St. Isadore's, not a day goes by that Charm doesn't think about the baby. Even though she knows he is well cared for and loved, she can't walk by the yellow Safe Haven signs in the hospital without remembering both the sadness and the relief she felt after giving him up, although he wasn't just hers to give away. In all honesty, she feels mostly relief. If she hadn't taken him to the fire station, she probably would never have been able to manage to finish high school, let alone go to college. And Charm is convinced that her mother would have somehow found a way to ruin that baby's life.

Charm rushes down a street lined with the venerable brick buildings that make up St. Anne's campus. The small, private college sits in the middle of Linden Falls and is surrounded by historical homes and cobblestone streets that are beginning to crumble. Out of breath, she joins a group of students walking to their Leadership and Contemporary Issues in Nursing class. Sophie, a tall, gangly girl who wants to work in pediatric oncology, is in the midst of insisting that she has a psychic link with her mother.

"Seriously," Sophie says as they enter the classroom, "I can just be *thinking* of my mother and she'll call me a minute later."

"No way." Charm snorts. "I don't believe you." Charm looks at her classmates for support but they are all smiling knowingly, nodding their heads and saying things like, "It's true, I've got that with my sister."

"Try it," Charm tells her, crossing her arms and leaning back in her chair.

"Okay." Sophie shrugs her shoulders and digs into her purse, pulls out her cell phone and sets it on the desk in front of her.

"Now what?" Charm asks.

"Nothing, we just wait. She'll call in the next minute or so," she explains.

Charm shakes her head in disbelief but in a matter of minutes Sophie's phone begins to vibrate, doing a little dance across the table. Sophie picks up the phone and shows everyone the display screen. *Mom.*

"Hey, Mom," Sophie says into the phone. "I was just thinking of you." She smiles in triumph at Charm.

Charm is impressed but saddened, too. She can recall no one with whom she has such a profound connection. Certainly not her mother. Reanne always needs to be the center of attention. Charm was never enough for her, her brother wasn't enough, Gus wasn't enough. Reanne Tullia was always on the search for something better, more exciting. Charm has no idea where her brother is and her father could be dead for all she knew. Charm did have a boyfriend last year who called her all the time, but that had more to do with his crazy insecurity than any supernatural bond.

Gus, she thinks. She may have that bond with Gus. He's the one who taught her to ride a bike, how to multiply fractions, the one who sat in the audience and blinked back tears when she walked across the stage to receive her high school diploma.

Everything Charm has learned about being a good parent, a good person, she learned from Gus. One thing she knows for certain, when she gets married and has children, she will be there, day in and day out. She won't leave when things get hard or sad or just plain boring.

That's something her mother or her brother never learned.

Brynn

It's my first class of the term and even though I know all my teachers and most of my classmates, I'm nervous. A familiar feeling creeps into my chest like thick dust rising and settling on my breastbone. I try to take big, deep breaths, like Dr. Morris said I should, and it does help.

I'm looking forward to my classes this semester; I'm taking Animals in Society and Humane Education with Companion Animals. I also get to do an internship off campus. Since I already volunteer at the animal shelter, I think I'm going to request that I get to work on a horse farm. I've never ridden a horse, but I've read that horses have been used to help people who have behavior problems, eating disorders, even autism. Despite what most people think, horses are incredibly intelligent. In the late 1800s there was a horse named Beautiful Jim Key who traveled the country with his trainer, Dr. William Key. Beautiful Jim Key could identify different coins and use a cash register to ring up amounts and give the correct change. He could also spell, tell time and was said to have the IQ of a sixth grader. I don't know if that is actually true, but I'd like to think so.

I hear my cell phone vibrate and I dig around in my purse to find it. For a second I think Allison has gotten my cell phone number from someone, but I haven't even given it to our parents and I know Grandma wouldn't have given it to her. I smile as I look at the display. It's my friend Missy. I flip open the phone and bring it to my ear. "Hi, Missy, what's up?"

"Party tonight, my place, eight o'clock," Missy says.

"What's the occasion?" I ask as I pull my car into a spot in the parking lot of Prairie Community College.

"Just a back-to-school gathering. Can you make it?"

"Sure," I tell her as I grab my book bag from the backseat and make my way to the Animal Science building. "I work until nine. I'll come right after."

I met Missy the November after I moved to New Amery. I came to live with my grandmother in September. I was so sad and lonely; I spent the first two months in New Amery sitting in an extra bedroom in my grandmother's house, crying and sketching in my journal, and trying not to kill myself. Finally, my grandmother had enough. She couldn't stand to see me like that anymore.

"Come on, Brynn," she said, coming into my room and sitting on my bed. "It's time to get up and start living your life." I peeked up at her from beneath my covers but didn't answer. My grandmother was so different from my own father; at times I couldn't believe she'd given birth to him. "I want to show you something," she said, pulling the quilt off of me.

"What?" I asked grumpily. All I wanted to do was

pull the blanket back over my head and sleep. Forget that I was such a failure, a loser, a no one.

"Come on, you'll see," she said, holding out her hand to help me up. My grandma herded me into her car and drove through the streets of New Amery until she pulled up in front of a long, squat metal building. Outside was a large sign, with the words *New Amery Animal Shelter* painted in bright red letters.

I sat up straighter in my seat and turned to my grandma. "Why are we here?"

"Come on, I'll show you." She smiled at me and I reluctantly followed her into the building. We were greeted by a friendly black lab and a girl my age wearing a red vest, with a name tag that said *Missy.* She was standing behind a tall counter holding a small orange kitten. I heard the muffled yips and whines of dogs being kenneled in another part of the building.

"Hello, ladies," the girl said brightly. "What can I help you with today?"

My grandmother looked at me "What can she help you with today, Brynn?"

"Really?" I asked in disbelief. "Grandma, are you serious?"

"Go on and take a look." She nodded her head toward the kennels. "There is some little critter in there, waiting for you… Go find him."

"Come on," Missy said. "I'll show you the way." Missy opened a door and we were met with yelps and barking that echoed against the walls. The long, narrow room was lined with kennels filled with all kinds of dogs—a beagle, an English setter, labs and lots of mixed breeds. I stopped in front of a puff of reddish-brown fur that looked at me with bright, pleading eyes.

"What kind of dog is this?" I asked Missy.

"That's Milo. He's a mix of German shepherd and chow chow. Two months old. He was found out on a gravel road south of town. Poor thing was starving and dehydrated. He's a busy little guy, but a sweetie."

I looked at my grandma. "Can I have him?" I asked her, not daring to get my hopes up. He was only a few months old and already had huge paws, and Missy had said he was busy. "I think he needs me."

"Of course, Brynn. He's yours," she said, sliding her arm around my waist.

It was through Missy that I became a volunteer at the animal shelter and learned about the Companion Animal program at the community college. I'm still not sure why pretty, fun-loving and free-spirited Missy befriended safe, boring me, but I'm glad she did. I remember when I was thirteen, my mother made me go to the same sleep-away soccer camp that Allison attended. I was terrible at soccer and screwed up every single time the ball came my way. Allison didn't acknowledge me once that week. Whenever I tried to talk to her, whenever I tried to join in with her group of friends, she completely ignored me. When I finally couldn't take it anymore and started blubbering like a baby, Allison rolled her eyes and laughed. I ended up spending the rest of camp in my cabin insisting that I sprained my ankle.

Having a friend, especially one who loves animals as much as I do, is such a relief. I drop my phone back into my purse and my hand grazes the bottle that holds the medicine I've been taking for the past year. I haven't taken my dose for the day. Didn't take it yesterday, either. I've been feeling better. Stronger. Even the news that Allison is out of jail doesn't bother me as much as it would have a year ago.

Maybe it's time to stop taking the pills. Maybe I'm ready to try things on my own for a while.

Allison

I look down at the baby doll, its lifeless eyes looking up at me, and I feel weak. It's been five years and one month and twenty-six days. She would have been five years or sixty-one months or 269 weeks or 1,883 days or 45,192 hours or 2,711,520 minutes or 162,691,200 seconds old. I've been keeping count.

Many of the women at Cravenville had children. Some even gave birth to their babies behind bars. I used to run circle after circle around the prison courtyard, my tennis shoes pounding against the cement, the air heavy in my lungs. "Where you running to, Baby Killer? You running from yourself?" I would hear this from a corner of the yard and then a cackle of laughter. I ignored them. When they weren't calling me baby killer or bitch or worse, they didn't talk to me at all. They looked through me as if I was just a part of the putrid air on our cell block. Those were women who themselves were killers; they murdered their husbands or stabbed their boyfriends or shot a clerk in a robbery.

But I'm worse. A helpless baby, a few minutes old, was tossed into the river to be swept away with the current, to be battered against the bank.

The women at Gertrude House are no different than the women at Cravenville. I have never felt more alone than I do right now. I know how hard it has been for my parents to witness how far I've fallen. But all I want is for them to come and see me. It's been so long since I've held my mother's hand, felt my father's touch. Heard my sister's giggle. We were never a touchy-feely family, but sometimes, when I hold very still, I can recall the weight of my father's large, capable hand resting on my head. Sometimes, when I close my eyes, I can imagine that things are like they were before everything went wrong. I can imagine that I am back in high school, running on the track and trying to beat my best time, sitting in my room doing my calculus homework, helping my mom with dinner, talking with my sister.

I had a plan. I would ace my college entrance exams, play volleyball for the University of Iowa or Penn State, major in prelaw, go to law school. I had my future all mapped out. Now it's gone. It's over. All because of a boy and a pregnancy.

I was in the hospital, hooked up to an IV, when I first met Devin. She told me I was going to be charged with first-degree murder and child endangerment. "Did you think the baby was dead before she went into the river?" she asked me at that first meeting. I shrugged my shoulders and didn't answer.

"Did you think she was dead?" she asked again, pacing back and forth in front of me. She was relentless. All I wanted to do was curl up in a ball and die and she kept trying to reexamine everything that had happened.

"Sure," I finally said. "Sure, I thought it was dead."

She spun on her heel. "Never call her an *it*. Do you understand?" she said severely. "You call her *the baby* or *she* or *her,* but never *it*. Got it?"

I nodded. "I really thought *the baby* was dead already," I said, wanting to believe it, but knowing nothing I said was the truth. The medical examiner had already proved I was wrong.

Eventually, Devin had me plead guilty to involuntary manslaughter, a class "D" felony that carried a five-year sentence, and child endangerment, a class "B" felony that meant I could be confined for more than fifty years, although Devin assured me that there was no way I would serve that kind of time. I didn't have to take the stand in my own defense. It never got that far. I've never told anyone what happened that night, and no one seems very interested in hearing the exact details. I think I remind everyone of someone they could know. A sister, a daughter, a grandchild. Maybe even themselves. Everyone knows the basics of what I did. That's enough for them. Devin was right. I ended up being sentenced to ten years at Cravenville. As horrible as that sounded at the time, it was much better than the fifty-five years I could have faced. I asked Devin why it was such a short sentence.

"There are many factors," Devin explained. "Prison overcrowding, the circumstances of the crime. Ten years is a bargain, Allison."

Then, a month ago, Devin came to see me at the prison. I was running around the courtyard, the July heat radiating off the concrete. I could feel the warmth seeping into my tennis shoes and through my socks. Breathing heavily, I watched as Devin walked quickly over to me, dressed in the gray suit she wore like a uniform and high heels. I've never worn a pair of high heels, never went to a school dance, never went to the prom. "Allison, good news," she told me by way of greeting. "The parole board is going to review your case. You'll go before the board next week for an interview."

"Parole?" I asked dumbfounded. "It's only been five years, though." I hadn't dared to think about getting out earlier.

"With your good behavior and all the steps you've taken to improve yourself, you qualify for a parole hearing. Isn't that great news?" she asked, looking questioningly at my worried face.

"It *is* good news," I told her, mostly because it was what she wanted to hear. How could I explain to her that after getting used to the confinement, the horrible food, the brutality of prison, after coming to terms with how and why I got here in the first place, I actually found comfort there. For once in my life I didn't need to be perfect. I didn't need to plan for my future. It was all laid out for me in prison. Ten long years of just being.

"We need to sit down and talk about the kinds of things the members of the parole board will most likely ask you. The most important thing for you to do is to express remorse for what happened."

"Remorse?" I asked.

"Remorse, regret," Devin said tersely. "It's crucial for you to say you're sorry for what you did. If you don't do that, there is no way they are going to grant you parole. Can you do that? Can you say you're sorry you threw your newborn baby in a creek?" she asked me. "You are sorry, right?"

"Yes," I finally said. "I can say I'm sorry." And I

did. I sat in front of the parole board as they reviewed my file. They complimented me on my good behavior while I was incarcerated, my work in the prison cafeteria, the fact that I earned my high school diploma and credits toward a college degree. They looked expectantly at me and waited. "I'm sorry," I said. "I'm sorry I hurt my baby and I'm sorry she died. It was a mistake. A terrible mistake and I wish I could take it all back."

My parents didn't attend the hearing, and I worried their absence would make the parole board think that if my own parents wouldn't even come to support me, there was no way they could recommend my release. But Devin told me not to worry; my grandmother was at the hearing and my chances of early release were excellent. "It's all about what you've done to make things right while you were in prison. How you've tried to better yourself." Devin was right. She always is. The parole board voted unanimously to release me.

I meet my roommate, Bea, a recovering heroin addict, at dinner. There are only five of us at the table. The rest of the residents are working or at approved activities. I want to know about the different jobs the women have gotten—I want so badly to start earning some money of my own—but I'm hesitant to ask or even speak. Everyone looks at me like I have the plague or something. Except for Bea, that is. She doesn't seem to be bothered by my history. Either that or she hasn't heard the sordid details yet. Bea has the thin, pocked face of an addict and hard black eyes that look like they've seen hell or worse. She also has thin strong arms that look like they could knock the crap out of any one of us, so everyone seems to give Bea her space. Not that violence of any sort is allowed at Gertrude House. Bea gleefully tells everyone about her first night at Gertrude House, anyway.

"Two ladies got in an argument over who got to use the phone next. There's a sign-up sheet for a reason. This woman who had been in jail for embezzlement smacked the other gal across the face with the phone." Bea laughs at the memory. "Blood and teeth flew everywhere. Remember that, Olene?" Bea asks as she stabs a green bean with her fork.

"I do," Olene says wryly. "Not one of our finer moments here. We had to call the police."

"Yeah, and because I was new to the house, I had to clean up all the blood and teeth." Bea shivers at the memory.

"Oh, Bea," Olene chides her gently. "I helped you."

After dinner and helping with the dishes, I try to call my parents and then Brynn again. No one answers. I sit numbly on the sofa, the telephone in my hand, listening to the dial tone until Olene comes into the room, pulls the telephone gently from my hand and tells me I'm on my own until seven, when we meet as a group. I'm not surprised when I go up to my room and find another battered doll, headfirst in a tin bucket of water, there to greet me. I swallow hard and a solid knot of rage forms in my chest. How dare these women who themselves have done terrible, terrible things judge me? With a kick perfected during my second year at soccer camp, my foot connects with the bucket, sending it clanking across the hardwood floor, water splashing and spreading in a puddle at my feet. I hear feet on the steps and snickers coming from the hallway and I turn swiftly and slam the bedroom door, the walls trembling with the force and echoing through the house.

After a few minutes there's a knock at the door. "Go away," I say angrily.

"Allison?" It's Olene. "Are you okay?"

"I'm fine, I just want to be left alone," I say more softly.

"Can I come in for a minute?" Olene asks. I want to say no, I want to climb out the window and run away, but I can't go home and I can't leave the area. "Allison, open the door, please."

I crack open the bedroom door and I see Olene's green eye looking in at me.

"I'm fine," I say again, but the water from the bucket is pooling around my feet and inching into the hallway. Olene waits, not saying anything, just looking up at me with her knowing eyes until I step aside to let her in.

Olene takes in the overturned bucket, the doll, the lake of water and sighs. "I'm sorry about this, Allison," Olene says. "You just have to let them get it out of their system. Lay low, do your work and then they'll treat you like everyone else." She must see the sadness on my face because she asks, "Do you want me to bring it up at our group meeting tonight?"

"No," I say firmly. I get that no good will come from confronting these women.

"I'll go get you a towel." Olene pats me on the arm and leaves me to my thoughts. I plan to keep my head down, check in with my parole officer twice a month, do my work and mind my own business, but I know they aren't going to let me off so easily. I know they hate me for my crime. They think they're better than me. They think they have perfectly reasonable excuses for doing the bad things they did. The drugs made them do it, their boyfriends made them do it, their rotten childhoods made them do it. But me? I had the perfect parents, the perfect childhood, the perfect life. I have no excuses. Olene returns and hands me a stack of towels. "Want some help?"

I shake my head. "No, thanks. I've got it." She comes into the room, anyway, and picks up the bucket and the doll, then closes the door gently behind her. I wipe up the water from the floor and lie down on the lower bunk bed and try to close my eyes, but each time I blink I see only the dull, dead eyes of the doll behind my own.

When I think back to that night, I remember that the baby didn't cry like you see in the movies and on television. First, there's the mother, gritting her teeth and groaning, bearing down for the long push, and then the baby appears and greets the world with a wail, as if angry at being brought from her warm, dim aquarium into the bright, cold world. That cry never came.

I could see the terror in Brynn's eyes as she offered the baby to me. I told her no. I didn't want to touch her. So with shaking hands, Brynn cut the umbilical cord and laid her gently in a little bundle on the floor in a corner of the room. "You need a doctor, Allison," she told me, her voice cracking with concern as she brushed my sweaty hair from my forehead. I was unbelievably cold, shivering so hard that my teeth clanked together. Brynn glanced over at the still, silent baby. "We need to call someone…"

"No, no," I chattered, trying to cover my legs, now conscious of my nakedness. I tried to control my mouth, forcing the words to come out smoothly, forcefully. If they didn't, I knew that Brynn would fall apart. "No. We're not going to tell anyone. No one needs to know now." I knew I sounded cold, cruel even. But, like I said,

I had a plan: valedictorian, volleyball scholarship, college, law school. Christopher was a mistake, the pregnancy an even bigger one. I just needed Brynn to keep a cool head, to go along with me.

"Oh, Alli," Brynn said, her chin trembling, tears running down her face. Barely keeping it together. "I'll be back in a few minutes," she told me, arranging the covers around me carefully. "I'm going to throw away these sheets." I wanted to sleep, so badly. I wanted to close my eyes and just disappear.

I used my arms to push myself up from the damp bed and slowly swung my legs over the edge of the bed, nearly crying out from the burning pain between my legs. I waited until the sting dulled into a throb and stood, reaching for my bedside table for support. I looked over to the far corner of the room where Brynn had left the baby. I can do this, I told myself. I have to do this.

As I steadied myself, I looked down and saw the rust-colored stains on my thighs. Brynn had tried to clean me up as best as she could, but blood was still dribbling down my legs and I moaned. There was so much blood. In the corner I saw the bundle of towels that Brynn had wrapped the baby in. It seemed so far away. I needed to get dressed and get things cleaned up. It would be dark soon, and there was always the chance that my parents would come home early. I had to make a decision. Through the sound of rain pounding on the roof I thought I heard Brynn downstairs and the slam of a screen door. I knew what I needed to do, where I needed to take her. It would be like she was never even here, like she never existed. After, I would rush to finish cleaning up my bedroom and I would pretend that

I had the flu for the next few days. Then everything would go back to normal. It would have to.

But it never seems to actually be finished, this thing. It has attached itself to me and to Brynn and even to my parents like some kind of malignant tumor, and we will never be free of it. I begin to cry. I've done everything right my entire life and then I made one mistake and my life was ruined. One mistake. It just wasn't fair.

Claire

As Claire steps into the old Victorian that she and Jonathan bought and restored twelve years ago, she makes a mental note to give Charm a call in a few days to see how she is doing. Over the years she has developed a fondness for Charm, a round, soft-spoken girl who has a fascination with self-help books. When she purchased *The Legacy of Divorce,* Claire learned that Charm had lived with Gus, her stepfather, ever since she was ten, even after her mother divorced him and moved on. Then when she bought *Brothers and Sisters: Bonds for a Lifetime,* Charm told her that she hadn't seen her older brother in years, but wanted to be prepared if he ever came back. When Charm was ready to start college she came in with a textbook list and Claire learned she wanted more than anything to be a nurse and that Gus had been recently diagnosed with lung cancer. Charm came to the store and bought books for her friends, a book about baseball for her first boyfriend.

Once, she even bought a copy of *Mother: A Cradle to Hold Me* by Maya Angelou for her mother, with whom she was trying to patch things up. "She didn't get it," Charm told Claire later. "She thought I was making fun of her by getting her a book of poetry and slamming her for her mothering skills. I just can't win with her." Charm said this so sadly that Claire takes comfort in the knowledge that she tells Joshua every single day how much she loves him. That even though she makes mistakes, like the time she wrongly accused Joshua of feeding Truman all of his Halloween candy, she is confident that he would never, ever doubt her love for him.

Claire finds Joshua rolling a tennis ball across the living room floor to Truman, who lazily watches it glide past him. "Go get it, Truman!" Joshua urges. "Go get the ball!" Instead, Truman heaves himself up on squat legs and leaves the room. "Truman!" Joshua calls disappointedly.

"He'll be back," Claire says as she bends over, picks up the ball and takes it over to him. "Don't worry."

"On TV there's this bulldog named Tyson that knows how to skateboard," Joshua says as he picks at the frayed hem of his shorts. "Truman won't even chase a ball."

"Truman does other cool stuff," Claire says, scrambling to think of something.

"Like what?" Joshua asks bleakly.

"He can eat a whole loaf of bread in three seconds flat," she offers, but Joshua doesn't look impressed. She sighs and situates herself on the floor next to Joshua. "You know that Truman is a hero, don't you?" Joshua looks at her skeptically. "When you came to us, you were pretty little."

"I remember," Joshua says sagely. "Six pounds."

"One night, after you were with us for a week or so, you were sleeping in your crib. Dad and I were so tired we fell asleep on the couch even though it was only seven-thirty."

Joshua laughs at this. "You went to bed at seven-thirty?"

"Yes, we did," she tells him, and reaches for his hand, which without her realizing had somehow lost its soft pudginess. His fingers were long and tapered and for a fleeting moment she wondered where he had got them. From his biological mother or father? "When you were a baby you didn't sleep much, so whenever you slept, we did, too. So there we were, sleeping peacefully on the couch, and all of a sudden we heard Truman barking. Your dad tried to take him outside to go to the bathroom, but Truman wouldn't go. Dad kept chasing him around the house, but he just kept running around and yipping and yipping. It was actually kind of funny to watch." They both smile at the thought of Jonathan sleepily stumbling after Truman. "Finally, Truman ran up the stairs and waited, barking, until we came up after him. When we got to the top he ran into your room. We kept whispering, 'Shhh, Truman, shhh. You're going to wake up Joshua.' But he kept right on barking. And then all of a sudden Dad and I knew something was wrong. Very wrong. With all that barking you should have been crying."

Joshua's forehead creases as he thinks about this. "I didn't wake up?"

"No, you didn't," Claire says, shivering at the memory, and pulls him onto her lap.

"Why not?" he asks while he twists her wedding ring off her finger and places it on his own thumb, moving it back and forth so that the diamond casts a mottled rainbow on the wall.

"Dad turned on the light in your room and you were in your crib and it looked like you were sleeping, but you weren't. You weren't breathing." Joshua's hands still, but he doesn't say anything. "Dad snatched you up out of the bed so quickly he must have scared the breath right back into you because you started crying immediately."

"Whew," Joshua says with relief, and begins rotating the ring again.

"*Whew* is right," Claire says emphatically. "Truman saved the day. So he might not know how to skateboard, but he's pretty special."

"I guess so," Joshua murmurs. "I'll go say sorry." He slides the ring back onto his mother's finger, springs from her lap and runs off to find Truman. What she doesn't tell Joshua is how, during the endless seconds between when Claire and Jonathan saw him lying in his crib, blue and still, to when they heard his angry cries, her own breath escaped her. *How could I lose him already?* she had wondered. *Did God change His mind?* It wasn't until air filled his tiny lungs that she breathed again, too.

Claire slowly gets to her feet, mindful that she is every bit of her forty-five years. When Joshua celebrates his tenth birthday she will be fifty. When he is forty she will be eighty. Motherhood is the hardest, most terrifying, most wonderful thing she will ever do. Perhaps the greatest joy she's gotten from having Joshua coming into her life, besides hearing him call her Mom, is watching Jonathan and Joshua together. Together they pore over home restoration magazines and, entranced, watch old episodes of *This Old House*. Claire has to laugh when Joshua, asked what he wants to be when he grows up, answers Bob Villa or his dad. As they scrape, sand and varnish together, refurbishing fireplace mantels, armoires, banisters, when she watches as Jonathan teaches Joshua how to hammer a nail or twist a screw, her heart swells with pride.

Even though Joshua is their only child, Claire knows that he isn't quite like other children. For the longest time she thought of him simply as a dreamer. His head is so full of creative, imaginative ideas, she can almost ignore the fact that he often doesn't appear to hear them when they speak to him. They can tell him to do something many times and Joshua will seem to understand, but he rarely follows through. There are times when he seems to leave their world completely, can stare into space fully absorbed by she doesn't know what, and he's gone until they bring him gently back to them. It's as if there is a buffer that surrounds him, keeping the harshness of the world away. Without it, she believes, he would be left exposed and vulnerable. Claire doesn't know if it had to do with those moments when he was deprived of oxygen or if something traumatic happened before he came to them. Sometimes she fears their love hasn't been quite enough to renew Joshua's trust in the world around him.

Claire runs a finger along the row of photos that line the sofa table. The pictures capture the day they brought Joshua home, the day he was legally theirs, the first time he ate pureed squash, his first Christmas. Every single day Claire says a little prayer of thanks for the girl who left Joshua at the fire station five years ago. Because of her, she and Jonathan have their son. Sometimes she wonders about her, the woman who gave birth to Joshua. Was she from Linden Falls or did she come from far away? Was she young, a teenager who just didn't know what to do? Was she an adult who already had several children and couldn't take care of one more? Maybe Joshua has brothers and sisters out there somewhere who are just like him. Maybe his mother is a drug addict or abused. Claire doesn't know and doesn't really want to. She is grateful that the girl chose to give him up. In that single act of altruism or selfishness—she'll never know which—that girl gave her everything.

Brynn

There are dozens of us crammed into Missy's one-bedroom apartment, which she shares with two other girls. The only person I know is Missy, who is on the couch, making out with some guy. I'm standing awkwardly in a corner, trying not to watch their frantic kissing, the way his tongue pokes into her mouth, the way he has his hand up her shirt. I gulp from the glass that someone has pressed into my hand and welcome the pleasant numbness that begins to spread throughout me. I'm not supposed to mix alcohol with my medication, but it's okay because I haven't taken my pills in days. A boy I think I recognize from campus squeezes through the bodies and comes up to me. "Hey," he says loudly, trying to be heard above the pounding music.

"Hey," I respond, and mentally roll my eyes at the lameness of my social skills. He is short, but still taller than I am, and his blond hair stands up in gelled spikes.

"I think I know you," he says, leaning in toward me. His breath smells sweet, like wine cooler.

"Oh," I say carelessly, trying to act as if this happens to me every day. I take another swig from my cup and find it empty. The skin on my face feels loose and I touch my cheeks to make sure they are where they need to be.

"Here, you can have mine," he says, and gallantly wipes the mouth of the bottle with his T-shirt. He has a sprinkle of brown freckles on his nose and I want to reach out with one finger and count them. I feel dizzy and lean back against the wall to keep my balance.

"Thanks," I tell him, taking the wine cooler and drinking from it because I can't think of anything else to say.

"I'm Rob Baker," he says with a grin.

"It's nice to meet you," I say, smiling back. "I'm Brynn."

"I know," he says. "You're Brynn Glenn." My smile widens. He knows my name.

"Yes, I am," I say flirtatiously, and take a woozy step closer to him, wondering what it would be like to kiss him. To feel his tongue against mine.

"I'm from Linden Falls," he says, and my heart seizes. "We used to go to the same church." I can see it coming. He isn't looking at me because he's seen me around campus or because he thinks I'm pretty. "Your sister is Allison Glenn, right?" I can't answer. I stand there blinking wordlessly back at him. "Allison is your sister, right?" he repeats. I see him glance back over his shoulder at a group of boys who are watching us.

"No," I say, and from the look on his face he knows I'm lying. "Never heard of her." I peer over his shoulder as if I'm looking for somebody.

"We went to the same church. Our moms volunteered at the bake sale together. You're Brynn Glenn," he says forcefully.

"Nope. Not her." I shove the wine cooler back at him, sloshing the contents all over his shirt, and step past him through the crowd. Unsteadily, I push my way through the sweaty bodies until I reach the door. Once outside, the mild night air cools my face. I make my way to my car and climb in. I know I can't drive like this. My head feels heavy and I rest it on the steering wheel and close my eyes. Growing up, teachers were always saying, *You're Allison Glenn's little sister, aren't you? Are you as smart, athletic, funny* (you can insert your own adjective here) *as your sister?*

Well, no, I'm not. *I'm not my sister,* I want to shout. I am nothing like her and never will be. But no matter how hard I try, no matter how far away I go, Allison is always there. It always comes back to Allison.

Allison

In the dark of night I still question how the police found out the baby was mine. Someone had to have called them and it sure wasn't me. In the back of my mind I know it was Brynn, even though I can't believe she had it in her to actually pick up the phone. Brynn couldn't even order a pizza on her own. Five years have passed and I still have trouble picturing her making the call.

The strange numbness that I had felt after giving birth the day before was gone, replaced with burning pain that brought tears to my eyes. I was actually glad for the officer's steadying hand. Brynn reached out to touch my face. "Alli," she cried. I pulled away from her fingers. I felt so sick, like I would combust if anyone touched me. I know that pulling away from Brynn hurt her feelings. She was always so sensitive. In an odd way, I could understand why she did what she did. This was way more than a fifteen-year-old girl, especially one like Brynn, should have had to shoulder. I prayed that for her sake she didn't tell anyone she had helped me through the delivery. There was no reason why we should both get in trouble for what really was my own fault. As I carefully slid into the back of the police car, I could hear Brynn's awful cries.

I haven't spoken to or seen Brynn since.

I ended up fainting in the police car, so our first stop was the hospital, where I got thirty stitches and spent the next three days hooked up to an IV full of antibiotics. The way the nurses and the doctors looked at me while I was in the hospital was new. Everyone took adequate care of me; they were all too professional to do anything else. But there were no gentle touches, no cool hands laid against my hot forehead, no plumping up of pillows. Just anger and disgust. Fear. My parents' original shock at me being led away by the police was replaced with outrage. "Ridiculous," my mother hissed when the detective who came to the hospital to interview me asked if I was the one who threw the baby in the river. I didn't say anything.

"Allison," my mother said, "tell them it's all a big mistake." Still I didn't say anything. The officer asked me why there was a black bag full of bloody sheets stuffed into the garbage can in our garage. I didn't answer. She asked me how I came to be nearly ripped in half, my breasts swollen and leaking milk.

"Allison. Tell them you didn't do this," my father ordered.

Finally, I spoke. "I think I need a lawyer."

The detective shrugged her shoulders. "That's probably a good idea. We found the placenta." I swallowed hard and looked down at my hands. They were puffy and swollen; they didn't look like they belonged to me.

"Inside a pillow case at the bottom of a trash bag." She turned to look at my father. "In your trash can. Call your lawyer." As she was leaving my hospital room, she turned back to me and said softly, "Did she cry, Allison? Did your baby cry when you threw her in the water?"

"Get out!" my mother screeched, so unlike her usual composed, proper self. "Get out of here, you have no right. You have no right to come in here and accuse and upset us like this!"

"Huh," the detective said, nodding in my direction as she moved toward the door. "She doesn't look so upset."

Charm

Gus is fading quickly. "Where's the baby?" he asks Charm when she comes home from the hospital.

"He's safe," she reassures him. "Remember, he's with that nice family now? They are taking good care of him."

Charm hears a rap at the front door. She lifts the pot of mashed potatoes from the stove top and goes to the door. Jane stands on the front steps, her black hair pulled back in a ponytail, carrying her bag of tricks, as she calls it.

"Hey, how're you doing?" she asks as she steps into the house. "Fall is in the air." She shivers slightly and Charm takes her coat from her.

"I know, and it's only the end of August. We're doing fine," Charm responds. "Gus is in the other room watching television."

"Ah, food for the mind." She smiles.

Charm shrugs. "It helps pass the time."

"How's he doing?" Jane asks, her tone turning serious.

"He's okay. Some days are better than others."

"How about you? How's school going? Are you juggling everything okay? It's a lot of responsibility for a twenty-one-year-old to be going to school and taking care of an old man."

"Hey, don't call Gus old, it will hurt his feelings. We're doing just fine," Charm says, stiffening a little. She knows where Jane is heading with this. Jane brings up the subject of a hospital or skilled care facility nearly every time she comes to the house. "I call him three times a day and check up on him at lunch."

"I know, I know." She holds up a hand, trying to placate Charm. "You're doing a great job. I'm just saying there are always options for you and resources. You let me know if you think Gus is taking a turn for the worse or if you need more help. Okay?" She looks her levelly in the eyes.

"Okay," Charm answers, knowing that Gus would never stand for being moved from his home.

"I saw your mom the other day," she says casually as she scans the kitchen. Charm is aware that, as a nurse, it's Jane's job to make sure that Gus is getting the care he needs. She's not worried—the house is always clean and she always makes sure to have food in the refrigerator.

"Oh?" Charm says as if she doesn't care. But she listens, greedy for any snippet of news of her mother.

"Yeah, I saw her at Walmart in Linden Falls. She looks good. Said she is working as a waitress at O'Rourke's."

Charm doesn't respond. Her mother has had many jobs over the years and Charm doubts this one will last long.

"She's still with that guy, Binks."

"For now," Charm says bitterly.

"She asked about you. I said you were doing great," Jane says gently.

"She could ask *me* how I am on her own, she knows where I am. She lived here long enough for her to remember."

"She wondered if you've heard from your brother," Jane asks tentatively.

"No," Charm says guardedly. "Not for years. Last I heard he was doing drugs and participating in other highly illegal activities."

"You *are* doing great, you know," she tells me again. "You hang in there. Soon you'll be done with college and can begin your own life." She hoists her bag over her shoulder and calls out to Gus. "The lady of your dreams is here, Gus. Turn off that junk on the television!" Gus's laughter rings out from the other room and then they hear the click of the television being shut off.

Charm sees how gentle and caring Jane is with Gus and knows she's like that with all her patients. She gives him medication that relieves the pain and finds a way to make him smile through the pain the morphine can't reach, treating Gus with the dignity and respect that is so important to him. Because in the end, that's all he really has left. He knows he is going to die, but Jane is easing the way for him. She talks to him like he was the man he remembers himself to be—the firefighter, a respected member of the community, a good friend and neighbor.

She thinks about someone finding out what they did five years ago. If anyone learns of the law she had broken, her dream of becoming a nurse would disappear.

I want to do what Jane does for others, Charm thinks. *I hope that I get the chance.*

Brynn

I wake up shivering. The windows of my car are fogged over and it takes me a minute to figure out where I am. I wipe away the condensation with the heel of my hand. The sky is black and I see that I'm still parked in front of Missy's apartment. No lights shine in the apartment and the street is quiet.

My neck is stiff from sleeping with my head against the steering wheel and my mouth feels dry, like it's stuffed with cotton. I think back to the night before, about how I thought for a second that boy could possibly be interested in me. Just me. I had thought that by leaving Linden Falls I would be able to start over in a place where no one would know where I came from, who my sister was. But I was wrong.

I turn the car ignition and flip the heat as high as it will go, so that warm air blasts against my face. The display on the dash says it's three-thirty. I hope my grandmother isn't waiting up and worrying about me. I try to gauge whether or not I'm sober enough to drive back to my grandmother's house or if I should knock on Missy's door and crash there for the rest of the night. I can't bear the thought of facing her, though, of explaining why I left in such a hurry. I'm sure word has already made the rounds. Soon I'll be right back where I was when I lived in Linden Falls. That girl. Brynn Glenn. That girl whose sister went to prison for drowning her newborn.

I decide that it's safe for me to drive home. The world isn't spinning like it was last night, even though my head is pounding and my stomach churns. I flip on my headlights and carefully pull out into the street toward home. I don't know what I'm going to say to my grandmother. The truth, I guess. She's just about the only person in the world I can be honest with, at least to some degree. She knows that I felt like an outsider in my own house. My grandmother understood. She told me that she felt the same way living with my grandfather and my father. They were both perfectionists, both incredibly smart, both interested in finance and astronomy. She said that try as she might, she always felt like she was on the outside looking in, wanting to be a part of their circle but never finding the space to squeeze in.

When I was fourteen I took a sketching class at the community center. One of our first assignments was to do a self-portrait. I sat in front of my mirror for hours with my sketch pad and pencil, just staring at myself. The nib of my pencil didn't touch the paper, my hand floating above it like a butterfly trying to find a place to land. Eventually, Allison wandered past my room and poked her head in.

"What are you doing?" she asked me.

"Nothing," I answered. "Just an assignment for my art class. I have to draw a self-portrait."

"Can I see?" she asked, stepping into my room. I remember thinking, *My sister is so beautiful. She should be the one I sketch a picture of,* but I didn't have the nerve to ask her. I tilted my blank sketch pad toward her and she looked at me, a troubled frown on her face. "I think that must be the hardest thing for you to do, for an artist to do. To draw yourself. For the whole world to see what you think you look like." She shook her head at the thought, as if impressed. "Maybe start with your eyes," she suggested. "And go from there." Then she was gone, on to the next activity, the next school project, the next workout.

I sat there for a long time, all alone in my room, smiling. Not just because Allison graced me with her presence—which rarely happened—but because she called me an artist. For once I wasn't the little sister, the nobody. I was Brynn Glenn, the artist.

I still have that portrait I ended up drawing of myself. It shows me sitting in front of a mirror, looking at myself, paper and pencil in my hand. And if you look closely at the pad of paper that I'm holding, you'll see another girl looking in a mirror holding a pencil and paper, and on and on until the girl in the mirror is so small you can barely see her. I thought it was pretty good and my art teacher did, too. I got an A. I showed my mom and dad and they told me I did a nice job. I asked if I could get a frame and put the sketch inside it and hang it in the living room or somewhere, but my mother said no. The picture didn't really go with the decor of the house.

I never showed the picture to Allison. I was afraid of what she might say. For that one moment, Allison considered me an artist. I wanted her to keep that thought, remember me that way.

As I pull my car into my grandmother's driveway, I see that she has left a light on for me. As quietly as possible, I unlock the back door and step into the kitchen. The light above the stove is on and there's a note on the table. *Hope you had fun with your friends. There's cake on the counter.* I smile. This is another reason I love my grandmother. There's always cake. My stomach still feels queasy so instead I get a glass of water and make my way to my bedroom. Milo is curled up on my bed, fast asleep. I nudge him to the side and crawl under my covers but sleep doesn't come. I get up again, swallow my medication, adding an extra two pills to make up for the doses I missed the past few days and pull out my sketch pad. Climbing back into bed, I begin drawing, my hand moving as if on its own. Dark clouds, a river, my sister, a baby…and me. Watching it all.

Allison

I'm on for cleaning bathrooms today at Gertrude House and then later I'm going to meet with Olene about a possible interview for a job at a local bookstore. I'm very excited about the job prospect and nervous, too. Olene is active in several community groups and many of her *girls,* as she calls us, get jobs at local businesses near Gertrude House. I set my bucket of cleaning supplies on the floor, grab the toilet wand and lift the lid of a toilet. Inside, I find a particularly realistic doll with wide, staring eyes looking up at me from the toilet bowl. I can't breathe when I see it. It has the same smooth pink scalp of the baby I gave birth to and its arms are reaching out for me as if begging me to pick her up. I don't stomp out of the bathroom wielding the toilet brush, ready to fight; I don't yell or scream obscenities, or promise revenge. I sink to the floor of the bathroom and lay my forehead against the blue tiled wall and cry and cry.

Finally, Olene comes into the bathroom—there are

no locks on any of the doors in the house—and sits on the floor with me, holding me as I cry as I haven't done in years. No one has ever seen me cry this way. Not my mother, or father, or even Brynn. I hold on to Olene's thin frame, her knobby shoulders digging into my cheek, and cry.

"Shhh now, Allison, shhh," she whispers into my ear, her stale cigarette breath a welcome breeze against my cheek. "It's going to get better," she promises. "Do you hear me, Allison?" I snuffle and nod into her neck. "Then let's get you up and wash your face." She places her rough, leathery hands on my shoulders. "It's not going to be easy," she says, looking up at me. "It's probably going to get a lot harder before it gets easier. No one can change what you did or what has happened in the past." I lower my head and start to cry again. "But—" she says so sharply that I have to look at her again. "But you do have control over who you are now and how you carry yourself. Do you understand?" I can't answer her. "Do you understand?" she says again, and I bob my chin up and down.

"Meet the world with hope in your heart, Allison," Olene says gently, tears gathering in her own eyes. "Meet the world with hope and it will reward you. I promise," Olene says in a way that I know she's said the exact same thing to dozens, maybe hundreds, of girls over the years.

I nod my head and rub my eyes.

"Are you going to be okay?" Olene asks.

"I'm fine," I tell her stupidly, nodding my head up and down and sniffling. It is so obvious I am anything but fine. "I just need a few minutes."

"Okay." She pushes herself up from the floor and

stands over me for a moment as if trying to decide if she should say more. "I'll see you later at the group meeting." She glances down at the baby still floating in the toilet. "You want me to take care of that?"

"No, I've got it," I say, and I hear the door click softly shut when she leaves. I look into the mirror at my swollen eyes and blotchy face. I can't let the other women see me this way, I tell myself, and bend over the sink to splash cold water on my face. For a brief moment I think about how shockingly cold the river water would have felt on my baby's face and a strangled gagging sound comes from my throat. I force myself to look in the mirror one more time and smooth my hair. It's still long and shiny, a sunny yellow. I hate it. I grab a fistful of it, take a deep breath and look through the medicine cabinet for a pair of scissors but find none.

I pull an old towel from the linen closet, reach in and lift the dripping doll from the toilet by its arm and wrap it up tightly. This is my test, I suppose, my initiation into the halfway house sorority, Phi Beta Felon. Well, I'm a kick-ass test taker. I open the bathroom door as the other residents sidle up to doorways to watch as I walk past them, my head raised, my back straight. I move purposely through the hallway down the steps, ignoring the snickers and comments as they follow behind me. I stomp through the kitchen and out the back door to where the large black garbage cans are stored. I wrench off the plastic lid and nonchalantly toss the bundle in. It lands noiselessly among the scraps of stinking food, the soiled paper towels, the garbage discarded by women who did bad things.

Hope. Olene had said to meet the world with hope. I want to do this. I need to do this, but I don't know how.

As I move through the hallways of Gertrude House I hear the whispers of *"killer"* and see the angry, disgusted faces of the other residents. I will never be free of my past as long as I stay in Linden Falls. I have to get this job at the bookstore and I have to do my time at Gertrude House and then I'm going to move away. But first I have to see my sister face-to-face and make her talk to me.

Claire

The lights that line Sullivan Street sputter on at nine-thirty even though the sky has been midnight-black since seven. Watching the rain fall in silvery sheets, Joshua stands with his fingers pressed against the front window of Bookends, leaving sticky fingerprints that Claire won't have the heart to wipe away. *Look,* the smudged impressions seem to say, *look who has been here—a little boy of five who loves sour gummy worms and chocolate-flavored soda.* Both of which Claire, in a rare moment of indulgence, allowed Joshua to have. They weren't supposed to be at Bookends this late on a Monday evening, but Ashley, Claire's seventeen-year-old part-timer, called in sick. Then the ceiling began to leak, causing a flurry of rearranging and mopping. Distressed, Truman slunk into the back room and Claire gave in to Joshua's pleadings for his favorite sugary snacks.

Now, two hours later, an exhausted Claire climbs the old rickety stepladder that Jonathan is convinced she will break her neck on one day, to finish the inventory that should have been completed hours earlier.

"Mom," Joshua says fretfully, "I saw lightning. I think it's going to thunder."

"Just give me a few more minutes, Josh, then we'll pack up and go home. I'm almost done. Are you tired?" Joshua shakes his head no. "We're going to have to start getting you to bed earlier. You start school next week," she tells him as she scans the upper levels of the bookshelves, noting what titles need to be ordered on her clipboard.

"Can I go upstairs?" Joshua asks. Above the bookstore is an unoccupied but furnished efficiency apartment that Jonathan has been updating in hopes that they can rent it out to a college student one day.

"Nope. Sorry," Claire tells him. "Dad still has a bunch of his tools up there. There's nothing fun up there, anyway, except for a leaky ceiling. I promise I'll be ready to go in…" She lifts her wrist to check her watch and nearly tumbles off the ladder. "Whoops," Claire says, steadying herself. "We'll leave in fifteen minutes."

Joshua sighs heavily as if he doesn't quite believe his mother. "Okay. I'm going back there." He hooks his thumb in the direction of the children's section and walks wearily away.

Such a little old man, Claire thinks. She hears the jingle of bells as the front door opens and two young men slouch in. "Sorry, we're closed," she tells them, truly apologetic. She hates to turn readers away—not just for the money, although there's that, of course, but she knows that yearning feeling of wanting the weight of a new book in her hands. "We open tomorrow at nine," she adds over her shoulder, not becoming suspicious until they pull the hoods up, their faces hidden in the recesses of their oversize hooded sweatshirts. It's the end of August and despite the rain it's still warm and humid in the evenings. Dread fills her chest and only one thought comes to her mind. *Joshua.*

The shorter of the two glances up at Claire, his hood slipping back, his dark eyes flickering toward hers. The second boy, taller and leaner, makes a beeline to the cash register. With a bony, nail-bitten finger he jabs at the register and the drawer opens with a clang, striking him in the stomach so that the sound of the coins clanking against one another echoes through the store. "Hey," Claire calls in disbelief. "What are you doing?"

The tall boy ignores her and begins stuffing bills and rolls of coins from the register into the pockets of his sweatshirt. Claire starts down the wobbly ladder, thinking of only placing herself between Joshua and the thieves.

"Stay there," the taller boy orders. She moves down one more rung, saying a silent prayer that Joshua won't come out of the children's section in the back. "I said, stay there!" he shouts, and he moves toward Claire. His hood slips back to reveal brown wisps of hair, framing a face that could be very handsome if his lips weren't curled in an angry sneer, revealing stained teeth. Meth mouth, Claire thinks. The boy has lifeless, dark eyes. *Where is Truman?* Claire wonders. *Where is that dog when I need him?*

Again, Claire thinks of Joshua, hoping he'll stay tucked away, but as she looks over her shoulder he is standing there, staring up at her with fear in his eyes. He looks so small and fragile. His face creases with worry and his hands are clenched together in front of him. The thieves haven't seen him yet. Claire imperceptibly shakes her head at him, willing him to go back into the children's section and hide, but Joshua is frozen in place. Claire takes another tentative step down the ladder and the boy reaches into the pocket of his sweatshirt. A few bills flutter to the ground and she sees the glint of metal. "Don't fucking move," he spits as he pulls a knife from his pocket.

"I'm… I'm not moving," Claire assures him, her eyes darting from Joshua to the knife.

"Jesus." His partner moves toward the cash register. "What are you doing? Put that away." This boy is smaller, more compact, built like a gymnast or a wrestler. Black curly hair springs out from his hood and his eyes are gray, the color of slate.

"Shut up," the tall thief orders his friend and then says to Claire, "Where's the safe?"

"There is no safe, just the cash register." Her legs are beginning to cramp and she resists the urge to shake them out, afraid to move.

"Where's the safe?" he demands again, his voice rising in frustration.

They all hear the whimper at the same time and Claire's stomach plummets. *Joshua.*

"What the hell?" the shorter of the thieves asks no one in particular.

"Mom?" Joshua says. "Is it time to go home?" He looks fearfully from his mother's face to the knife the tall thief is holding.

"It's okay, Josh," Claire tells him, panic forcing her words to come out in breathy puffs. "Go back. It's going to be okay. Go back and wait for me." Josh takes a cautious step backward.

"No! You stay right there!" the tall boy shouts. Joshua blinks rapidly and hesitates just for a second, then dashes to the back of the store. The tall thief makes a move to run after him and Claire instantly begins to rush down the ladder when she feels it begin to shift beneath her feet.

The hinges on the ladder buckle at her quick movement and she loses her footing. It isn't a long fall—she's not really up all that high, five feet or so—and she tries to twist her body midair so she won't fall flat on her back. When people described time slowing down in situations like these, she had always laughed, shrugged it off as a silly trick of the mind. But it's true; during her short journey to the hardwood floor below, she notices an amazing number of details.

Midspin, she finds herself looking straight at the taller thief, who has decided Joshua isn't worth chasing. "Come on," the other boy calls out nervously. Except it comes out as "Cooommme oooonnnnnn." Slow and stretched out like taffy. He is scared; Claire can see it in his eyes. He can't be more than fifteen, Claire thinks, and wonders if these boys' mothers know what they are up to. "Let's get out of here!" he cries in long, drawn-out syllables, and then they are heading for the door. They are leaving. Thank God. And everything speeds up, back to normal time.

Claire's right shoulder hits first. An explosion of pain radiates through her arm, then her head hits the floor and a burst of warm yellow light explodes behinds her eyelids. From the doorway she can hear the taller boy shouting, "Hang it up! Hang up the phone!"

Then she hears his voice, small and hesitant. "They made my mom fall," Joshua says into the phone, his voice shaky, scared. "They took the money," Joshua adds in a rush.

"Run!" Claire tries to yell, but all her breath has been pressed from her lungs.

"Hang up the fucking phone!" the thief says between clenched teeth.

Claire begins to army-crawl across the bookstore floor toward Joshua, the pain in her shoulder and head secondary to reaching her son. "Run," she gasps desperately.

Joshua releases the phone and it clatters to the ground and instead of running away he goes to his mother and drops to the floor next to her. She can hear a siren in the distance and, in her ear, Joshua's frantic breathing. The thieves hear the sirens, too, and quickly rush from the store.

"It's okay, Joshua!" Claire says to him weakly. "It's okay, buddy." He is sitting cross-legged next to her, his small hand wrapped tightly around her wrist as if he's afraid that if he lets go she will float away. The pain that pulses through Claire's shoulder and the throbbing in her head churn her stomach and bile creeps into her throat. She turns her face to the side, away from Joshua, and vomits. Claire hears his sobs and can feel the shudder of his body next to hers, but still he grasps her wrist, clutching even tighter. "Don't cry, Joshua," Claire whispers, her own tears sliding down her cheeks. "Please don't cry." Finally, Truman lumbers over to them, nudges Claire's face with his wet nose, sits down, and the three of them wait for help to arrive.

It isn't until the ambulance arrives and the EMTs convince Joshua that they are there to help that Joshua releases Claire from his grip, leaving five perfectly circular imprints of his fingers like a red wreath around her wrist. "It's okay, Josh," Claire tells him over and over.

"One of the police officers will stay with your son until your husband arrives," the EMT promises Claire. "You took quite the tumble. We need to get some X-rays and have you checked over by a doctor. Are you in much pain?"

Claire nods. "Can't he stay with me? I don't want to leave him alone," Claire says as she tries to lift her head to see Joshua, wincing at the movement. He is sitting on the reading sofa with Truman's head on his lap. A young police officer approaches him, kneels down and says something to Joshua that makes the corners of his mouth rise in a reluctant smile.

"We really need to get you to the hospital, ma'am. The officer will stay and take care of him."

"I feel like I'm going to throw up again," Claire admits with embarrassment.

"It's okay." He nods at Claire. "I'm sure you got a doozy of a concussion. Vomit away."

When Claire arrives at the hospital and is wheeled into the emergency room, Jonathan is already there, standing at the door, waiting anxiously.

"Claire?" he asks as the gurney comes to a stop. "Claire, are you okay?"

"Joshua," she says. "Where's Joshua?" She sits up quickly and pain shoots through her skull as she lifts her head to search for her son.

"He's fine," Jonathan assures her, tears welling in his eyes as he looks down at his wife. "An officer is bringing him here right now." He runs a hand gently across her head. "How are you? What happened?"

Claire tries to describe the robbery as the EMT rolls her down the corridor, Jonathan holding her hand as they move, but her eyes are heavy and keep closing. All she wants to do is sleep but she fights the urge. "You should have seen Joshua," she says, her voice filled with awe and pride. Claire glances down at her wrist, the one that Joshua had held so tightly while they waited for help. She feels a surge of panic when she sees that his fingerprints have faded from her wrist. For a moment she has the sense that Joshua is gone, torn from her forever. But then she hears the familiar cadence of Joshua's steps coming near and then he is at her side.

"My brave boy," Claire whispers, and reaches for him before finally surrendering to sleep.

Allison

At group meetings I'm trying to decide whether to speak up or not. We each have the opportunity to talk about relationships that may have played a role in our poor decision-making. I mull this over. I don't think anyone in the history of Linden Falls has fallen as far and as fast as I have. I was the perfect daughter to perfect parents, but looking back, I don't know. My parents fed and clothed us and made sure we had everything we needed academically, athletically, socially. We even went to church every Sunday, but something was missing. Between swim meets, volleyball tournaments, the SAT prep courses and church youth activities, there wasn't much there. We didn't really speak to one another or laugh together, and I can't retrieve one memory that wasn't scheduled into a one-hour time block and marked on the calendar that hung on the wall on our kitchen. So I could talk to the group about my parents and our lack of communication and how I didn't feel like I could tell them that I was pregnant, certainly.

But really, the source of my very steep downfall was Christopher.

I met Christopher by chance, at St. Anne's College. I was taking the SATs again, trying for an even better score. My goal was a perfect 2400. Only about three hundred students per year scored a 2400 and I was going to be one of them.

It was a Saturday afternoon and I walked out of the classroom into the bright sunshine after taking the test in a daze, my mind whirling with exam questions and answers. I was tired and hungry and sick with worry over how I had done. Now came the hardest part, the waiting. I had to wait a month to find out the results. My stomach flipped at the thought and I froze in place, just stood there. I must have looked lost or sick because the next thing I knew a boy was at my side, peering worriedly into my face. He was taller than I was—that was what I noticed first. Not very many boys are taller than I am. The second thing I noticed was that he was older. He had to be twenty-two or twenty-three. He had copper-brown hair that curled around his ears and sharply angled features that were only softened by his eyes, which were such a deep brown and so beautiful it hurt to look at them. He wore a Cubs jersey and I later learned he was a huge fan.

I was used to guys looking at me, boys from school with their idiotic sexual comments that were for the benefit of their friends. I didn't waste my time even thinking about them. Grown men even stopped to look at me—my father's friends, the manager at the grocery store—though they were much more subtle about it. I was flattered. Don't get me wrong, it's nice to know that someone thinks you look good. I just didn't have time for it.

Every waking minute of my day was spent studying, cramming as much knowledge into my head as possible. I was sort of like one of those binge eaters who sit in a closet, with their packages of doughnuts and bags of potato chips, and stuff food in their mouths, not understanding why, just needing to do it. That's how I felt. I needed more and more information and I didn't know why. Well, of course, there were obvious reasons—to get good grades so I could get into a good college so I could get a good job and make good money. But there was more to it. I studied once for a history test on the Revolutionary War for ten hours straight. I knew the material, but I had to keep reviewing it, memorizing meaningless names and dates and battles. Finally, my father, who always tiptoed about as if he were afraid to startle the air around me, came into my room and took the book from my hands and insisted that I come down and eat something. I tried to balance things out—I joined all the sports teams I could—but it was the same kind of endless circle. I had to run farther, run faster— not to beat some competitor. No, it was something else. I'm not sure what, but I know I was miserable.

"Are you okay?" the boy with brown eyes asked me. "You don't look so good."

I blushed and stared up at him, not knowing what to say.

"You just look like you're in shock or something," he explained. "You're not going to pass out, are you?"

"No, no," I assured him. "I'm fine."

"Well, that's good. I wouldn't want you to die on me or something terrible like that."

Well, I didn't die, though a little more than nine months later I wished I would have. We walked to a nearby café, had coffee and talked and laughed. He was the one person who could distract me from myself and for the first time ever I was actually having fun. He told me he was a junior at St. Anne's College, working on a business degree. We spent the next three weeks together, every spare moment. I really loved Christopher, but it was too much, too fast. I considered lying to him about my age, but although I may have been many things, a liar wasn't one of them. At least, not at that time. Christopher raised his eyebrows at my age, but it didn't stop him from taking my hand at the restaurant. I didn't mean to keep him a secret, but I did. I didn't introduce him to my parents or Brynn, didn't even tell them about Christopher. I'm not sure why. He was twenty-two, way too old for a just-turned sixteen-year-old, and I knew my parents would have forbidden me from seeing him. Maybe deep down I knew it wasn't going to last—that while there wasn't anything wrong with a sixteen-year-old falling in love with a twenty-two-year-old, there was something definitely wrong with a grown man falling in love with a teenager. So I kept us a secret.

In the three weeks that I was with him, I didn't crack open one book outside of school. I rushed through my homework before school and during study hall. My grades dipped. I went to volleyball practice, but my mind wasn't on what the coach was saying. My mother asked me if I was feeling okay. Brynn looked at me suspiciously, but didn't say anything. Neither did my teachers. I'm sure they were thinking, *No one's perfect, even Allison Glenn.* I think they were secretly pleased to see me this way. As for me, I was gloriously happy.

That first week we met in ordinary places—the movies, restaurants, the park—but the next Saturday he took me to his house. We had met at the city park and then I climbed into his car and he drove us out of Linden Falls across the Druid River into the country. "You don't live in town?" I asked him, surprised.

"No, just outside of Linden Falls," he explained.

It was a sweet house, plain and small but clean.

He opened the refrigerator and pulled out a soda.

"Come on, I'll show you my room." I raised my eyebrows slyly at him. "Don't you want to?" he asked, sliding his arms around my waist and pulling me to him.

"I want to," I said as I kissed him.

He led me to his bedroom. It was a small, dark room with a plaid comforter and blank walls. "Not much for interior decorating, are you?" I teased.

"A man's gotta travel light," he responded, slipping his hands into the waistband of my jeans.

"Are you planning on going somewhere?" I asked, pulling his shirt over his head.

"Yeah, I am," he said, grinning at me. "If you'll let me."

"Oh, I'm going to let you," I whispered. And I did. I let him. And as he slid into me, I wasn't scared or worried. It wasn't painful. It was like coming home and all I could do was say his name over and over. "Christopher, Christopher, Christopher…"

Charm

The newspaper doesn't reveal many details about the robbery at the bookstore, just that Claire Kelby and her five-year-old son were there and that Claire was taken by ambulance to the hospital. After reading the article, Charm rushes over to Bookends to check on Claire and Joshua.

Through the years, Gus had heard the gossip from his friends at the fire station. They shared the news they gathered about the little boy that was left at the firehouse and in turn Gus would come home and share the tidbits with Charm, who listened greedily, hungrily. He was healthy, was adopted by a nice couple, the mother owned a bookstore, the father was a carpenter, they named him Jacob or Jeffery or Joshua.

There were only four bookstores in town and it wasn't difficult for Charm to find the one owned by a woman who had a husband who was a carpenter. Bookends. She liked the name. It sounded strong, sturdy, safe.

The first time Charm got the nerve up to go into

Bookends, she was eighteen. She figured the store would be closed, maybe not even be there anymore. She slipped in unnoticed and went back to a spot in the self-help section. She only needed one look, she told herself, only needed to see his face, look into his eyes, then she could leave. A woman walked by a few minutes later, carrying a stack of books, a little boy toddling closely behind her. He was small and had blond hair the color of corn. She quickly dropped to a sitting position, making it even more difficult for anyone to see her among the stacks of books about how to get a lover, keep a lover and live without a lover. If she was discovered, she figured it would appear that she had settled in to look through the books that would somehow save her from herself. The squat little bulldog that roamed the store waddled up to her and she patted his head, hoping he wouldn't give away her hiding spot. The woman passed by without a glance. But Charm saw the little boy's face. His beautiful face that was his father's. The same nose that turned delicately upward, the same ears that poked out a little too far from his head. His eyes were dark brown, the color of chocolate. She had found him.

Their eyes, mirrors of each other, latched on to one another. Was there a flicker of recognition? Charm wanted to think so, wanted him to wade back through the days, months, years that they had been separated and find a memory of her. But the moment was too short.

She thought that she would be able to just walk away once she saw him. That after she saw his face and knew that he had a family that cared for and loved him, she would be able to waltz right out without looking back.

She was wrong. She couldn't just leave. Who were these people who had ended up with him? Who were the Kelbys? No, she couldn't walk away just yet. Maybe never.

After seeing Joshua that first time in the bookstore with Claire, it took her three weeks to gather enough nerve to return. She planted herself in the self-help section because it was located in a far corner of the store behind the cash register and gave her the best spot to secretly watch the front door to see who came and went. She pretended to read through a book about moving someone's cheese that she actually found quite good and ended up buying.

She wanted to get close enough to make sure he was okay, well taken care of. She wanted to say with a single look, *You were a boy who was well loved. You were born on a cool summer night and when I held you in my arms for the first time I wasn't a child anymore, but a mother—your mother, even if it was only for a short time. You were a baby who liked to have your bald head rubbed, loved to be sung to by a sick man and rocked to sleep by a young girl. You would cry until all the tears that could be were squeezed from your body. But then you'd look up at me like I was the only person in the world and it didn't matter that I only got two hours of sleep the night before. The secret of you was too heavy. I wanted you to have an excruciatingly boring childhood with a mother and father.* That's what her look would have said.

And the boy's look would have said, *I know you. I'm not sure how, but I knew you once somewhere and that place was warm and good.*

From behind a book about a man who thought his wife was a hat, Charm continued to wait. Out of the corner of her eye, she saw a small boy in a white T-shirt dash into the children's section. She moved slowly to get a better look. It was him, she was sure of it. He was smiling; he looked happy. The little boy was fine.

She now knows that Claire and Jonathan are the perfect parents for him. She doesn't seek him out to mourn over him or to reassure herself that she did the right thing. She comes, she thinks, to watch. To learn. To witness what she never had as a child, to experience what her mother could never give her. That's what a mother should be like, she thinks as she watches Claire bend to give Joshua a hug or wipe away a tear or whisper in his ear. *I had a hand in this,* Charm tells herself. He is safe.

Now, as she steps through the front entrance of Bookends, Charm finds Virginia working at the counter. "Hi," she says breathlessly. "I heard about the break-in last night—is everyone okay?"

"Claire and Joshua had quite a scare, but they're both fine. Decided to stay home today, of course. Claire has a slight concussion and a sore shoulder but Joshua wasn't hurt. The little guy called 9-1-1 all by himself." Virginia shakes her head at the thought of it.

"He did?" Charm asks. "Joshua did that?"

"Yes, he did." Virginia nods as if she can't believe it herself. "The robbers told him to hang up the phone, but he wouldn't. Told the 9-1-1 operator that there were 'bad guys in the bookstore.'"

"Good for Joshua. When will Claire be back at work?" Charm asks.

"Oh, tomorrow, I imagine. She's going to hire another part-timer. Doesn't want any of us working solo anymore. Know anyone who needs a job?"

"I'll check with the other nursing students and see. Did they get much money? Did the police catch them?"

"A few hundred dollars. And no, no one was caught yet, not so far as I know. Claire and Joshua were going down to the police station today to give their statements," Virginia says as a customer brings her purchases up to the counter.

"Will you tell Claire I stopped by? Tell her to let me know if she needs anything?"

"I will, Charm, honey." Virginia stops with a sudden thought. "Why don't you take the part-time job? Claire would love to have you here. So would Joshua."

"I wish I had the time, but I don't. I'll put the word out, though. Thanks, Virginia." Charm says goodbye and steps out into the hazy sunshine, imagining what it would be like to work in the bookstore alongside Claire, being able to see them every day. She knows it isn't practical, isn't safe. Isn't the right thing to do.

If I do nothing else in my life, she thinks, *I will have played a part in giving a little boy a home that isn't fractured or incomplete.* She basks in the knowledge, takes comfort in the certainty that Joshua will never know the hurt a mother is capable of inflicting.

Brynn

I wake up to hear the phone ringing and I realize that it's probably Allison again. I sit up. I can still taste the wine coolers I was drinking last night in the back of my throat and smell cigarette smoke on my clothes. I should have never driven home this morning—I was in no condition. I try to focus my eyes on the alarm clock. Nine-thirty. I've missed my eight o'clock class. Great. As I make my way to the bathroom, I feel as if I'm moving through sludge. My head still throbs. I expect my grandmother to holler that Allison is on the phone for me, but she doesn't. Maybe she told her I was still sleeping. Maybe it wasn't even Allison. But I know that it was. I have some kind of sixth sense about when she's going to call that makes me feel sick. Maybe I can talk to my grandmother again about getting our telephone number changed. We've had this conversation before, but she always says that she can't shut Allison out of her life, that she is her granddaughter, too. I bend over the toilet just as I begin to dry heave. Loud, wet-sounding barks erupt from my throat but nothing comes out, just the bitter taste of bile tinged with the strawberry wine coolers.

When I was six, my parents took Allison and me to the Minnesota Zoo. I was in heaven, even though my dad pulled me as quickly as he could through all the exhibits so he could get back to the hotel and check his work emails. I dragged my feet, determined to snatch up the image of each animal with my eyes. The zoo had this amazing rain forest ecosystem. One minute we were standing in the middle of the Midwest and then we stepped over a threshold and were smack-dab in the center of a rain forest. The air was steamy and hot and we were surrounded by huge trees and vegetation. A fine mist clung to our skin. We traveled across a swaying suspension bridge and the roar of a huge waterfall filled my ears.

My senses couldn't take it all in—the smells, the heat, the animals scurrying through the treetops and across the forest floor. At first I didn't know exactly what I was seeing. Above us, in a thick-limbed synthetic tree, was a spider monkey, with its white-whiskered chin and long, narrow hands. I thought it was holding a small blanket, wrapped around its neck like a superhero's cape. I pointed and laughed. "Look," I said to my mother, who had a hand pressed to her nose as if trying to block out the musty smell of the forest. "Look at that monkey."

She looked and her hand fell from her face and reached for mine. "Don't look, Brynn," she said softly. "You don't want to see that."

"What?" I asked, wanting to see even more. "What?"

Then I saw. The blanket I thought the monkey was

carrying was actually the limp body of a much smaller monkey. The larger monkey—the mother, I figured—gently pulled her lifeless child from her shoulders, laid it on the branch and poked it with one long finger. The monkey didn't move.

I gasped at what I was seeing. The mother grabbed the infant by one thin arm and swung her onto her back, only to have her slide helplessly down to her side. Still the mother persisted, prodding and lifting and shaking. Even at my young age I knew this mother was in denial, not accepting that her child was dead. "Oh," I said, tears streaming down my cheeks.

"Don't look at it," my mother said, trying to shield my eyes with one hand and pulling me away with the other. "It's too sad." Allison didn't even bother to look twice. She just wrinkled her nose in disgust and scooted ahead of us across the bridge with my father.

Nine years later, when Allison was sixteen, it was the same thing. I was the one who saw. Saw the baby with its blue lips and limp arms and her head flopping to the side. I'm the one who saw and suffered because my sister didn't want to face the fact that she'd had a baby. Still I pay for it. Still I see that baby girl, night after night in dreams, her little face pasted on the body of a dead monkey, her arms wrapped around the mother's neck, flopping uselessly against her back.

I shower and dress, knowing that I'm going to be late for my ten o'clock class. I rush down the stairs, my shoulders damp from my wet hair, pass my grandmother and say a quick goodbye. I reach into my purse for my medication and grab a bottle of water from the refrigerator. Driving toward the college, I fish out one pill, then another, swallowing them both with one gulp of water, willing the tiny beads of medicine within the capsules to travel to my brain, to carry the images of dead babies—primate and human—away from me.

Allison may have gone to jail, but I'm the one in prison and will never be free.

Allison

I did love Christopher, more than anything, and maybe a part of me still does. He was sweet and handsome and he made me feel like I was the most beautiful girl in the world. He was smart. So smart. Said he was working on his business degree, described how he was a whiz at day trading. He certainly appeared to have the money, always paying for things, flashing large bills, buying me things. After our first week together he gave me a gold bracelet that looked very expensive. As he fastened the bracelet, his fingers brushed against the thin skin on the inside of my wrist and I trembled.

"Just the bracelet," he murmured in my ear. "I want to see you wearing only the bracelet." He pulled off all my clothes. "Let me look at you, I just want to see."

I wasn't embarrassed, wasn't ashamed. There was a wildness in his eyes that scared me, but excited me, too. For the first time in my life I wasn't worrying about school or sports or my parents. I felt free and loved. I felt normal.

It wasn't until my high school adviser pulled me aside and told me I was losing my place at the top of the class rankings and was in danger of losing scholarships if I didn't start getting my act together that reality started to creep back into my life.

"Is there something going on at home?" she asked me. I assured her things were the same as they always were. "Is it a boy?"

She raised her eyebrows at my reluctance to answer. "No boy is worth it," she said sternly. "Do you really want to throw away all you've worked so hard for over a boy? Do you really want to end up staying in Linden Falls for the rest of your life?"

I did not.

"Coach Herrick is worried about you, too. Tell the boy you need to focus on your schoolwork and your sports. Tell him anything, but get your priorities straight. You have a lot riding on the next two years, Allison. Make the right choice."

The night I broke up with Christopher I told my parents I was at my friend Shauna's house, studying. Christopher drove me out into the country and we sat looking through the windshield at the stars.

"You're quiet tonight," Christopher said, fingering the bracelet on my wrist.

I took a deep breath. "My parents are getting suspicious. If they find out about us there is no way they are going to let me keep seeing you. They'll say you're way too old for me." I looked up at him through the shadows to gauge his reaction. He sat in stony silence. His fingers pulled away from my hand. I went on. "My grades are dropping. My adviser thinks I could lose scholarships if I don't—"

"What are you trying to say, Allison?" Christopher asked. His voice was cold.

"I think we should..." I paused. I was good at almost everything I'd ever done, but this was hard. "I think we should slow things down a bit. See less of each other."

"Is this what you want?" His hands were resting on the steering wheel, shoulders slumped, head down.

"I'm sorry," I said, tears burning my eyes.

"Get out," Christopher whispered.

"What?" I asked, thinking I couldn't have heard him right.

"Get out of the car," he said forcefully.

"What? You're just going to leave me here?" I asked with a nervous laugh.

He reached over my lap and pushed open the door. "Get out," he ordered.

"Christopher..."

"Out!" He gave me a shove—not hard, but still a shove. I scrambled from the car into the cold November night and he pulled the door shut with a slam and drove away.

I cried for a week and had to force myself not to call Christopher, but I quickly pulled my grades back to where they belonged. Studied harder, worked out more, became more intent on graduating at the top of my class. My teachers stopped worrying, my parents stopped worrying. It was going to be okay.

Sometimes I had to really concentrate to remember what Christopher looked like. I could picture only parts of him, his brown eyes, his upturned nose, his long, slim fingers, the way his foot would tap nervously, always in motion. I couldn't bring to mind his entire being and sometimes I wondered if he was even real, if we had ever happened.

I should have known I was pregnant. And if I'm perfectly honest with myself, the idea crossed my mind a few times in the months leading up to when I gave birth. But I didn't want to be pregnant, so the best thing for me to do—the *only* thing for me to do—was to ignore it. Otherwise, I had turned into one of *those* girls. One of those moronic, stupid girls, and as a result I had completely screwed up my entire life. I could have just killed myself and I would have, if that wouldn't have sealed my fate as becoming one of them—a helpless, weak nothing. I'd seen them walking the halls of my high school, beautifully dressed and perfectly made up. Those were the girls who spent more time picking out their outfits and putting on their makeup than doing their algebra. These girls weren't even in algebra, they took basic math and giggled up at their teacher, Mr. Dorning, who they thought was so hot.

But come on, it's pathetic, really. It took me seven months to figure it all out. The upset stomach, the bloating, the unending fatigue. I fell in love with a boy and look where it got me—a prison cell in Cravenville, and now to a halfway house.

I can't change the past. I can't undo what's been done, I can't bring back that baby girl, but I can be a good daughter again. I can be a good sister.

Claire

As the three of them approach the playground of Joshua's new school, Claire presses her fingers against the side of her head, finding the tender spot where her skull struck the floor after she fell off the ladder. It's been a week since the robbery and Joshua has awakened each night calling out for her. Though Jonathan goes to him, tries to comfort him, it's not enough. He has to see his mother, makes his father walk with him to the bedroom where his mother lies. He has to crawl into their bed, bringing his face close to hers. "You're here," he says, his sweet breath filling her nose. He says this as if it's a surprise, as if he was certain that the two thieves from the bookstore had stolen her away during the night. During the day he is fearful of having his mother out of his sight and stays near, a shadow following her about.

"Don't worry," Claire tells him, but Claire herself is apprehensive. She hasn't been able to bring herself to return to the bookstore since the robbery, relying on Virginia to keep it open for part of the day.

Jonathan pulls open the doors of the old redbrick building and a stifling heat greets them, reminding Claire of her own school days in an almost identical building just a few miles from here.

"Who's going to protect you?" Joshua asks, looking anxiously up at his mother, his eyes tired and red from another restless night. Claire and Jonathan glance at each other with worry. They've discussed taking Joshua to see someone, a doctor, a counselor. Someone who can help him with his fears.

"I'm hiring another worker for the bookstore, Joshua," Claire tells him, trying to keep her voice light. "That way I will never be alone while I am working."

"You still got hurt and I was there," he reminds them.

"We put in an alarm, Josh," Jonathan tells him. "If bad guys come, the alarm will scare the bejeezus out of them and then the police will come."

Joshua nods, his face serious. He has to think about this for a while. "What's the name of this place?" he asks for the third time this morning as they walk through the empty, quiet halls of Woodrow Wilson Elementary School.

"It's Wilson School," Jonathan tells him, and tries to take his hand. Joshua pulls away and slides his fingers into Claire's sweaty palm.

"It's so big," he says, looking around, his brown eyes woeful.

"Don't look so sad," Jonathan tells him. "You're going to love it."

"I'm not going to school," he says with a finality that Claire has come to know too well.

The Kelbys missed the school's scheduled registration day, which was held three days ago. They intended to go, had gotten in the car, had driven the five blocks, had pulled up in front of the school building. But it was all too overwhelming for Joshua. Streams of excited, rambunctious children of all ages and their families were entering and leaving the school. Josh tearfully clung to his booster seat and refused to exit the car. They left, went straight home, Joshua checking to make sure the doors were locked behind them after they went inside.

A little boy shouldn't have to think about locking doors, Claire thinks as they stop in front of a classroom. A child shouldn't have to worry about keeping his mother safe.

"You must be Joshua!" a woman coming to the doorway says in a loud but friendly tone, and Claire feels Joshua flinch beside her. "I'm Mrs. Lovelace." She holds out a hand for Joshua to shake that he shrinks shyly away from and Jonathan reaches for it instead.

"It's nice to meet you," Jonathan and Claire say in turn. Mrs. Lovelace looks to be in her fifties, which Claire takes to mean that she is a seasoned teacher. She has short no-nonsense steel-wool-gray hair and sharp blue eyes that appear to miss little. Claire searches Mrs. Lovelace's face for any indication that she might have a soft spot for timid, anxious children like Joshua who need a little more help navigating their way through the precarious world of kindergarten. "Joshua is nervous about starting school," Claire explains, resting her hand on Joshua's shoulder.

"We'll figure things out together, won't we, Joshua?" Mrs. Lovelace bends down to his level to speak to him and Joshua scurries behind Claire and presses his face into the small of her back.

"Joshua," Claire says, trying to keep her voice soft and patient, "Mrs. Lovelace is speaking to you." He wanders away from them and into the classroom toward a set of cardboard blocks, designed to look like bricks.

"Go ahead and build something, Joshua," Mrs. Lovelace tells him. "I'll visit with your mom and dad for a few minutes." Joshua looks hesitant, but after an encouraging nod from Mrs. Lovelace, he begins to methodically place the bricks side by side, one on top of the other, building a rust-red wall around him.

"Oh, Joshua, did you bring a baby picture to add to the bulletin board?" Mrs. Lovelace calls to him.

Joshua is so completely engrossed with building his wall that he doesn't seem to hear Mrs. Lovelace and Claire bites her lip with worry. "Here you go." Claire holds out a copy of the first photo she had taken of Joshua after they brought him home from the hospital. Grinning broadly, Jonathan was holding Joshua, who was staring, eyes wide and watery from a bout of crying. His bottom lip curled in an adorable pout.

"Oh, what a nice picture, Joshua," Mrs. Lovelace exclaims, walking over to Joshua's wall. "Who do you look like? Your mother or your father?"

"I'm buhdopted," Joshua says, peeking out from behind the red bricks.

Mrs. Lovelace doesn't miss a beat. "And your mom and dad picked you! How lucky they are." She steps more closely to the cardboard fortress and asks in her soothing voice, like milk being poured into a glass, "May I join you, Joshua?"

Joshua considers, and Claire sees for a fleeting moment the possibility, a faint light in his dark eyes, but it is quickly doused out and replaced with doubt.

"No, thank you," he finishes politely, placing another brick on top of his wall, completely blocking off his face from view.

Mrs. Lovelace tries again. "I see you like to build things, Joshua. I'd really like to help you." She takes away the top brick so she can see his face again.

Joshua startles and accidentally knocks down several bricks, causing the structure to collapse in a heap around him. "Oh, no!" He moans in despair at the pile in front of him.

"Oh, Joshua," Mrs. Lovelace says soothingly, "it's okay. We can put it back together. See?" Mrs. Lovelace begins to rearrange the blocks again, one on top of the other. Joshua sniffles, but begins to help rebuild the wall. In a few moments Joshua is once again safely ensconced behind the barrier.

Mrs. Lovelace leads Jonathan and Claire to a table surrounded by exceptionally small chairs and invites them to sit. "Tell me about Joshua," she says.

"Joshua is a very sweet, caring little boy, but he can get very anxious at times. Especially when he is asked to try something new," Claire admits. "Sometimes he seems like he's off in his own little world and it can be really hard for us to pull him back to us."

"That's not unusual in a kindergartener, Mrs. Kelby," Mrs. Lovelace says. "I promise to keep a close eye on him and let you know of any issues that come up."

"Joshua also had a very traumatic experience recently," Claire explains, trying to keep the tremor from her voice. Jonathan squeezes her hand. "Last week, the bookstore that we own was robbed and Josh was right there and saw everything. It scared him, and me, terribly." Claire shakes her head at the memory of the thieves and the glint of the knife in the tall boy's hand.

"The police haven't caught them," Jonathan continues, "and Joshua's very worried about not being with Claire at all times. He feels like he needs to be her protector."

Mrs. Lovelace furrows her brow with concern. "Thank you for telling me about this. Let's see how Joshua does the first few days of school and then touch base again. We can always bring in the school counselor to visit with him, if needed. All new kindergarteners have an adjustment period when starting school. Some adjustments take longer than others." She stands and walks over to where Jonathan is sitting in his fortress. "It was nice meeting you, Joshua," she says to him.

"Nice to meet you," Joshua replies, his voice barely audible.

Mrs. Lovelace turns her attention back to Claire and Jonathan. "It was nice meeting you, too, Mr. and Mrs. Kelby. If you're interested in chaperoning any of our amazing kindergarten field trips, just let me know." Her voice noticeably louder, she continues, "This fall we get to visit the fire station, the apple orchard and the pumpkin patch. In the winter we go sledding down the hill behind the school and make gingerbread houses, and in the spring we get to go on the very best trip of all!"

"Oh, what's that?" Claire says in an affected tone she reserved specifically for trying to get Joshua excited about something.

"We don't tell anyone that until the first day of school. It's just too special." The three glance covertly at Joshua. He is still sitting behind the wall, but his toes, clad in sandals, peek out, inching slowly forward.

"Hmm, I guess we'll just have to wait until then to find out. Come on, Josh," Jonathan says. "What do you say to Mrs. Lovelace for letting you play with these great blocks?"

"Thank you," comes Joshua's squeaky, timid reply.

"You are welcome, Joshua," Mrs. Lovelace says warmly. "The blocks will be here waiting for you on the first day of school."

Jonathan holds out his hand to help him up from the floor, but Joshua ignores it and scrambles to his feet on his own and moves out of the room ahead of his parents, his footfalls echoing off the newly waxed floors. He is walking slowly, head down, his shoulder hugging the painted cement wall.

"Oh, Josh," Claire whispers, knowing he can't hear her. "It's going to be okay."

Allison

I'm nervous about my upcoming interview at the bookstore. I've never had a real job—I never had time when I was in high school. Oh, we practiced interviews in Cravenville and Olene did a mock interview with me last night. But I'm still sick with worry. I'm not sure why the owner of the bookstore would want to hire a convict, but she's giving me a chance. Olene told me that there are some pretty good tax incentives for businesses who hire people like me.

"Does she know what I went to prison for?" I ask Olene before I leave. Bookends is only a few blocks from Gertrude House and if I get the job I'll be able to easily walk back and forth to work.

"She knows the basics," Olene explains, "but she wants to help, plus it helps that the government is footing the bill for your paycheck."

"How do I look," I ask, holding out my arms and spinning around. I dressed up, borrowing an outfit from Bea. The skirt is a bit too short, the sleeves stop just above my wrists and the shoes pinch my feet, but I look somewhat professional and I hope to make a good impression. I need to go to my parents' house and retrieve some of my old clothes, but I haven't been able to get ahold of them just yet. My father travels a lot for work and my mother has all her projects and causes. They're very busy people.

"You look just fine," Olene tells me. "You sure you don't want a ride?"

"No, thanks, I don't mind walking," I say. I have a newfound appreciation for being able to step outside whenever I want to, for being able to feel the sun warm my face, the night air on my skin.

I arrive at Bookends just after it opens. I see the woman I assume is Mrs. Kelby through the window. She is smiling at something one of her customers has said as she slides the purchase into a paper bag stamped with the store's name on the front of it. I study my reflection in the window. Then I take a deep breath and push open the door.

"Hi," I say with more confidence than I actually feel, while I walk up to her. The woman is tall, but not as tall as I am. She is solid, strong and fit-looking, with olive skin and thick golden-brown hair that hangs loose around her shoulders. She wears a chunky, hip pair of glasses with tortoiseshell frames. "My name is Allison Glenn," I say, reaching out to shake her hand, just like I practiced. "I'm here to interview for the part-time position." This was where things got tricky. Do I remind her that my parole officer helped set this up? Do I bring up my past? Olene and I discussed the pros and cons of being the first to mention my conviction. I'm still not sure what to do.

Mrs. Kelby smiles at me. A real, genuine smile. Not the kind that looks like it has been spackled on with a trowel. A good sign. "Allison," she says. "Thank you for coming in. It's nice to meet you. Have a seat and we can chat. I'm sorry if we get interrupted, but we're a little shorthanded around here."

We sit and I cross my legs, fold my hands in my lap and wait for the first question.

"Why don't you start by telling me a little bit about yourself?"

"Well, I'm twenty-one years old," I begin nervously. "When I was in high school, I was a straight-A student and a member of the National Honor Society..." I stop. My voice is high and I must sound ridiculous. Mrs. Kelby is looking at me expectantly. I take a deep breath. "Mrs. Kelby, I would really like to work for you. I've made some terrible mistakes in the past, mistakes that won't ever happen again." I lean forward and look her straight in the eyes. "I'm starting over and I would be so grateful if you..." My chin begins to wobble and tears fill my eyes. "If you just gave me one chance."

Mrs. Kelby is quiet for a moment and looks at me, her face impossible to read.

"You know, Allison, I think this might work out well for the both of us. Olene thinks highly of you and I could really use the help." Mrs. Kelby smiles and there is such kindness in her eyes. A kindness I haven't seen in a very long time.

I clear my throat and quickly brush away the tears. "Thank you," I say with relief.

"Great," she says brightly, and stands. "Can you start the day after tomorrow? Come in at nine and stay until four or so?"

I nod. "That will be great. Thank you, thank you so much!" I reach out to shake her hand again and she takes it without hesitation.

"You're welcome. This is a great place to work. You'll get to meet my little boy tomorrow, too. His name is Joshua."

"I look forward to it. And, Mrs. Kelby," I say, emotion threatening to spill over again, "I'm going to do a really good job for you. You won't be sorry."

I catch myself practically skipping back to Gertrude House. I want to tell someone about my job interview. Want someone to feel the same excitement I do. But the only person I can imagine calling is Brynn.

For years, I've kept having this dream—a nightmare, really—even before I went to jail. The same dream over and over again. It's not what you'd imagine someone like me would be dreaming about…you'd think babies and rivers. No, you'd be surprised. In my dream I'm at home, studying for the SATs. I'm bent over my books and writing furiously in my notebook when an alarm goes off. This is it. It's time. I need to go take the tests. I carefully place my books and notebooks in my book bag and I sharpen seven number-two pencils. They have to be number-two pencils; it has to do with the computer being able to read the answer sheets. I calmly walk to my bedroom door. I'm ready, I'm confident that I'm going to ace these tests. My hand reaches for the door-knob. It doesn't turn.

I try and try to twist it, but nothing. I'm locked in. Panicking, I go to the window and try to lift it open; it's stuck, too. Air gets locked in my chest—I can't breathe. I have to get out of my room; I have to go take that test. I pound on the door, calling for my mother,

my father, my sister, anyone to let me out. I return to
the window and knock on it, trying to get the attention
of those down below. No one notices. I beat harder on
the window with my hands. My fingers are tingling and
cold from lack of oxygen; I see them turning blue. I'm
dying. I need to break the window and in desperation
I begin to strike my head against the glass. It shivers
and cracks. I feel the blood warm and wet on my forehead. It doesn't matter. Again I smash my head against
the window and again it cracks a bit more. It doesn't
hurt and the need to escape takes over everything else.
Over and over I pound and pound my head, until I can't
see through the blood and I can feel the little slivers of
glass in my skin.

Then I'd wake, in my bedroom or in my cell, drenched
in sweat but shivering from cold.

I don't give up. Ever. I'm going to get Brynn to talk
to me, no matter what it takes.

Claire

Joshua's first day of school starts out hopefully. Since his visit to the classroom and meeting Mrs. Lovelace, Joshua did not balk about going to kindergarten. In fact, he seems excited.

He frets over what he is going to wear and finally settles on a plain red T-shirt and his favorite pair of khaki shorts. "You look very nice, Joshua," Claire tells him. He smiles and rocks proudly back and forth in his new tennis shoes.

Claire isn't prepared for the sight of hundreds of children lingering outside its doors, waiting for the bell to ring. "Organized chaos," she says, and looks back at Joshua, who is staring, mesmerized, at the crowd.

"Wow," Jonathan mutters. "What do we do? Do we just drop him off and send him into…that?"

"No, we can walk him in," Claire says. "Let's wait, though, until the bell rings and most of the kids are in."

"I'm not going in there," Joshua calls fearfully from the backseat. "Let's go home."

"It'll be okay," Jonathan says soothingly. "Let's do a backpack check."

"I don't want to," Joshua says again, the anxiety building in his voice.

"Come on, buddy, let's go through your gear, make sure you've got enough crayons." Item by item, Jonathan and Joshua search through his backpack, making sure that he has all the supplies he needs to start school. Claire smiles at the two of them, heads bent over the school supplies. By the time they are finished the bell has rung and all but a few students are still milling outside the building.

"Look now, Josh," Claire tells him. "See? All the other kids went inside. You can't be late for your first day of kindergarten. It looks like you're all set." Together the three make their way to the front entrance of the building. Joshua walks slowly, dragging his feet. When they stop just in front of Mrs. Lovelace's classroom, Joshua peeks inside, wistfully watching the mostly happy din of twenty kindergarteners beginning their first day of school. He looks up at his parents, his lips twitching nervously.

"I'm off, then," he says, like the forty-two-year-old soul in a five-year-old body that he is. "I'll see you later, after kindergarten." Sadness tinges his voice and Claire feels her heart breaking. She scoops him up into a tight hug. Grabbing the bulging, heavy book bag from Jonathan, Joshua steps cautiously into the classroom as if meeting an untimely demise. Claire bites her cheeks, trying to keep the tears from coming. Why does everything have to be so hard for Joshua?

Claire hooks her arm through Jonathan's and they watch Joshua sidle into the classroom where Mrs.

Lovelace greets him and helps him find his cubby. "Look at him go," Claire whispers.

"Yeah, look at him go," Jonathan agrees.

The two stand in the doorway of Joshua's class-room until Mrs. Lovelace gives them the thumbs-up and shoos them politely away. As they walk to the car, Claire turns back several times to look at the building, half expecting Joshua to come dashing out, begging her not to leave him. She knows she shouldn't be, but she is a little sad. Joshua is never going to need her in quite the same way again. Other people, teachers and friends, will fill his life. And that's a good thing, she tells her-self. She wants to be happy that the morning had gone so smoothly, that he had walked into the classroom on his own accord with no major meltdowns, but Claire isn't exactly happy. Relieved maybe, but definitely not happy. "He'll be fine," Jonathan says as he reaches for his wife's hand.

"I know," Claire answers stiffly, settling herself into the passenger seat of the car. "I just can't believe he's actually in kindergarten. First, I didn't really think this day would ever come, and second, I didn't think it would go so well. I guess I tired myself out fretting about it so much."

"Let's go get some breakfast," Jonathan says sud-denly.

"Oh, I can't," Claire protests. "I've got to open the store, I'm running late as it is," she says, checking the clock on the dashboard. Eight-fifty. Ten minutes until opening time.

"Let's swing by the house, then," he whispers sug-gestively, sliding his hand between her thighs.

"Jonathan!" Claire laughs, pushing his hand away. "I don't have time."

"Come on, how often do we get the house to ourselves?" he asks, placing his hand back on her knee.

"Really?" Claire asks, surprised at Jonathan's impulsiveness.

"Yes, really," he says, sliding his hand up her shirt.

Claire gently kisses the soft skin below his jaw and turns his face toward her, kissing him and running her tongue along his lower lip. A sense of longing enters her. Sweet and nameless.

"Please," she whispers in his ear. "Take me home."

Brynn

When I finally get to school, I see Missy standing with a group of girls at a coffee kiosk. She looks right through me. When I come up to her, she says hello but immediately returns to her conversation with the other girls. It is as if I don't even exist.

The boy from the party must have told her about me. About Allison.

So this is the way it's going to be. Just like Linden Falls.

At first I didn't think anything could be worse than not having Allison at home anymore. The house was so empty, so quiet. In the days just following Allison's arrest, I made the mistake of going into her bedroom and lying on her bed, wrapping myself in her comforter and pressing her pillow against my face so I could breathe in the imprint of her scent. Allison's trophies and awards were beginning to gather dust but still gleamed with her lost potential.

My father found me in Allison's room, sitting on her bed, fingering her blue ribbons. For a moment I thought he might come in and sit down next to me. How I wanted him to pull me close and tell me everything was going to be all right. I wanted him to hold my hand in his and ask me about the night that Allison gave birth. I wanted to tell him how I was there, how I wiped her forehead and encouraged her to push and held her baby girl in my arms. But on Allison's orders, I'd told my parents and the police that I was in my room listening to my iPod, that I never heard a thing. I wanted to talk to my father about these things, but he just stood in the doorway and looked at me, deep disappointment on his face. And I knew then that I would never, ever be the person my parents wanted me to be. The next day, when I tried to go into Allison's bedroom, I found the door locked. My parents didn't even find me worthy enough to sit among my sister's things.

My parents wandered around the house in a daze. My mother cried all the time; my father worked longer hours, sometimes not coming home until late into the night. Dinner was a silent nightmare. Without Allison, there was nothing to talk about. No discussions about volleyball games or college plans. The few friends I had rarely called. I didn't blame them really. What was there to say? My friend Jessie tried. She called and stopped over, tried to be cheerful, tried to get me to go to football games and movies, but I felt numb and lost. I was a junior at Linden Falls High School. Allison would have been a senior. I learned to ignore the stares and the whispers as I passed in the hallways.

It wasn't until the first progress report of the school year was sent home that my parents were spurred into action. I was barely passing my classes and was failing gym. The minute the letter hit the mailbox, my parents had me in the principal's office. Mrs. Buckley was this crazy, energetic principal who prowled the hallways of the high school making sure that students were behaving the way they were supposed to be. She was married to her job, staying at school late into the night and arriving early in the morning. She was strict, could be sarcastic and gruff, but she knew each and every one of the students at Linden Falls High School.

"Why didn't anyone tell us that Brynn was failing?" my mother demanded angrily. "This is absolutely unacceptable."

"Mrs. Glenn," Mrs. Buckley said. "We did send letters. We called. There was no response."

My mother sent me a searing look. "I didn't see any letters. I didn't get any phone calls. Did you?" she asked my father, and he shook his head wearily.

"We are all very worried about you, Brynn," Mrs. Buckley said, addressing me for the first time. "We know this has been a very difficult time for you and your family and we want to help you." I slunk lower into my chair and didn't say anything. "If you'd like to talk to someone, we can certainly arrange that."

"She doesn't need to talk to someone," my mother said impatiently. "She needs to get focused and start studying."

"We'll get Brynn a tutor," my father added. "We'll get things turned around. It has been a difficult time, but nothing we can't handle."

"Sometimes," Mrs. Buckley began carefully, "having an outside resource to help work—"

"We don't need an *outside resource*," my mother said

sharply, standing. "From now on, I'd like weekly reports from each of Brynn's teachers on her progress. We'll arrange for a tutor for her. Thank you for your time." She turned on her heel and stormed out of Mrs. Buckley's office, with my father and me following behind.

As promised, I did get a tutor. Every day after school, for ninety minutes, a local college student from St. Anne's came over to our house and we would sit at the kitchen table, reviewing algebra equations and Spanish vocabulary. My tutor, a boring philosophy major with zero personality, was relentless. While she was very good at explaining things so I could understand them, she was impatient, clucking her tongue and snapping her fingers at me when my mind wandered.

Eventually, my grades improved to all Bs and a C in gym. I graduated smack-dab in the middle of my class and the day after graduation my mother enrolled me for summer courses at St. Anne's College.

I tried, I really did. But whenever I stepped into the classroom an overwhelming feeling of dread would wash over me. My chest would tighten and the pounding of my heart would thump in my ears. I rarely lasted more than five minutes in the classroom and then I would run.

I had been so hopeful the day I turned eighteen. I had planned on telling my parents that I was going to drop out of St. Anne's and get a job working with a local veterinarian. It didn't pay much, but it was a start. We had just come home from celebrating my birthday with dinner at a restaurant and were eating cake and ice cream when I saw the letter on the kitchen counter. My pleasure at having a halfway nice evening with my parents dissolved. It had been more than two years since Allison was arrested and even though my parents rarely spoke of her, there were always reminders. Her beautiful face beamed at me from photos that still held a major spot in the house. Allison's letter stared up at me and my earlier resolve left me. It didn't matter that Allison was in jail; it didn't matter that she would be locked up for eight more years. She was always *there*.

I left my plate of cake and ice cream on the table, next to the letter from Allison, and went upstairs to my bedroom. I stared at my mother's bottle of sleeping pills for several hours until I finally got up the nerve to twist off the cap and pour the capsules into my hand. They were smaller than I thought they would be, and I had to smile at the thought that something so lightweight could end the pain. I left no note. What would I say? I'm sorry I'm not my sister? That I was tired of tiptoeing around the edges of my world trying to please everyone, but pleasing no one, especially myself? That I still couldn't get the vision of that baby girl's soft bluish skin out of my mind, of her tiny fingers and toes, and that haunted me more than anything?

I swallowed the pills one by one. As I laid each one on my tongue it was like a communion of the wrongs I felt were done against me. Never smart enough, never pretty enough, never athletic enough—never, ever enough. I buried myself under my covers to die. Briefly, before I drifted off to sleep, I wondered if my parents would miss me. I didn't think so. Their grief in losing Allison had consumed them.

I think I would have been successful in killing myself if my mother hadn't come in search of her sleeping pills. She found me unconscious in bed, the pill bottle next to me. When I awoke I was in the emergency room, having my stomach pumped. After a few days I was on my way to New Amery to live with my grandmother.

A year later, I thought that things were going so much better. That all I needed to do was to keep Allison away from me, my parents away from me, forget the past, focus on the future. I was wrong.

I have a class at noon but I climb back into my car and drive back home. My grandma isn't around. Milo looks at me hopefully, wanting to go for a walk. Instead, I go to the cabinet above the refrigerator where my grandmother keeps her alcohol. I know it's stupid, I know I shouldn't do it, but I pull down a bottle, grab a tall glass and fill it to the rim with the sweet-smelling red wine. My stomach is still upset from last night's drinking, but I don't care. I want to go back to those few wonderful minutes when I thought I was just another college girl with friends, with the possibility of a cute boy being interested in me, when no one knew my past.

I take the bottle and go into my bedroom. I sit on my bed, take a big swallow of wine from the glass and wait. Wait for the effect of the alcohol's smooth warmth to spread to my legs, my fingertips. Wait for it to numb my thoughts. It was stupid, really. To think that I could start over.

Claire

As Claire watches Allison leave after the interview, she is struck at the lightness in her step. When she had first entered the store, Allison looked downtrodden and weighted with her history, though she was trying to stand tall and appear confident. Allison Glenn seems like a nice girl, despite her past. Everyone needs a second chance. Claire firmly believes this. If she and Jonathan had been given only one chance at parenthood, Joshua would never have come into their lives.

It was a bitter cold January night seven years earlier, just one week after they had received their foster parent license, when Dana had called Jonathan and Claire. A three-year-old girl had been found wandering down on Drake Street at midnight. She wasn't wearing a hat or coat, couldn't tell the group of college boys who found her outside the bar nearby where her home was, whom she belonged to. The boys called the police and the Department of Human Services stepped in and called them. "We'll be right there," Jonathan told Dana. He didn't ask Claire if she wanted to take in a child. He knew. Claire wanted a child more than anything. It didn't matter if the child was a boy or girl, how old she was, where she came from, the color of her skin. It didn't matter. And Claire knew that Jonathan just wanted to hold a small beating heart next to his and tell the child over and over that everything was going to be all right.

It *was* right for a long time and then it wasn't. Ella's mother, Nicki, a twenty-year-old part-time college student, had been drinking and doing drugs in her apartment with her friends the night that Ella wandered away. Nicki didn't even know that Ella was missing until nearly twelve hours later, when she had sobered up enough to realize that Ella wasn't in the apartment.

That morning when Claire and Jonathan went to the hospital where Ella was being checked over for any signs of frostbite or abuse, Dana explained to Ella that she would be coming home with the Kelbys for a while. Ella just looked up at them in confusion. "Where's my mom?" she asked over and over again. "I want my mom." She didn't throw a fit when she was placed in their car but looked out the window, twisting her head as they passed people walking along the street, as if she was looking for someone. Once they pulled up to the front of the house, Ella seemed to figure out that she wasn't going home anytime soon. Her tired eyes filled with tears and she began to shake and shiver so much that her teeth kept clanking together. She just couldn't seem to get warm.

"It's okay, Ella," Claire told her as she wrapped her in a big blanket and set her on the sofa. "Are you hungry?"

Ella didn't say anything at first, her eyes fixed on the strangers' puppy, who was snuffling at her feet.

"That's Truman," Jonathan told Ella. "He's a bulldog. We just got him last week."

"He bite me?" she asked in her surprisingly gruff voice.

"No," Claire reassured her. "He's a good dog. Do you want to pet him?"

Ella pinched her lips together and closed her eyes as if deep in thought. After a moment she opened her eyes and looked up at Claire and took a deep breath, as if mustering all her courage.

"He won't bite," Jonathan promised as he lifted Truman onto the cushion beside her. "He might slobber on you, but he won't bite."

She tentatively reached out a plump little hand and swept it quickly across Truman's head and giggled. She did this over and over, a fast pat and a laugh, until Jonathan and Claire were laughing with her. Truman looked at each of them in turn with an expression that let it be known he was simply tolerating the lot of them. Twenty minutes later, Ella had fallen asleep, her face buried in Truman's neck. Jonathan and Claire just sat there watching, falling in love with her.

It wasn't long before Claire considered Ella hers. She knew it was dangerous, thinking this way. Knew that she really had no true claim to call Ella her own. But she loved that little girl. Loved her as if she had been the one to carry her in her own, scarred womb for nine months. Ella was the most beautiful child she had ever seen, with her big brown eyes that could in one minute be full of mischief and in the next be filled with tears.

She called Jonathan "Dad" right away, although she seemed to miss her mother terribly.

It was obvious that Nicki wanted her daughter back, but didn't quite have the skills to pull it all together. She was defiant and argumentative with her caseworker, showed up late to supervised visits and case facilitation meetings. She kept blowing it, and try as she might, Claire couldn't understand it. How, *how* could someone possibly not move heaven and earth to be with this amazing miracle of a child? Still, during supervised visits, Nicki got right down on the floor with Ella and insinuated herself seamlessly back into her life. Seeing Nicki with Ella filled Claire with jealousy, although she was ashamed to admit it. They would look at each other and smile and touch like they'd been together forever. Claire would watch Nicki cup her palm gently around Ella's plump cheek and Claire imagined that Nicki once cradled her swollen belly the same way when she was pregnant. It was such an intimate, protective, possessive gesture that Claire would have to turn away; it hurt to look at them.

Jonathan and Claire had Ella with them for just over a year. Jonathan didn't think that Nicki would be able to make the necessary changes to actually earn Ella back, but she did. Claire still remembers the stark, naked look of disbelief on his face when they made the final handoff that February. It was a frigid afternoon, much like the night when Ella had come to them, but now she was more than adequately dressed in the puffy lavender parka with matching hat and gloves that they had bought her. Her brown eyes flashed excitedly up at them. "I get to go see Mommy?" Ella asked over and over.

"Yes, Bella Ella," Claire said, using their pet name

for her. *Beautiful Ella.* "But this time you get to stay with your mommy for..." She couldn't bring herself to say forever. Who knew, Claire thought, she might make another mistake and Ella might return to them, though she didn't truly believe that. Nicki really wanted Ella back. "For a very long time," Claire finished. Ella carefully thought about this before responding.

"Dad is coming," she stated. It wasn't a question. A soft hitch erupted from Jonathan's throat and Claire bit back her own tears.

"No, Dad's not coming," Claire told her, trying to keep her voice cheerful. It was the least she could do, she thought. Why send her own distress along on this journey with Ella? "You get to go live with your mommy, Ella," Claire said for perhaps the hundredth time. "Isn't that exciting?"

"Yessirree, it is," Ella agreed. "But Dad's coming, and you, too, Mama Claire," she insisted.

"No, Ella. Not this time," Claire said. Next to her in the driver's seat, she heard Jonathan sniff and she placed her hand on his knee. When they arrived at Dana's office, Jonathan unhooked Ella from the car seat and emerged from the car holding her tightly to his chest, trying to protect her from the cold wind. Claire realized then what a mistake this had been. She thought they would be able to handle the transition. They had done what they had said they would. For one year she and Jonathan sheltered, clothed, fed and showed genuine affection for Ella. Loved her. And now they had to give her back. Back to a woman who had allowed her little girl to wander the streets all alone in the middle of the night, who would rather drink and party with her friends than spend hours reveling in the glory that was Ella, as they had. The cold air scoured at Claire's cheeks as they made their way inside the Department of Human Services building, the place they had always brought Ella to visit with her mother.

"Ella, you get on over here and give me a kiss goodbye." Claire forced a light note into her voice.

"Goodbye, Mama Claire," Ella chirped as she trotted over. She kissed her stoutly on the lips and Claire gathered her up into a tight hug.

"I love you, Bella Ella," Claire squeaked, tears falling freely.

"Bye, Dad," Ella said as she slipped from her grip toward Jonathan. "See you later, alligator," she quipped as she held tight to Jonathan's leg. Jonathan stood still for a moment and Claire watched helplessly as he struggled with what to do next, his chest rising and falling heavily.

"See you later, alligator," Ella repeated forcefully.

Jonathan sank to his knees and, with a smile that didn't reach his eyes, responded, "After a while, crocodile."

Ella giggled at the familiar game. "See you soon, you big baboon." She wrapped her arms around Jonathan and nuzzled her face into his neck.

"I love you, Ella. Always remember that, okay?" Jonathan croaked so piteously that Claire had to shut her eyes to it.

"Love you back." Ella pulled away from Jonathan and turned back to Nicki. "Let's go, Mommy. Let's go. Bye, Mama Claire, bye, Dad."

"Come on, Ella," Dana said. "Let's go put your bags in your mom's car." And before she could blink Ella had already left them behind.

Claire and Jonathan walked away from Ella, hand

in hand, and drove home in silence. The house already seemed so empty, abandoned. Even Truman didn't know what to make of it. He sniffed at corners and wandered warily from room to room, searching for Ella.

Claire remembered that they tried to make love that night. They undressed each other tentatively, a shirt pulled gently over a head, pants unzipped and lowered. They stood naked in the middle of their darkened bedroom, the frost on the windows, lacy shades concealing them from the street below, Jonathan's calloused fingers catching on the tender skin on the inside of her thigh. Claire's lips brushed his neck, lingering on the rough spot just below his chin that he missed shaving. In the end they stopped, grief and exhaustion dropping their hands to their sides. Claire laid her head on Jonathan's shoulder and he rested his cheek on her head. The house was quiet, too quiet. The realization that they had nothing to listen for anymore. No worries that Ella might crawl from her bed and toddle to their bedroom door, standing on tiptoe to turn the burnished brass doorknob and throw the door open to Claire and Jonathan in various states of nakedness. Ella's little cartoon voice would come from the shadows. "Whatcha doin? Can I come in?" And they would hastily pull themselves together and she would clamber in between them.

Standing there, the dark sitting heavily on their shoulders, Claire felt Jonathan's first tear as it slid hotly down her temple and along her cheek. Claire resisted the urge to brush it away as she tracked its journey down the length of her body, from her collarbone, between the swell of her breasts, until it finally plopped onto her toes. Claire took Jonathan's hand and led him to the bed. Gently, she pulled on his boxers and slid a thick pair of woolen socks onto each chilled foot. She drew an old T-shirt over his head and threaded his arms through each sleeve. All the while Jonathan cried silently. "I know," Claire said over and over. "I know." She pulled the covers up to his chin and crawled unclothed into bed next to him. Jonathan's sleep was fitful and restless. Claire didn't sleep at all.

For a long time Claire couldn't talk about Ella. She would remember last Halloween, when they had Ella, and how she dressed up as a princess in a shimmery silver gown and little plastic high heels that she ditched after a block. "These things are killer bees," she said, kicking them off her feet. Or how they would find her curled up alongside Truman on his round fleece dog bed, the two of them breathing heavily in sleep, foreheads touching. Sometimes she would see a wisp of a smile emerge on Jonathan's face, just for a moment before it would fall away, and knew he was thinking of Ella, too.

They tried to start over, tried more fertility treatments and talked about beginning the process of trying to adopt. They had set their hopes on Ella. And there they were again, an empty womb and empty-handed. Childless.

But less than a year later, Joshua came to them. He's ours, Claire thought. Forever. She was given a second chance at motherhood.

Now she feels the need to do the same for someone else. Claire will give Allison Glenn that second chance. A new start, a new beginning. A new life.

Charm

Charm is running late at the hospital. When she tries to call Gus to let him know she'll be home as soon as she can, there is no answer. He seemed fine when she left him this morning. She had talked with him at noon and though he sounded tired, he requested mashed potatoes for supper. Charm keeps punching the redial button as she drives, but still there is no answer. She pulls up in front of the house and comes to a screeching stop, wrenches open the car door and finds a pile of Gus's gardening tools lying on the ground next to his flower beds. "Gus!" she calls out in desperation as she opens the back door. "Gus! Are you okay?" Charm makes her way through the small house, throws open the door to his bedroom and there she finds him fast asleep in his bed. His chest rising and falling, rattling noisily.

Charm retreats quietly back into the living room and sinks down on the sofa. It's the same couch they had when Charm moved in. The cushions sag and the blue-

and-green plaid fabric is worn and faded. But it's comfortable and smells like home. She is so tired. So tired of worrying about Gus and school. She lies down on the couch and pulls an afghan over her and closes her eyes. She is only twenty-one and feels ancient, like her bones are brittle, like gray hairs are springing up from her follicles. The phone rings and she's too tired to rise from the couch. Let the answering machine pick it up, she tells herself, save your strength.

"Just checking in with you." Her mother's voice fills the room. She sounds very innocent, very motherly. But over the years Charm has learned that there is nothing innocent in what her mother says or does. Reanne rambles on a bit more about her job and Binks. Remarkably, they are still an item. She signs off with an invitation to dinner the next week. "I've got to work the next four nights, but Binks and I are both off on Monday evening. We'd love for you to come over and have dinner with us. Nothing fancy."

Charm considers picking up the phone before her mother hangs up in order to get the conversation over with, but decides not to. If everything is normal—at least, normal for her family—Reanne won't call back. But if she has a less than pure motive, she will call back within the next twenty-four hours. Almost instantly the phone rings again. Afraid that the ringing will wake up Gus, Charm picks it up.

"Charmie," her mother says sweetly.

"Hi, Mom," she answers, trying to match her enthusiasm.

"I just called and you didn't pick up the phone." She sounds wounded.

"I'm sorry, I just got home. I haven't even had a

chance to check the messages." Charm tries to sound sincere.

"Listen, can you come on over for dinner on Monday night?" Reanne asks.

"Oh, huh," she says, stalling for time. "Let me just go check my schedule at the hospital. My hours have been crazy there." Charm sets down the phone, walks over to the refrigerator and pulls out a can of soda. She pops the top, takes a long drink and walks slowly back to the phone. "Mom, hey, I'm sorry. It looks like I'm on at the hospital. I start my rotation on the mental health floor. Maybe another time." Charm stifles a burp with the back of her hand.

"Check your schedule, what night are you free?" her mother persists.

"I've got a pretty busy next few weeks. How about over Thanksgiving?" Charm suggests.

She considers this. "That's two months away. I was really hoping to see you. It's been too long. Plus I have some good news to share with you."

Don't ask, don't ask, Charm says silently. "What is it?" she says, despite herself.

"No, you'll just have to wait," she says tauntingly. "Now tell me a night that works for you, and Binks and I will make it fit our schedules." *See how flexible I'm being and how rigid you are?* her tone suggests.

"Okay, then, how about tonight?" Charm throws right back at her.

"Tonight? But that's such short notice."

"I'm free tonight, Mom," Charm tells her patiently. "After then, I'm pretty booked for the next three weeks."

"Well, all right, then," she says, annoyed.

"What can I bring?" Charm asks, surprised that her mother truly wants to see her.

"How about dessert? Come by at about seven or so. I've got a lot to do to get ready." She sounds excited, like a little girl preparing for her birthday party.

"Mom, it's just me. You don't have to do anything fancy," Charm tells her.

"Nonsense. I don't get to see enough of you as it is. I want tonight to be special."

That's the thing about her mom, Charm thinks. She says these amazingly simple, sweet things, and you can tell she means them. It throws Charm off every time. Still, she gathers her mother's words up like smooth, shiny pebbles and tucks them away for later, to be pulled out and admired, mused over.

"Oh, and before I forget," she says, "your brother called. Did Gus tell you?"

"He mentioned something," Charm says offhandedly.

"He was talking very strangely. Said he had to tell me something about you. Do you know what he was talking about?"

"No." It's all she can manage to say once her heart starts to beat again.

"See you at seven, sweetie."

Charm stands there, holding the dead phone, trying not to cry, when Gus comes into the room. He looks rested and his skin is almost a healthy pink.

Guiltily, she tells him about dinner at her mother's.

"Of course you should go, Charm," he tells her. "She's your mother. You should spend time with her."

"You're a lot more fun," Charm assures him. "And nicer."

"Maybe so," he says, pressing a handkerchief to his lips and coughing. "But I'm not going to be around forever."

"Gus," Charm says warningly.

But he smiles and pats her on the head. "Go and see your mother," he orders, and Charm feels like she's ten years old again.

Claire

After Claire's interview with Allison, the day passes slowly and every time the bell on the door jangles her heart skips a beat. She wonders if she'll ever feel safe in her own store again, despite the security system and the additional help. Every few minutes she checks the clock, watching the door for Jonathan and Joshua to come running in. She wishes she'd made arrangements for Virginia to work so she could have gone with Jonathan to pick Joshua up from school.

Finally, Jonathan and Joshua breeze through the front door at three-thirty. Jonathan is grinning broadly and Joshua looks exhausted. His fine hair is rumpled, his shirt is untucked; there is a stain on his shorts and his shoelaces are untied.

"Hey, kindergartener!" Claire greets him. "How was your first day?"

"Josh had a great day!" Jonathan exclaims, and Claire feels a rush of relief course through her.

"Of course you did," she says, pulling Joshua into a tight hug.

"I did," Joshua says with a ghost of a smile pulling at the corners of his mouth. "I got to play with the blocks *and* I got to swing during both recesses!"

"Jackpot!" Claire matches his enthusiasm. "Did you find out what field trip you're going on next spring?"

"The zoo!" he shouts. "We get to go to the zoo and see the elephants and monkeys!" Joshua bends down, arms akimbo, and morphs his face into his best monkey impression and chatters, scuttling around the store. Jonathan and Claire look at each other and laugh. After Joshua makes his rounds through the store, he comes back to where they stand at the checkout counter and, as if unloading a deep, dark secret, blurts out, "There were bananas, though."

"We talked about this, Josh," Jonathan tells him. "We told you there would be some things at school that you didn't like. Do you remember what we told you to do?"

"Say 'no thank you,'" Joshua says sadly. "But it didn't work. The passer-outer kid still gave me one. I didn't plug my nose and I almost threw up," he admits. "But I didn't—I swallowed it back down."

"You did fine, Joshua," Claire tells him. She holds her hand, palm down, at Joshua's height and he steps directly under her spread fingers. She firmly rubs his head, his hair like satin under her fingertips. She can feel each slope and bump in his skull, has memorized them as she would a map. This area here, just above his left ear, she imagines, was where he stores his love for music. He is very particular about his music, as he is with most things. Nothing loud and pulsing—that agitates him, causing him to cover his ears and retreat either into another room or into himself. He likes soft, soothing music.

She feels the top of his head, just where his cowlick swirls his yellow hair into a stubborn peak. This is where the ideas for his buildings take shape. He can spend hours constructing huge, gravity-defying structures from Legos or Lincoln Logs. His bedroom is strewn with the nubby pieces and periodically they find the brightly colored plastic amid Truman's droppings in the backyard.

She moves her fingers slightly south on Joshua's head to the small bulge just above the tender groove behind his right ear. This is where he has amassed all of his memories from the time before he came to them. Before he was theirs. Here, she thinks, could be where his stockpile of grief and fear lies, stagnant and festering, manifesting itself through Joshua's shyness, his frequent trips into himself and phobias. Claire kneads that little knob, trying to massage it out of him until he wriggles away from her, saying, "Don't." As if admonishing her for trying to take away the only things his first mother had given him. She must have loved him in her own way, Claire thinks, and he is trying to hold on to it as tightly as he can.

"We need to celebrate," Jonathan announces. "What would you like for supper, Josh?"

"Pizza," Joshua answers immediately. "Pizza at Casanova's," he says with finality.

"Pizza, it is. Why don't you go in the back and get a snack to tide you over until Virginia and Shelby get here." Claire holds out her arms. Joshua leaps into them for a brief hug and she lowers him to the floor and he trots away, his shoelaces slapping against the hardwood floor.

"Whew," Claire says to Jonathan after Joshua is out of earshot.

"Whew is right," Jonathan agrees. "One day down, about two hundred left to go."

"Maybe everything will be okay," Claire says hopefully, wrapping her arms around Jonathan's middle.

"He'll be just fine. Try not to worry. Listen, I gotta go," Jonathan tells her, planting a kiss firmly on her lips. "I'll stop by at five-thirty and we can go to Casanova's."

After helping Joshua make peanut butter cracker sandwiches and pouring him a glass of milk from the small refrigerator kept in the storeroom, Claire goes back out front to wait on customers. After the break-in, she doesn't want anyone to have to work in the store alone. She knows that it will be more expensive having the extra staff, but with the tax breaks provided by the state for employing a parolee, it can be done. She really needs another part-time worker, anyway; with the revitalization of Linden Falls's downtown area, there has been a surge of foot traffic along Sullivan Street and the other historic streets that run parallel to the Druid. One of the high school students that has worked at the store the past three years is heading off to college. The other, Shelby, is sweet but active in school activities and can only work a few evenings a week. Virginia, the retired woman who works most weekends, will be heading to Florida for the winter.

Claire really hopes that things work out with Allison Glenn. Olene Jurgison didn't give her the exact details about Allison's past, but Claire has known Olene for years through the Linden Falls Downtown District Organization. They've worked on fundraisers and civic activities together and every once in a while Olene recommends one of the residents from her halfway house. Claire has always said no, until now.

* * *

At five Jonathan pulls up in front of Bookends and Joshua and Claire say goodbye to Virginia and Shelby. Casanova's is only a few blocks from the store and they walk hand in hand down the street. The early September sun is just beginning to soften, the way it does when the summer is fading into autumn.

Jonathan and Claire settle into a booth while Joshua trots off to join a group of children who have gathered to watch pizza dough being rolled out and tossed behind a Plexiglas window. "It doesn't make sense to me to hire an ex-con as a form of security," Jonathan comments when Claire tells him about hiring Allison Glenn.

"I know, I know," Claire concedes. "But Olene highly recommends this girl. Says she's very bright and has a real future in front of her."

"What'd she do? I mean, do you really want Joshua hanging around some girl who has been in prison?" he asks.

"I don't know the specifics," she admits. "Just that she was convicted of a serious crime, but she was released early for good behavior. Part of the deal is that she gets to have a fresh start, without the baggage of her past. But Olene reassured me that she doesn't have a history of violence and she's not considered a threat by the state." Claire sees the look of doubt on Jonathan's face. "I know," she says again. "It doesn't make sense, but I've got a good feeling about her. Joshua would never be in the store unless I was there with him. At least meet her. Please."

Jonathan sighs. "Okay. I'll meet her."

"Thank you," Claire says, leaning over the table and kissing him on the lips. "It will be just fine. Plus, it's a good move financially. You'll see."

"Mom, Dad," Joshua calls as he runs back to their booth. "The pizza guy threw pepperonis at the window while we were watching him make it, and they stuck there! Can we have pepperoni pizza?"

"Sure," Jonathan says. "We'll make sure to ask them to use the pepperoni that's stuck to the window on our pizza."

The excitement of Joshua's first day of school has exhausted him and by the time Claire and Jonathan get home his eyes are heavy and he's yawning. Jonathan carries Joshua into the house and upstairs so he can wash his face and brush his teeth.

Claire tucks Joshua into bed, arranging his bedcovers just so around him so there are no lumps. The soft light peeking in his drawn shades casts a dim halo about his head and brushes purple shadows beneath his eyes. "Do you think you're going to like school, Josh?" Claire asks him as he methodically strokes the head of his stuffed bulldog, the once-furry toy now nearly rubbed bald. Joshua considers the question and then shrugs. "Do you like Mrs. Lovelace?" she asks.

"Yes," he responds, but there is that familiar cadence to his voice that means "yes, but…" Claire sits, waiting him out. "It's loud. The kids are really loud." He finally adds.

"There are a lot of kids in your class. I imagine it does get very noisy," Claire says, smoothing the hair from his forehead, and he brushes her hand away in irritation.

"I miss you." He glances up at Claire to gauge her reaction, his hand rubbing the stuffed dog in more frenetic circles. "It makes me want to leave."

Claire takes a breath before answering. "Josh, I miss you, too. But I've got my job at the bookstore and your job is to go to school." He doesn't answer. "Right, Joshua?"

Joshua doesn't say anything but nods. His lower lip pokes out and his chin quivers.

"Josh," Jonathan says tenderly. "You can't just leave school. You're in kindergarten now, the big leagues."

"I know," Joshua mewls, plump tears sprouting in his eyes.

"What's the matter, Josh?" Jonathan asks, but Claire already knows the answer.

"I'm scared. I want to sleep with you."

"Josh, you need to sleep in your own bed. You'll get a better night's sleep," Claire says, knowing that Joshua will crawl into their bed in the wee hours of the night.

"Where do you think those bad guys are?" he asks.

"They're far, far away, Joshua," Claire assures him, and looks to Jonathan for help.

"They don't dare come back," Jonathan says. "They know the police are looking for them and they know there is a brave little boy who made them run away."

"I was the brave boy," Joshua informs them, as if they didn't know this already.

"Yes, you were, Joshua. You were very brave," Claire tells him. "But you don't need to worry anymore, remember? We've got the alarm at the bookstore now."

"And the new girl is coming," he pipes up. "What's her name?"

"Her name is Allison. And yes, we will have Allison, too. You'll get to meet her tomorrow. So don't worry."

"We have Truman, too," he murmurs sleepily, and snuggles more deeply under the covers.

"We'll keep you safe, Josh," Jonathan whispers. "Don't worry."

Brynn

I wake up to my grandmother leaning over me, gently shaking my shoulder.

"Brynn, wake up," she is saying over and over. "It's eight-thirty. You've been sleeping for so long, are you sick?"

I jump out of bed in a panic, wondering if I slept through the whole day and night, missing class again. The room sways and I have to grab on to my grandmother to keep from falling over.

"The flu," I manage to say before lurching out of my room and into the bathroom where I vomit into the toilet. When I finally open the door and step shakily into the hall, my grandmother is there, a look of concern on her face.

"I was getting worried," she says, taking me by the elbow and guiding me back to my bed. "I tried to wake you up for ten minutes. You were out cold."

"The flu," I mumble again, not able to look her in the eye. I get back under the covers and see the glass on my nightstand. A small amount of wine sits at the bottom. If my grandmother noticed, she doesn't let on.

"Can I make you toast or some soup?" she asks as she sits down next to me.

"No," I say, burrowing my head underneath the covers so I don't have to look at her. "I just want to sleep."

She sits in silence for a long time. All I want her to do is leave, to go away and leave me alone. Finally, she speaks. "Brynn, are you okay? Did something happen?"

"No," I say from beneath my quilt. I can smell my breath, stale and sour. "I'm sick."

"Are you taking your medication?" she asks carefully, as if she'll offend me for asking.

"Yes, Grandma," I say impatiently. "Please, I just want to sleep. I don't feel good."

"Did you take your medicine today?" she asks.

I throw the covers away from my body and sit up. I snatch the pill bottle and unscrew the lid, making a big production out of holding one capsule up so my grandmother can see it. I toss it into my mouth and give an exaggerated swallow, opening my mouth wide so she can see that it is gone. I know I'm being mean, know my grandmother is just worried about me. I flop back down and cover my face with a pillow, feeling sick and miserable.

After several minutes, I feel my grandmother pat my leg, rise from the bed and tiptoe out of the room. Then I spit the pill out from under my tongue.

Allison

I can hardly believe I got the job at Bookends. Every time I think about getting teary-eyed in front of Mrs. Kelby, I cringe. I have cried more in the past few days than I have in the past twenty-one years. I start tomorrow and I have absolutely zero clothes to wear that would be appropriate for work. Mrs. Kelby has only a few rules about dress code—no jeans, T-shirts or sweatshirts, but that's all I own. All afternoon I've been dialing my parents' phone number. Finally, my father answers.

"Hello," he says. The familiarity of his confident, resonant voice sweeps over me and I clutch the phone more tightly to my ear.

"Hi, Dad," I say, the words catching in my throat. "It's Allison."

There's silence on the other end and I know he's thinking about what he should do. Should he hang up or talk to me? "I got a job, Dad," I say in a rush. "In a bookstore, and I was wondering if I could stop home and pick up some of my old clothes. I don't really have anything dressy enough to wear to work and thought maybe I could go through my closet and see if anything might still fit me. I haven't really gained any weight and I probably could still wear my old khakis and I had some nice…" I realize I'm rambling and suddenly stop talking. I can hear my father's breathing from across the line. "Dad, can I please come over?" My hands are sweating and I've twisted the phone cord so tightly around my finger it's turning blue.

"Dad?" I can hear the pleading in my voice.

He clears his throat and speaks. "Of course, Allison. Why don't you come over tonight around six. We'll see what we can find." He sounds distracted, faraway. Not cold, but not warm. Not how you might sound if you haven't talked to your daughter in months.

"Thanks," I say. "I'll see you then. Bye." I wait for his goodbye but only hear the soft click of the receiver. They just need time to get used to the idea of me being out of prison, of my return to Linden Falls. They just need a little more time.

As Olene drives down the street I grew up on, it strikes me how little has changed in the five years I've been gone. Everything looks just the same. The same well-manicured lawns, the same large, redbrick houses with two-car garages and window boxes. She pulls up in front of my childhood home and a flood of memories rush through me. My mother sitting at the kitchen table, reading through cookbooks, my father working at his desk in the den, me in my room, studying. Brynn tiptoeing through the house, trying not to be noticed.

"You want me to wait out here for you, Allison?" Olene asks me.

"No, no, that's okay," I tell her. "My dad will give me a ride back." But I don't make a move to leave the car. Olene looks at me expectantly.

"Allison?" Olene pats me on the knee. "Go and see your parents. It won't be as bad as you think."

I give her a faint smile. "Thanks, Olene. You don't know my parents."

"They were tough on you? Knocked you around a bit?" Olene questions. "You're an adult now. They can't hurt you."

"They didn't beat me," I tell her with a laugh. "Not with their fists."

"Then what?" she asks.

"It's hard to explain," I say, putting my hand on the door handle. "I was perfect."

"And…"

"And then I wasn't." I push open the car door, step out and wave goodbye. Then I trudge up the path, feeling all of ten years old again.

When I get to the front door, I hesitate. I don't know whether I should ring the bell or just walk in. I haven't been here in five years; I don't know my place anymore. If I even *have* a place here. Finally, I press the bell. After a few moments I hear footsteps and my father opens the door. "Hi, Dad," I say shyly and step forward to hug him. I feel him go rigid and I drop my arms. He looks at me uncomfortably. He's still the same tall, handsome man I remember, but I'm surprised at the amount of weight he has gained, the way his belly pushes against the fabric of his dress shirt. His brown hair has grayed and thinned and there are sagging pouches of skin beneath his eyes. I peer over his shoulder, looking for my mother. "Is Mom home?"

"She's not here right now," he says, shifting uneasily from foot to foot. I see several cardboard boxes on the floor behind him.

"Oh," I say in a small voice, realization dawning on me. There isn't going to be any dinner with my parents, no rummaging through my closet with my mother for my clothes. I think of my old bedroom, with its walls painted soft lavender and my polka-dotted comforter. I loved that room. It was a refuge for me. A place where I could just be.

"Can I help you carry the boxes to your car?" my dad asks with forced cheerfulness.

"I don't have a car, Dad," I say shortly. "I just got of prison. I don't have a car, or clothes or anything."

"Oh, well." His face becomes pained. "Can I give you a ride somewhere?"

"Don't bother," I mutter, and turn away from him, feeling my heart pinch. Then I quickly turn back toward him. "I want to see it," I say. My father looks confused and I continue. "I want to see my room."

"Allison," my father says with an awkward chuckle. I push past him, step into the house and look around. I move into the formal living room and everything appears to be the same as it was five years ago. The same floral wallpaper on the walls, the same sofa and love seat, the same grand piano. Even the smell is the same. A mixture of rose petals and cinnamon. But something is off, something is different—I just can't see what it is yet. "Allison," my father says again. This time his voice is hard, cold. "What are you doing?"

I ignore him and begin to climb the staircase that leads up to my bedroom. The carpet is soft beneath my feet and the mahogany banister feels smooth and cool against the palm of my hand. I stop suddenly and I know—I know what's different. The pictures. The pictures are all gone. Every single photo of me is gone. I continue to move slowly up the stairs. My legs feel heavy and my heart is hammering in my chest.

"Allison," my father calls after me. "You can't just come in here…" His voice trails off as I reach the top of the steps and turn down the hallway that leads to the bedrooms. The air up here feels stale and presses on me even more heavily than when I was in prison and I push down the urge to dash back down the stairs and out into the fresh air. The door to my bedroom is shut. I reach out for the knob, twist, and it opens with a click. The weak evening sun doesn't soften the shock. Gone are the lavender walls, replaced with stark white paint, gone is my polka-dotted comforter, gone is my desk for studying, gone are my soccer trophies, my blue ribbons, my team pictures, my bookshelves, my stuffed animals. All gone. I choke back a sob and lunge toward my closet and fling open the door. Empty. No clothes, no shoes, no boxes filled with keepsakes. I've been erased.

As I stumble from my bedroom and into the hallway I see the door of my parents' bedroom, open a crack, and catch a glimpse of my mother, her face mostly hidden in the shadows.

As I rush down the block I keep expecting to hear them call my name or feel a hand on my arm. But nothing. They're just letting me walk away. I'm angry at myself for being so heartbroken, but I am. I walk for several blocks. Gertrude House is about five miles from my parents' home and I wonder if I can make it there by eight o'clock, the time Olene is expecting me. I hear a car creeping up behind me and I turn. It's my father and my stomach flips with hope even though I'm irritated with myself for caring.

"Allison," he says through the open window, "I'll give you a ride." Even though I want to open the car door and get in, I don't want to make it too easy for him.

"It's obvious you and Mom don't want anything to do with me, so don't bother." I begin to walk in the direction of Gertrude House again.

My father follows me slowly in his car. "Allison," he calls, "I'll only say it one more time. Please get in the car." I look at him long and hard, then climb in beside him. He turns off the ignition and looks over at me, rubs his face. "Allison, please look at this from our point of view. This has been very hard on us."

"But I'm—" I begin, and he cuts me off.

"Let me finish. This has been very difficult for your mother and me. We've finally found some…" My father looks at me pleadingly. "Some peace."

He wants me to let them off the hook, to say I understand why they have completely written me off. In a way, I do, but it doesn't make it hurt any less. They are done with me. Finished.

"Okay, Dad. I get it." I smile sadly. "Tell Mom I understand." My father breathes out a stream of air and begins to drive. When we pull up in front of Gertrude House my father pops open the trunk.

"Do you need help with the boxes?" he asks.

"No, I can do it," I say, and I can see he is relieved. I pull out each of the boxes filled with clothes and set them on the curb next to me. "Thanks, Dad," I tell him. "Say hi to Mom for me."

"I will," he assures me as he retrieves his billfold

from his pocket and pulls out several bills. "Here, take this."

"You don't have to," I say.

"No, please. We want you to have it." He presses the wad of cash into my hand. "Good luck with your new job."

"Thanks," I manage to say, and my throat aches with emotion as I watch him pull away. I stand there for the longest time until I feel a hand on my arm. I turn around, expecting to see Olene, but it's Bea. With her is Tabatha, piercings and all.

"You okay?" Bea asks.

"I'm fine," I say, brushing away tears, hoping that they couldn't see them. Bea bends down and with her wiry, strong arms picks up a box and then Tabatha does the same. In fact, I'm *not* fine. Not at all.

Charm

Charm stops at the grocery store and picks up an apple pie from the bakery case and a carton of vanilla ice cream. She considers buying the cheapest generic brand of ice cream she can find, seeing as she'll probably end up leaving Reanne's before dessert. But her mother will be all light and air and will wonder sweetly out loud if Gus and Charm are having financial difficulties and what a shame that would be, since Gus got the house in their divorce. Charm knows she couldn't splurge for the expensive ice cream, either; her mother would think she was putting on airs. No Häagen-Dazs tonight. Charm settles on a midpriced half gallon of French vanilla.

Reanne greets Charm at the door with a big hug. Binks takes the pie and ice cream from her hands and pats her awkwardly on the shoulder.

"It's so good to see you, Charm," Reanne says. She has put on weight. Her curves have turned to chub and her hair, rather than sun-streaked, looks brittle and overprocessed. Fine lines have settled beneath her eyes and her makeup has bled into the crevices. Charm resists the urge to wet her finger and wipe it away.

Her mother has gone to a lot of trouble. The small kitchen table is covered with a floral cloth and candles are lit.

"Wow," Charm says, taking it all in. "What's the occasion?"

"Just you come in and sit down. Dinner is ready. Let's eat it while it's hot," she says, nudging her toward the table.

"Okay, okay." Charm laughs guardedly as she takes a seat. "It smells really good," she offers charitably.

"You'll have to thank Binks for the chicken. He made that. But I made the potatoes. Mashed, just the way you like them!"

Charm feels a sudden pang of regret. Gus is at home with only the hospice volunteer to look after him. "Those are Gus's favorite, too."

Reanne quickly glances at Binks to see if he caught the comment, but he's busy forking the chicken onto plates. She waits until he sits down and the dishes of food have been passed around. Charm takes a few bites. The chicken is dry and she struggles to swallow. Binks smiles and nods at Reanne and she wiggles in her seat as if bursting to speak.

"What?" Charm asks, fearful of the response.

"Binks and I are getting married!" Reanne screeches with happiness, and Charm finds a smile frozen to her face. She tries to make her lips move but nothing happens. Binks and Reanne look at her expectantly.

"Wow," Charm says softly. Suddenly the need to

get out of this tiny apartment with its greasy, cigarette-infused air and kitschy knickknacks is overwhelming.

"And...?" Her mother leans toward Charm, waiting for more. Binks is looking down at his plate. Mashed potatoes are stuck to his mustache.

"And... I'm happy for you," Charm says, the quivering ripple in her voice betraying her. All she can think of was how badly Gus wanted to marry her mother. This amazingly kind, responsible, handsome man loved her mother, but she had walked away. "Congratulations," Charm finishes weakly.

"You're not," Reanne says petulantly. "You're not happy. You cannot stand to see me doing well."

"Mom," Charm says tiredly. "That's not it. I am happy for you. I'm just surprised."

"Surprised? Surprised at what, Charm?" She is angry now. "Surprised that I am in love and getting married? After all I've been through, I thought at least you'd be understanding!"

"What you've been through?" Charm says incredulously, though she knows it will do no good to get upset. Her mother will twist it, make Charm seem like the ungrateful, spiteful one. "What you've been through," Charm says again, more softly this time. "You are absolutely unbelievable, Mother. Pardon me for being a little skeptical about you finally settling down with one man. It's not exactly what you're known for."

"Now, Charm," Binks says reasonably. "No need to be disrespectful."

"You know what's disrespectful?" Charm says in a dangerously low voice. "Disrespectful is bringing man after man into your home so that your children have no idea who will be sitting at the breakfast table the next morning. Disrespectful is allowing men into your house who make moves on your nine-year-old daughter!" Reanne looks confused for a moment, as if running through each of her former boyfriends, trying to figure out which one preferred Charm to her. "Disrespectful is raising your child to believe that men are stupid cattle that can be tossed aside like garbage. Disrespectful is divorcing the one decent man who loved you and your children, breaking his heart completely. *That* is disrespectful." Charm pushes her chair back from the table and stands.

"You're leaving?" Reanne asks in disbelief. "We haven't finished eating. We haven't talked about your brother yet."

"I'm through talking," Charm says, looking levelly at her mother. She moves to the door and changes her mind. She knows it's childish, but she can't stop herself. She walks to the refrigerator, calmly opens the freezer door and retrieves the half gallon of ice cream. She and Gus will eat the ice cream tonight. She won't tell Gus about her mother's upcoming wedding. Instead, she'll tell him that her mother seemed miserable, lonely, that she asked after how he was doing. "Have a happy life." Charm tries to muster as much goodwill as she can, but it comes out bitterly. She leaves, her mother and Binks staring after her, mouths gaping open.

Charm is still shaking with anger when she arrives home, not sure why the news of their upcoming marriage has made her so upset. She suspects that it has to do with how the news will hurt Gus's feelings. She peeks in on Gus, who is fast asleep, and then decides to go for a walk along the Druid River. She loves this place. In the fall, she sits under the locust trees, their small yellow leaves falling around her like canary feathers. In the winter she would walk for miles, the cold air making her eyes water, her boots leaving bigfoot-size prints in her wake.

Years ago, when Charm was twelve, she made an army of snow angels, one for each of the men her mother had brought home—the ones she could remember, anyway. With her finger she wrote the initials of each man next to the angel. If she couldn't remember the man's name, she wrote down what she remembered about them. *C.B.* stood for the man who wore cowboy boots. She was six, and didn't even recall seeing the actual man. Just the boots lying at the floor of her mother's bedroom. Gray and scaly, in the dark they looked like they were guarding the room, ready to strike. When she stood and looked down at her work, the rows and rows of angels imprinted in the snow, Charm felt satisfied somehow. The only thing that was missing was a little red spot in the center of each angel. A broken heart. Charm's mother was always the one who left, never the guy. She kept them wanting more.

After walking along the river until her anger cools, Charm goes back into the house and once again looks in on Gus. He doesn't stir. She tiptoes to her bedroom and pulls out the shoe box she has kept hidden in her dresser drawer for years.

In the shoe box, she keeps the few mementos of their time with the baby. Less than three weeks. A lifetime ago. Every once in a while she sits on her bed and fingers each of the items. First there's a pair of tiny baby socks that are a soft periwinkle blue. They were too big for his tiny feet and looked clownish on him. When he kicked out his legs, the socks would slide off his feet and he would wriggle his toes as if saying, Ahh, this is better. But they were his socks and he had worn them, even for a short time, so they were special. Also in the box is the wrist rattle shaped like a bumblebee and a tiny blue Chicago Cubs baseball cap. Finally, there are the two small, framed photos. One shows Charm, looking incredibly young and incredibly exhausted as she holds a crying, red-faced baby. The other is of Gus, smiling, holding a quiet, sleeping infant. She knows she will never be able to tell him about the first two days of his life. That he was loved by a fifteen-year-old girl and a sick man who had no idea what they were doing, but who tried and tried until they couldn't.

Allison

I'm so nervous. More nervous than when I took my SATs and more nervous than when I had to wait for the results. I really want to do well in this job. My life is starting over and this is just the beginning.

Though it is only early September, the air is crisp and cold and the leaves on the trees that line the street are just beginning to become edged with vibrant yellows and reds. I arrive too early at the store and wait anxiously outside. Mrs. Kelby waves as she pulls into a parking space.

"Good morning, Allison," she calls out to me as she climbs from her car. "Are you ready for a great day?"

"I am," I tell her. "I'm a little nervous," I admit.

"You'll do just fine," Mrs. Kelby assures me. "If you have any questions, just ask." She unlocks the door, enters the store and flips on the lights. It is beautiful, warm and cozy. I turn in a circle and scan the rows and rows of books that extend from the floor to the ceiling. The library at the prison was inadequate, but while I was there I read everything I could get my hands on, even though the books were dog-eared and stained, some of the pages falling out. But here every book had shiny, gleaming covers and I want to grab one, open it and press my nose into the crisp, clean pages. Mrs. Kelby is watching me, an amused look on her face.

"I know," she says. "I have to pinch myself every day. Seeing all these books never ceases to amaze me. Come on, I'll take you on the grand tour." She leads me around the store, showing me the children's section with its beanbag chairs and miniature table and chairs set for a tea party.

Brynn and I used to have tea parties when we were little. We would dress up in my mother's old clothes and jewelry and gather our favorite stuffed animals and dolls, setting them in chairs around the table that was in our playroom. I would always play the hostess and Brynn and the dolls were my guests.

"Please sit," I would order in a pompous voice that wasn't much different than how I usually sounded. Brynn would sit, her small, thin body enveloped in a floral Laura Ashley dress, a castaway of my mother. Her brown eyes peeking out from beneath the tattered straw hat she wore.

Once, I smuggled red Kool-Aid and cookies into the playroom, which was expressly forbidden by our mother.

"Tea?" I asked.

"Yes, please," Brynn answered, trying to mimic my own affected voice.

I poured the Kool-Aid into the teacups and we settled into munching and sipping, pausing once in a while to comment on the weather or gossip about the neighbors as we had seen our mother and her friends do. Brynn reached over to grab another cookie from the plate and her elbow caught the teapot. A stream of red Kool-Aid spilled to the pale carpet below. A look of panic crossed Brynn's face and she began to cry, knowing how angry our mother would be.

"*Shhh,* Brynn," I ordered. "She'll hear."

"I'm sorry." Brynn started crying even harder.

"Stop crying," I demanded, pulling hard on one of the dark curls of her hair.

"Ow," she squeaked, but her cries stopped. She didn't look angry at the yank I gave her, but even sorrier, if possible.

Our mother came into the room and stood looming over us. She was tall, like I would become, and had sleek blond hair that she always wore pulled back. She regarded the Kool-Aid dripping from the table and blooming into a crimson stain across the carpet. Next to me, Brynn started to sniffle.

"I did it," I said automatically. "It was my fault."

Wordlessly, my mother grabbed my arm and gave me two quick swats on the behind. It didn't hurt, but I was embarrassed, my pride wounded. Brynn covered her eyes, not wanting to see. Then my mother turned and did the same to Brynn. The suddenness of it sent Brynn tumbling, her little body not able to maintain balance against the force of the blows.

"But I did it," I told my mother indignantly. "It was my fault."

"Your spanking was for lying," my mother said icily. "And yours," she said, turning to Brynn, who was still sprawled on the floor, "was for letting your sister take the blame. Clean this up," she snapped, and left the room.

"Allison," I hear a voice say. I blink and see Mrs. Kelby looking at me curiously. "Come on, I'll show you the storage area."

I spend the day familiarizing myself with the store, the books, the cash register. At noon, Mrs. Kelby runs across the street to a small restaurant and picks up sandwiches for us and we spend half an hour chatting about growing up in Linden Falls. There's something so beautiful about the way she carries herself. I wish I still had that confidence but somewhere along the way I seem to have lost it. I think I'm really going to like working with Mrs. Kelby. This is going to be a good thing. She is showing me how to use the computer to order books that a customer requests when a blond-haired boy bursts through the door.

"Hey, Josh, come on back here. I want you to meet someone," Mrs. Kelby calls to him.

"Hi, Mom. Gotta go." He sweeps past us and dashes into the bathroom.

"He doesn't like to go to the bathroom at school," she explains. "The sound of the toilet flushing kind of freaks him out and he tries to hold it."

"How old is he?" I ask, just to be polite.

"He turned five in July. He's in kindergarten." She beams with pride. We return to the computer and she begins keying in a title.

A tall man comes through the door, steps up to the cash register and leans over the counter to give Mrs. Kelby a kiss on the cheek. "Allison, this is my husband, Jonathan."

"Nice to meet you, Mr. Kelby." I reach out to shake his hand, which is rough and calloused.

"Nice to meet you, and call me Jonathan," he says pleasantly.

"And call me Claire. Enough of this Mrs. Kelby nonsense."

"Mom," the little boy says coming up behind us. "I'm thirsty."

"Did you wash your hands?" Claire asks.

"Yep. Can I have some juice?"

"Come here, first. I want you to meet Allison," she tells him. I raise my head from the computer screen and turn to greet Claire's son. "Joshua, this is Allison." Claire smiles broadly. "And, Allison, this is my son, Joshua."

The little boy before me has dark brown eyes and an upturned nose set onto a sharp, angled face. But it isn't until he smiles that all of his features fall into place. I can hear Claire talking, chattering on about Joshua, and I swallow hard, trying to keep any of the emotions that I am feeling from reaching my face. My mind is whirling.

"Excuse me," I say to Claire and Jonathan. "I just have to use the bathroom." I try to keep my steps slow and casual but my face feels hot and I try to catch my breath. I lock the bathroom door and lower the lid on the toilet so I can sit down. I close my eyes and it's Christopher's face that beams up at me.

Joshua Kelby is a miniature version of the boy I fell in love with.

Brynn

Even though alcohol is more effective than any antidepressant in helping me forget the night Allison gave birth, I still remember running back toward the house, Allison calling after me. It was pouring down rain by then. Any mud from the river's edge had been washed away. I felt so strange, my legs heavy and shaky. But still I ran toward the house. Just get to the house, I kept telling myself. I wasn't sure what I had just seen, didn't want to know. It was supposed to be over. Done. But I knew it was really just the beginning.

By the time I made it back into our house my clothes were drenched and I couldn't stop shivering. I looked through the back door toward the yard and through the rain I could see Allison coming my way. Every few seconds she would stop, clutch at her stomach and bend over at the knees. I knew I should go to her, help her back to the house, but at that moment I truly hated my sister. Hated everything about her, hated her for being perfect, and smart and beautiful, for getting pregnant and expecting me to keep it a secret. Beyond Allison and me no one would ever know about that baby girl, no one would know that she ever existed. Most of all I hated her because I was sure she was going to get away with it and would be able to go back to her perfect life without a backward glance. I turned away from her and kicked off my soggy tennis shoes and squelched to the linen closet to get a towel.

I heard the squeak of the screen door and over the sound of rain beating against the windows I heard Allison weakly call out to me. "Brynn, *please*."

Don't go, I told myself. *It's all her fault. Let her clean up her own mess.*

"Brynn," she called again. I could hear the panic in her voice. "Something's wrong. Please. Help me."

Ignore her, I ordered myself again. *Go up to your room and shut the door. Pretend this never happened.* I was halfway up the stairs when I heard the unmistakable sound of someone falling to the ground. *Leave her there. She'd do the same to you.*

Her moans traveled from the kitchen to the stairwell and I sat down on the steps. I covered my ears with my hands and began rocking back and forth. *Don't go down there, don't do it,* I told myself over and over. *Leave her there. She's not your sister, she's a monster.*

The moans suddenly stopped and all I could hear was the nonstop drum of rain on the roof. I strained to hear any sound, any movement, from the kitchen. Silence. Then the truth came to me, like the rain tapping against the window. Striking sharply, over and over and over. *Who's the monster? Who's the monster?* I stood quickly, knocking a photo of Allison standing with my parents and accepting some award from the wall. I watched as it tumbled down the steps and landed facedown at the bottom.

"Allison," I hollered. "Allison!" I skittered down the steps and into the kitchen and found her lying on the tiled floor trying to peel her pants from her legs. Her face was white and she could barely lift her head. *Please,* her eyes begged me. She had no voice left, couldn't even cry out in pain. *She's going to die,* I thought to myself. Our parents would find us there, in the kitchen. Allison, dead, blue, half-naked and bloodied. And me, just sitting next to her, doing nothing.

"It's the placenta," Allison managed to squeak. An immediate sense of relief came over me. It was going to be okay. She wasn't going to die. It was almost over.

Allison gave one puny grunt. I could see something begin to slide out from within her and I reached out with my damp towel to catch it. "It's okay, Allison," I said through my tears. "I'm here."

Allison

After I had given birth to the little girl, after Brynn gathered up all the bloody sheets and went downstairs to throw them away, after the trip to the river, I started to feel the contractions pull at my stomach again. I was expecting a purplish mass to emerge from between my legs, but the placenta wasn't what surfaced. I blinked twice and tried to wipe the sweat from eyes. I glanced at the clock on the microwave and saw that it was nearly nine-fifteen. *No,* I told myself. *No way.* It was all just too crazy. If what I was seeing didn't convince me, the strong squawk that came from what was supposed to be the afterbirth did. A baby. A tiny baby boy with a pointy chin and an upturned nose, just like Christopher's. Brynn, kneeling before me, caught the baby as it slid from inside of me and cried out in disbelief.

I reached out one trembling hand toward him and at the same time he seemed to reach out for mine. Our fingers grazed each other's and for the first time in a very long while I smiled.

Brynn

I stared at Allison in disbelief. She had this odd smile on her face, not really one of happiness, but of amazement. But it quickly fell away.

"No. Please," she whimpered, and she looked away from the red-faced baby that I held with shaking hands. "Please, we have to get him out of here."

"I don't understand," I said, looking down at the crying child.

"It's a baby," she said acidly. Seeing my eyes fill with tears, she apologized. "I'm sorry, Brynn. But Mom and Dad will be home in a few hours. We've got to hurry."

"They look the same," I said softly, thinking of the little girl, dead now. Gone.

"It's a boy," Allison croaked, her face full of anguish. "Come on. We have to get rid of it."

Allison

Somehow I force myself to leave the bathroom and return to the front of the store. I attempt to say a cheerful goodbye to Claire's husband and Joshua, who are on their way out the door. Though I don't have actual evidence, I know that Claire's little boy is my son.

I'm sure Claire is going to notice that something is wrong just by looking at me, and I'm right. After working side by side in near silence for almost two hours, Claire turns to me, a concerned look on her face.

"Allison," she says. "You're awfully quiet. You're not worried about how you did today, are you?"

"A little bit, I guess," I answer, grateful for an excuse for my behavior.

"Well, don't be. You did a great job," Claire reassures me. "So what do you think? You going to give this place another chance tomorrow?"

I almost tell her no, but I stop myself. If I quit, there's no way I'll ever find proof that Joshua is my son. "I'd really like to come back, if you want me," I tell her, not quite able to meet her eyes.

"Of course I do. Now go on home and get some rest. I'll see you tomorrow at nine." Claire walks me to the door. "Do you need a ride home?" she asks, looking out the front window at the gathering rain clouds.

"No, I like the fresh air," I explain. "Thanks again, Claire. I'll see you tomorrow."

As I walk back to Gertrude House, the sun is completely swallowed up by gray clouds and my mind is swirling with the possibility that Claire's son could be the boy I gave birth to five years earlier, could be Christopher's son, could be the brother of the little girl I was convicted of killing.

I need to tell someone. I could call Devin and ask her what I should do, but I *know* what the right thing to do is. I should tell Claire that things just aren't working out for me at the bookstore. Then I need to find a way to get out of Linden Falls.

I never wanted to see the boy I gave away before. I felt like I had done my duty by giving his father a chance to raise him. That obviously hadn't happened. I know I should run away from the Kelby family as fast as I can, but I can't. I have too many questions. I want to know what kind of people adopted Joshua, want to know the kind of person I gave birth to. How did Joshua end up here and what happened to Christopher?

When I arrive at Gertrude House, I open the door and meet Olene. "How was your first day?" she asks.

"It was good," I say, not making eye contact. I'm afraid to say more. Feeling Olene's curious stare on my back, I rush up the stairs and into my room where I find Bea sitting on the upper bunk bed.

"Hey," she says, her eyes never leaving the pages of her magazine. "How was work?"

I kick off my shoes and flop down on the lower bunk. "Good," I say. Then I add, "Weird."

"I know what you mean," Bea says from above me. "It's like you catch yourself in these moments and you think, This is normal. This is something a normal person would do."

"Yeah, that's exactly it," I lie. "I don't know if I want to go back there," I admit.

Bea is quiet for a minute. Then I see her legs swing over the side of her bunk. She is barefoot and the bottom of her feet are scarred and calloused. She leaps lightly to the ground and bends down to look at me. Up close I realize she's not as old as I first thought she was— maybe thirty—but already her forehead is creased with grooves, and lines as fine as spider webs frame her eyes. "Olene set up that job for you."

"Yes," I say.

"She goes to a lot of trouble to find us places to work. Puts her good name and reputation on the line." There is no accusation or judgment in Bea's voice, just stating the facts.

"I'll go back," I say in a small voice.

Bea smiles and holds out a hand to me and for the first time I notice a tattoo on the inside of her forearm, a beautiful bird with the initials *O.V.* dangling from its beak like an olive branch. I want to ask her what it means but I don't want her to think I'm being nosy. "Come on," she says, grabbing my hand and pulling me up. "It's spa night."

"Spa night?" I ask.

"Yeah, Flora's going to beauty school and likes to practice on us once in a while."

"Oh, no," I say, and pull away. "Flora still looks at me like she'd like to murder me in my bed. There's no way she's going to get her hands on me."

"Come on," Bea says, and it comes out like an order. "You can just watch. Flora's not that bad, just a little nervous around new people. She's been through a lot."

I give a little grunt. "Haven't we all?"

"I suppose so," Bea allows. "But you should give her a chance. You don't know her story."

"You know," I say with irritation. "I'll give her a chance once she gives me one. I know she's the one behind all the damn dolls that keep showing up. She doesn't even know me but her mind's already made up." I sit back down on my bed. "You go on without me. I want to try and call my sister."

"Suit yourself," Bea says, "but we're getting pedicures tonight." She looks down at her feet and wiggles her toes. "I've never had a pedicure."

The person I want to tell about finding Joshua is Brynn. Maybe it would help her to see that something good came of the terrible night I gave birth. But once again, I can't get ahold of Brynn. My grandmother tells me she is out somewhere. I feel a pang of jealousy. I should be away at college, spending time with my friends. Then my envy is replaced by guilt. Brynn deserves all the fun she can possibly get. I know she had to deal with the fallout from my arrest, that she was bullied and made fun of because of what I had done. That she almost ended her life over it.

"Will you tell her I called?" I ask my grandmother.

"Of course," she says. "How are you doing, Allison? Have you seen your mom and dad?"

"I'm okay," I say. "Mom and Dad aren't exactly welcoming me back home with open arms. But I started my job today. At a bookstore."

"Good for you," my grandma says enthusiastically. "See, you're already getting back on your feet."

"Grandma, does Brynn ever talk about that night? Did she ever tell you about it?"

There is silence on the other end and I'm afraid that we've been disconnected or, worse, that my grandmother has hung up on me. "Grandma?" I repeat.

"No, she never talks about it," my grandma answers sadly. "I wish she would, though. At least with her doctor. Keeping things bottled up inside doesn't do anyone any good. I'll tell her you called, Allison. You take care of yourself, okay?"

"Thanks, Grandma. Bye," I say, and hang up the phone. I guess I'm not the only one good at keeping secrets.

My hair feels heavy and scratchy on my neck and I wonder if I dare ask Flora for a haircut instead of a pedicure. Then I remember what Olene said about hope, and I make my way down the spiral staircase toward the sound of laughter.

Charm

No matter how many times Charm sees a mother holding her newborn baby—and at the hospital she sees many—she still thinks of that night five years ago.

Gus was snoring in his chair. The windows were wide-open and a cool breeze, unusual for July, blew through the screen door. It had rained off and on earlier that evening and everything smelled fresh and clean. Charm was sitting in the dark, watching TV with the volume turned down low so she wouldn't wake Gus. He hadn't been sleeping well lately. It was getting harder and harder for him to catch his breath and he would wake up several times during the night gasping for air. They didn't know it at the time, but that was just the beginning of his downward spiral into lung cancer.

Charm heard the crunch of gravel as a car approached and she rose from the couch to peek out the window. A small car, without its headlights on, stopped in front of the house and a person stepped from the passenger side. She couldn't tell if it was a male or female, but whoever it was moved slowly and shuffled toward the front door as if very old or in a great deal of pain. The tall figure was carrying something and stopped every few steps as if resting, regaining strength. "Gus," Charm called softly, suddenly afraid. He slept on. She flipped on the outside light.

It was Allison Glenn, a junior at her high school. Allison was beautiful, smart, athletic—nice even— and Charm had no idea why she would show up at her home. Charm wasn't even sure if Allison even knew who she was. Allison was dressed in sweatpants and a sweatshirt, her blond hair piled on top of her head. Though she looked sick and her face was as pale as the moon that had just started to peek through the clouds, she was beautiful. Charm strained her eyes, trying to see who was in the driver's seat of the car. Another girl, her dark hair hiding her face. Charm could hear her cries. "Gus," she called again, more loudly this time.

Before she could say anything, before she could even open the screen door, Allison spoke in a tired, scared voice. "Is Christopher here?" She glanced around nervously.

"I'll go get him. Come on in," Charm answered, and her eyes settled upon the bundle in her shaking hands. She was trembling so hard Charm thought she was going to drop it.

"No, I'll just wait here," she said, her teeth chattering.

Gus came up behind Charm and peered over her shoulder. "She's looking for Christopher," Charm told him.

Gus made an impatient noise, one that Charm was now used to hearing every time someone said Christopher's name. "Hmmph," he muttered. "Who's asking?"

The cries from the car grew louder, more desperate. "Is she okay?" Charm asked worriedly.

Allison looked wearily over her shoulder. "She'll be okay. Please, get Christopher."

Charm hurried to the back of the house and knocked on her brother's bedroom door.

"What?"

"There's someone here to see you," she called. "Hurry," she urged, rapping on the door again.

"Jesus, I'm coming. Who is it?" Christopher, tall and handsome, threw open the door and emerged from a fog of smoke.

"Christopher," Charm snapped. "You're not supposed to smoke in the house."

"Who is it?" he asked again, ignoring her lecture, running his hands through his thick brown hair.

"It's Allison Glenn," Charm said, and Christopher froze and she saw something new skitter across his face. Something she'd never seen before in her brother's eyes. A flash of hope. "How do you know Allison?" she asked, as she followed him through the house to the front door.

"Christopher," Allison said, trying to control her voice, but failing. She looked terrible.

"Are you okay?" Christopher asked, then recovered, his face transforming into an unreadable mask. "What are you doing here?" His voice was cold.

Charm and Gus watched them regard each other, Allison and Christopher both trying to appear cool and indifferent. Allison, Charm knew, was a girl who was used to getting her way, but she looked so sick, so miserable. No match for Christopher, she thought. But she was wrong.

"Here." She thrust the blanket toward Christopher. "He's yours. You need to deal with it." Christopher looked dumbly down at the bundle in his hands and nearly dropped it when it softly squawked.

"Jesus." Christopher paled. "What is it?"

"Be careful," she said, and her icy eyes fixed on Christopher's. "A baby," she said matter-of-factly. "He's yours and I can't… I can't keep him."

Charm moved slowly closer and leaned in, reaching for the infant.

The towel fell away, revealing a pinched, red face, and the baby started wailing, his cries joining the cries of the unknown girl who remained in the car, her shoulders convulsing with her sobs. "Why?" Charm asked.

"I just can't," Allison said, and began to limp back to the car.

"Hey!" Christopher yelled after her. "Hey, I don't want it. Get the hell back here." She ignored him and started to get into the car.

Gus and Charm looked at each other and then down at the baby, whose skinny, twiglike arms moved spastically about his head. "Shhh," Charm whispered to him, already falling in love.

Gus called out to her. "You don't really think he'll take care of this baby, do you?"

She stopped and turned back toward them, her face unbearably sad. "He has to."

Gus and Charm stood there looking at the tiny little boy in stunned silence as Christopher stormed out of the house, knapsack in his hand, into the rainy night, letting the screen door slam behind him without a backward glance. Gus shouted angrily after him as Charm looked down at the baby in awe. A mixture of terror and wonder filled her chest. How was she going to take care of this scrawny, red-faced child, when that was all she really was herself?

Brynn

I'm working with Milo in the kitchen, teaching him to stay even though it's his dinnertime and his food bowl is full and waiting for him. It seems so cruel, making him wait to eat, but it's crucial for his obedience training. I started out having him wait just a few minutes to eat and now we've worked our way up to twenty minutes. He is sitting there, each muscle twitching, his eyes looking hopefully at me for the signal that will release him.

Some people believe that dogs are psychic, that they have this paranormal knowledge of the world around them, allowing them to know their master is home well before they come to the door or that they can sense danger. Actually, this sixth sense has more to do with the dog's amazing sense of smell. They are known to be able to detect when an epileptic seizure or a heart attack is coming on. Some people believe dogs can sense certain kinds of cancers in humans even before a doctor can diagnose the disease.

This makes me think of Allison. I wonder if things might have been different if we'd had a dog growing up. Would a particularly intuitive golden retriever have been able to sense Allison's pregnancy? Would he have sniffed at Allison's nearly nonexistent belly long enough for our parents or for me to notice something was up? Or maybe, just maybe, in the time before the police came to take Allison away, he could have alerted my parents to how sick Allison was and I wouldn't have had to do what I did. I don't know.

It was bad enough having my sister taken away by the police, but what made it worse was that it was my fault that she was arrested. I was the one who panicked and called the police. I didn't mean to get Allison in trouble. But I hadn't slept since the night she gave birth. All I could think about was that baby. It just wasn't right that she was so cold and wet in that river, and I couldn't stop shivering and I couldn't catch my breath. Allison was burning up with fever and she was bleeding, there was so much blood. I tried to tell my parents that Allison was sick, but as usual they were caught up in their own lives. All my mother did was peek into Allison's room and say, "Are you okay, Allison?" And Allison said she was fine and then gave me hell when my mother went away.

I don't know why I picked up the phone but I did. When the 9-1-1 operator answered the call I started hyperventilating and she kept asking me if I was okay and did I need an ambulance. Finally, the words came. "My sister, the baby in the river, please," I cried. "You have to help her…" And then I started crying and couldn't stop. Five minutes later the police were at our door and even though my father told them no one called the police, there was no baby, it was all a big mistake, they still came into the house.

After they took her away I still couldn't sleep more than two or three hours at a time. Every time I closed my eyes I saw that blue-skinned baby in front of me and every time I opened my eyes I saw my parents' disapproving looks. They couldn't really say anything—the doctor said that Allison could have died if we hadn't gotten her to the hospital. But I know my parents were angry at me for calling the police and for revealing to the world that their perfect daughter wasn't all that pure.

I give Milo the signal that releases him and he runs to his food bowl and greedily gobbles up his dog food, then trots up to me, nuzzling against my leg as if to thank me. His ears perk up at the ring of the phone, followed by a soft growl that begins low in his chest. I absent-mindedly shush him as I reach for the receiver and he whines quietly when I order him into a down position.

"Hello," I say.

"Brynn, please don't hang up," she says in a rush. "Please just let me come see you. I need to talk to you. Please." I don't recognize the voice at first, but realization quickly dawns on me. I almost don't believe that it is her. Growing up, Allison always sounded so confident, sure of herself. The girl I hear over the line sounds desperate, scared, but it's her, it's my sister, and her voice pierces my heart. "I found him," she says in a rush. "I found the baby boy—"

Without answering her, I slam down the phone.

I feel my chest tighten with panic, although I haven't had a full-blown panic attack in months. Why can't Allison just let me be? I don't care that she's out of prison, I don't care that she wants to make amends. I'm better off without her; I'm better off forgetting what happened that night. "No, no, no!" I shout, and Milo answers me with sharp, loud barks. "No!" I yell again at the phone.

The phone begins to ring again, loud and high-pitched, and I sit weakly down on the cool linoleum floor and cover my ears.

Allison

I walk into Bookends like nothing has happened. Claire greets me with a cup of coffee and a doughnut. "You came back!" she teases. "I thought maybe I scared you away. Love your haircut, by the way."

"Oh, no," I protest, "it's great here. Thanks again for the chance." I self-consciously run my fingers through my newly shorn locks. "Thanks."

"Come on, a new shipment of books came yesterday afternoon. I'll show you how to check them in."

We work quietly for a while. I still can't get over all the books and I have to force myself to keep working and not stop to open them and begin reading.

"It must be very hard to be here," Claire says finally, breaking the silence. My stomach leaps. She can't know. There's no way. "Starting all over again. It must be very difficult."

I slowly nod. "It is," I whisper. "It's like the whole world moved forward and I'm stuck. I'm twenty-one, I'm supposed to be done with college, supposed to be starting a career…but here I am."

"You can't let that hold you back," Claire proclaims. "No one knows what they're really going to do with the rest of their life when they're twenty-one. I sure didn't. Do you know what I was doing when I was your age?" I shake my head. "I was a librarian."

"You were?" I guess I shouldn't be surprised, but I am.

"Of course," Claire continues, "most people don't just get out of college and open up their own business right away. I had so much to learn at the library and I had to meet Jonathan before it even dawned on me that owning a bookstore was what I wanted to do."

"How'd you meet Jonathan?" I ask.

Claire laughs. "In a flood, of all things."

"Really?" I ask, impressed. "What happened?"

"Come on, let's run across the street and grab something to eat and I'll tell you all about it."

"Can we do that?" I ask with surprise. "Can we just leave?"

"That's the beauty of owning your own business," Claire says wickedly. She locks the door behind us and we cross the street to a small restaurant. Once we are settled in our booth the waitress hands us our menus and we both order burgers and fries.

"This place has the best food," Claire explains. "Actually, this restaurant is one of the reasons I decided to buy the building across the street. The idea of being able to run over here whenever I wanted to was just too tempting."

"So you met your husband in a flood?" I ask, bringing the conversation back to the story of Claire and Jonathan.

"Well, sort of," Claire begins.

Claire

"The floods were supposed to come the spring I turned twenty-five," Claire explains as she pushes her plate away from her. "That spring started out beautifully, each morning a brisk fifty degrees, but by ten o'clock the temperature would rise to seventy degrees. We were all well aware that the flooding was heading our way from the north—towns and farms along the Mississippi in Minnesota and Wisconsin were already devastated—but it was just so hard to believe, because we hadn't received an unusual amount of rain that spring. And it was even more difficult to imagine the destruction that was making its way toward us."

"I remember my mom and dad talking about that spring. We... They live by the Druid..." Allison breaks off and lowers her head in embarrassment.

Claire pretends not to notice and continues on. "We had planned to sandbag the block surrounding the library. We had so many people who volunteered. The

Friends of the Library Organization, our local Red Hat Club, members of the Jaycees, even the homeless man who spent cold or rainy days in the library reading the *Des Moines Register* or dozing behind a huge world atlas. Everyone had gathered in front of the library, ready to help."

Claire smiles at the memory of seeing Jonathan for the first time. He was tall and had the face of an academic and the body of a laborer. Serious, thoughtful blue eyes looked out from wire-rimmed glasses. His forehead was furrowed, a permanent crease already set between his brows. His long, lean frame was powerful and sinewy. He was wearing work gloves and holding a shovel when Claire thanked the crowd for coming out to help. She could feel her skin burn with the weight of his gaze on her face as she described the thousands of books that they were trying to save, along with the computers and art collections that were also at risk. Inside the library, employees worked to move the contents of the library to the upper floors, but it was a daunting task.

"My job was to hold open a bag while Jonathan lifted shovelfuls of sand in. I'd tie the bag closed and put it into the waiting arms of the homeless man, who I learned was named Brawley, and it would be whisked down the assembly line that we formed. By the fourth hour I had blisters on my hands and the skin on the insides of my forearms was raw from being scoured with the sand that Jonathan poured into the bags. 'You should pace yourself,' Jonathan finally said to me." Claire remembers watching as Jonathan leaned against his shovel, wiping the sweat from his face with his arm and leaving granules of fine sand clinging to his sweaty cheek.

"Things just progressed from there." Claire shrugs. "The funny thing was that the floods never actually came. We did all that sandbagging for nothing. But Jonathan and I were married a few months later, bought a house, opened Bookends. Then came Joshua." Claire smiles thoughtfully at Allison. "It's funny how things work themselves out."

Claire notices the look on Allison's face. Allison wants to ask her something, but is too shy, too embarrassed. Too something.

Allison

I know I need to form the question carefully, to make it sound like it is a natural part of our conversation. "How long were you married when you had Joshua?" I ask, trying to sound normal, but inside I'm screaming.

A ripple of pain passes across her face. "Joshua's adopted. Someone else did the hard part, but we get to enjoy him."

"How old is he again?" I ask. My voice sounds too high.

"He just turned five last month," Claire said proudly. "We're not sure of the exact day he was born, but we don't think he was more than a month old when he was left at the fire station."

"Fire station? He was left at a fire station?" Still my voice doesn't sound like mine. I clear my throat and take a sip of my soda. This doesn't make sense. It isn't the way it happened.

"His mother left him at the fire station over on Oak

Street in the middle of the night. One of the firemen called Human Services and then took him to the hospital. Human Services called us the next day and we got to take Joshua home with us."

"Did they figure out who she was? The mother?" My heart is fluttering in my chest. She can't know, I tell myself. Only four other people in the world know that Joshua was mine.

Claire shakes her head. "No. We never found out. We figure it was a young girl who came from out of town and left the baby there, then took off again."

"What about the father?" I ask.

Claire shrugs. "No idea. Jonathan and I held our breath for a long time. We were sure that someone was going to come and reclaim him. But they never did. Six months after we brought him home, we legally adopted him." Claire pushes her plate away. "Ugh, that was good, but I'm stuffed. We should be getting back."

Suddenly, I realize I don't have any way to pay for my meal; I left the money my father gave me at Olene's. Claire must see the horror on my face because she reaches out to touch my hand.

"My treat," she says. "You can get lunch next time."

"Okay, thanks," I say with relief. We go back to the store and have a steady stream of customers the rest of the afternoon. It isn't until Joshua bursts through the front door and I see him for the second time that I'm sure. He looks just like Christopher, the same sharp-angled face, the same beautiful brown eyes. Except for his hair—like me, his hair is white-blond and stick-straight.

"Hi, Mom. Hi…" Joshua squints his eyes in concentration. I know he's trying to remember my name.

"Allison," Claire finishes for him.

"Hi, Allison," he says. I look carefully at his face and wonder if on some level he might recognize me. Maybe if he takes a good, long look at me and hears my voice. I know that it is ridiculous to believe that he will throw himself into my arms and whisper, *You finally came back for me, I knew you would.* But part of me hopes there will be a flicker of recognition, like the light from a firefly on a warm summer's night. Hopes for a special look that will pass between the two of us.

But his eyes barely land on my face and he's gone. "Can I have a snack?" he calls from the back room.

He doesn't know me. I'm no one to him. I should feel relief, but I don't. It makes me a little sad.

"Does he know?" I ask Claire once Joshua is out of earshot. "Does he know he's adopted?"

"He knows," Claire answers. "We've never hidden it from him. We celebrate his birthday and the day of his adoption each year."

"Does he ask about her? About his mother?" I'm almost afraid of the answer.

"Not really," Claire answers. "But we tell him she did a very good thing. That she wanted a better life for him and she must have loved him very much to give him up."

"Oh," I say. "That's nice."

"So," Claire says, pointing to a calendar. "How does Thursday, Saturday and Sunday look to you?"

I try to focus on the dates, but the calendar is one of those personalized ones. A large photo of Joshua, holding a soccer ball and wearing a bright green soccer uniform, is staring back at me. "Allison?" Claire asks. "Is that too many hours?"

I tear my eyes away from the calendar. "No, the more hours you have available, the better."

"Great. You'll work with Virginia on Saturday. She's only going to be here through October or so and then she and her husband spend the winter in Florida. You could probably take on some of her hours, too, if you want."

I can hear Claire, but all I can think about is Joshua in that little green uniform. He plays soccer. Just like I did. I wonder what else we have in common.

Charm

She has another two hours before she needs to be at St. Isadore's. As a student nurse Charm is expected to spend time in all departments in the hospital. Next week she is scheduled to begin her mental health rotation. *I'll fit right in,* she thinks to herself. Working with this population will be nothing new to her, between Charm's mother and her mother's boyfriends—probably three-fourths of them were mentally ill. All but Gus, of course. She feels a little bit guilty about storming out of her mother's apartment the other day. She called her mother and apologized for the way she left things. But at the end of the conversation Charm couldn't help but ask the question, though she really tried to hold the words back: Was she still planning on marrying Binks? Her mother responded by hanging up on her.

She's already completed rotations in community health geriatrics, internal medicine, pediatrics and maternity. Maternity was the hardest. Seeing all those beautiful newborns wrapped up tightly in the way that makes them feel safe and secure. Charm hadn't known how to wrap the baby up that way and neither did Gus. They just laid a blanket over the top of him and hoped for the best. *If only I would have known,* Charm often thinks. *I could have done so much better.*

After Allison Glenn left and Christopher took off, Gus and Charm just stood there in amazement. Charm held the crying baby close to her chest, swaying back and forth, trying to shush him.

"Did you know that girl?" Gus asked Charm over the howling baby.

"That was Allison Glenn," Charm said in disbelief. Allison Glenn and Christopher? Charm still couldn't reconcile the thought of her brother and Allison Glenn. Together. Having sex. "She goes to my school. She's going to be a senior. Her sister is in my class," she explained to Gus.

"We have to call someone. We need to get that baby to a hospital," Gus said, overcome by a spasm of coughing.

"Maybe they'll come back," Charm whispered. The baby's cries stopped and his cloudy eyes, an indiscriminate color, squinted up at the overhead light. His mouth curved into a small pink circle.

"I don't know," Gus fretted. "He should see a doctor."

"Allison Glenn is, like, the smartest girl in school. I didn't even know she was pregnant," Charm marveled. "She'll come back—or Christopher will. They can't just walk away from this. They have to come back."

Gus looked doubtful. Charm couldn't imagine taking the baby to a hospital, telling the world Allison Glenn's secret. "You were a firefighter, Gus. You said you delivered a baby once—"

"I *helped* deliver that baby and we got her right to the hospital," he interrupted, wheezing. "That girl should get to a hospital herself. We need to get this baby to the hospital."

"Can't we please wait a while?" Charm begged. "He seems okay."

Gus sighed and sat down heavily in a chair. "We need to get some things for him, some formula and diapers. We'll give them a few hours, Charm. That's it. This isn't a game." Gus went resignedly out into the night and returned a short time later with four sacks filled with everything they could possibly need to take care of a newborn.

"Look at all this stuff," Charm said in amazement, handing Gus the sleeping infant. "I didn't know a baby needed so much." She reached into the bottom of a bag and pulled out two receiving blankets, baby wipes, bottles, formula and tiny blue pajamas with a bear embroidered on the front, laying each on the counter. The last item she pulled from the sack was a blue-and-red Cubs baseball cap. "Gus?" Charm looked at her stepfather in surprise. "A baseball cap?"

He shrugged and smiled wearily. "Gotta get them started young."

The two sat up together that first night, taking turns trying to feed the baby, holding him, both falling a little bit in love with him, but knowing it couldn't last. They knew that if Christopher or Allison didn't come back they'd have to do something.

"Be brave," Charm whispered in the baby's ear. "Everything will be okay."

Now Charm makes her way into Bookends, wanting to see five-year-old Joshua and Claire for herself. Sitting in her car, she sees Joshua through the store's plate-glass window; he is dancing around in a circle, waving a dog treat over Truman's head, laughing. You are brave, Charm thinks to herself. So brave. Claire comes up behind Joshua and plucks the treat from his fingers and bends down to feed it to Truman. Charm smiles. They are fine. Through the window, a tall girl with chin-length blond hair steps into her line of vision. Though she can't see her face there's something familiar about her that Charm can't quite put her finger on, something in the way she carries herself, in the way she tilts her head. It isn't until she is driving home that she realizes who the girl reminds her of. Allison Glenn.

Charm laughs out loud and shakes her head. It's impossible, there's no way. It was years until Allison Glenn would be released from prison. She must be going crazy.

Brynn

After Allison was taken away by the police, I was trying to fall asleep when the phone rang. Biting back tears, I answered it, hoping beyond reason that it was Allison. It wasn't.

"I'm calling about the baby," a man said. I didn't know who he was at first and then it dawned on me. It was the man whose home Allison had driven us to that night. Where she left the baby.

He told me that Christopher had left and wasn't coming back. Ever. And Allison needed to come get the baby.

"She can't," I sobbed. "She's gone. You've got to keep that baby away from here," I said desperately, thinking about what my parents would do if they found out that Allison had another child out there. Selfishly, I thought of myself, too. There was no way my parents would believe that Allison drove to Christopher's alone with a newborn baby. They would figure out quickly that I had helped her, and I couldn't handle their wrath, not all by myself. "You have to take care of him. Please," I begged. He kept on insisting that I explain where Allison went and finally I spat out, "She's in jail. They took her away."

"Why?" he asked, obviously surprised.

"Just turn on the television," I said, getting choked up again. "But keep that baby boy away from here. My parents... No one can take care of him here. He's better off with someone else. Make sure he goes somewhere safe. Please," I begged.

When I least expect it, the thought of that little boy creeps into my mind. I wonder where he ended up. I know that Charm Tullia and her father don't have him anymore. When school started that next fall I saw Charm in the hallways. For two years we would look at each other out of the corners of our eyes, but never spoke about that baby boy. Except once.

After Allison was arrested, people whispered about me behind their hands, looked at me as if I was a freak. When the teachers weren't around, someone would say something obnoxious. I never got used to the comments, but I learned how to deal with them. I learned not to make eye contact, kept my head down. I made sure to move with the crowd, stayed to the edges of the hallway, but still the words felt like sharp blows. *How's the murderer doing in prison? You're sister isn't such hot shit now, is she? Are you a baby killer, too?* There was a twisted glee in their voices. They enjoyed every moment of Allison's very steep fall. It was always the same people—the girls she'd played soccer and volleyball with, the boys her group sat with during lunchtime.

Near the end of my junior year—nine months after Allison was arrested—I made the mistake of lagging behind to talk with my government teacher after the bell rang. You'd think that these morons would have moved on, found some other weaklings to bully, to try and make feel worthless. When I stepped out of the classroom, I found myself in a nearly deserted hallway.

I knew I was in trouble when Chelsea Millard, a senior who had been one of my sister's best friends, and two of her lapdogs stepped into the empty corridor. Though it was springtime and the temperature was warm, goose bumps sprouted on my arms and I shivered when I saw Chelsea straighten her back. A look of righteous indignation settled on her face.

My second mistake was my hesitation. I should have just kept walking, kept moving forward with my head down. But I didn't. My feet did a ridiculous stutter-step and Chelsea and her friends cackled at my awkward dance. They circled me, hands on hips with elbows jutting out like the wings of crows and looked down on me scornfully.

"How's your sister doing?" Chelsea asked snidely. "I bet the women there love Allison." Her friends laughed and I noticed how ugly meanness looks on girls, how it transforms their eyes into thin slits, their mouths into pinched crab-apple smiles. Bitter grins, like they just bit deep into something sour. I stared, transfixed on their grotesquely changing faces, and shuddered.

"Sour," I said before I could stop myself. Their laughter stopped suddenly. Their faces relaxed in confusion but then their eyes narrowed even more. Black angry slits. "Shhh," I said out loud to myself. "Shut up. Don't talk." I knew I was acting strangely, but I couldn't help myself.

"Did you just tell me to shut up?" Chelsea asked in

disbelief, and stepped more closely to me. Sweat began to gather at my forehead. Beads of perspiration pooled between my breasts and slid down my back. *Oh, good,* I thought with relief, *I'm beginning to evaporate.* I covered my mouth to hold back a giggle. I didn't think I said that out loud, but I couldn't be sure.

"You're crazy," Chelsea spat. "Just like your baby-killing sister." I looked down at my shoes and wondered if I was getting smaller and smaller. I hoped that I would continue to drip and melt until there was nothing left.

"Are you hiding something under there?" one of Chelsea's friends asked. She reached for my T-shirt. To avoid her hand, I stepped back, crashing into the bank of lockers behind me. "Are you hiding a baby, like your sister?" She grabbed for my shirt again, this time clutching a handful of fabric. In the process, she grabbed the soft, fleshy skin of my stomach and wrenched it upward. I cried out in surprise and pain.

"Leave her alone." A firm voice came down the hallway. The afternoon light was streaming brightly through the high windows that lined the hallway, making it difficult to see the figure that was moving toward us. As the person approached, I realized it was Charm Tullia.

"Just leave her alone," Charm said evenly. She didn't look afraid or intimidated by the older girls, just annoyed.

"What are you going to do about it?" the girl who still held fast to my shirt asked.

Charm ignored the girl and continued to peer levelly into Chelsea's eyes. The stare-down seemed to go on forever until finally Chelsea lowered her gaze and said to her friends, "Come on, let's go, we've got practice.

Freaks," she said loudly as she bumped past Charm, her entourage following closely behind.

"You okay?" Charm asked me, gently touching my arm. I stared at her small, nail-bitten hand, surprised it hadn't passed through my skin. I hadn't evaporated into nothingness.

"I'm still here," I said softly.

I meant to thank her. I wanted to thank her. But I simply drifted away.

Allison

I start with the phone book and look up the last name Tullia. There is only one entry—a Reanne Tullia who lived over on Higgins Street. No Christopher. I think of Charm Tullia. Christopher's little sister. Charm, her stepfather and Christopher are the only other people besides Brynn and me who know about Joshua. What was her stepfather's last name? I remember where they lived five years ago, but I have no way of getting there, even if that's still where they live. I need to speak with them. Do I dare call this Reanne Tullia? It couldn't hurt, I guess. I could just ask about Christopher or Charm and leave it at that, couldn't I? I take a deep breath and with shaky hands I begin to dial Reanne Tullia's number. Then I hang up.

I'll try to get a little more information and then I'll go to Devin, I promise myself. Deep down I know that it's risky, that it's stupid. But I pick up the phone again and dial the number I know by heart. It rings and rings and just as I'm about to hang up the ringing stops.

I'm learning all about being patient at Gertrude House. The women here are finally leaving me alone. I guess they figured that if I didn't completely freak out from finding all the dolls they put in sinks and toilets that I wasn't all that much fun to terrorize. Still, everyone pretty much ignores me there except for Olene and Bea and sometimes Tabatha.

Bea's a good talker and a good listener. She goes on and on about her four children who range in age from twelve down to nine months old. They live with her sister in a town about a half hour from here. She tells me how her oldest, a boy, is an honor student and a star pitcher on his baseball team and how her three girls are the smartest, sweetest things.

"Have you seen them lately?" I ask while we're preparing supper. "Can they come to Gertrude House to visit?"

Bea shakes her head and drops a handful of pasta into a pot of boiling water. "No. I don't want them to see me yet. I'm not ready."

"What's to be ready for?" I ask. "You're out of jail, they're close by. I'm sure they're dying to see you."

"Maybe," Bea says. "But I want to make sure I'm the mom I'm supposed to be first. I want to be healthy. I want them to be proud of me."

"You're their mom—of course they're going to be proud of you," I assure her.

She shakes her head again. "I showed up high at my daughter's second grade conference. I stumbled all around the room and threw up on her teacher's shoes. She most definitely was not proud of me. I want to make sure I stay sober and get a good job. Then I'll see my kids."

"I don't know," I tell her. "My parents, on the outside, looked like everything a kid should be proud of. But they didn't really seem to care a whole lot about us." I open the refrigerator and pull out the salad dressing. "Go and see your kids, Bea. All they really want is to be with you, for you to be truly interested in who they are and what they do. That will be enough."

"It's not the right time," Bea says in a way that I know I should drop the whole topic, but I can't.

"Do you think they'll remember you?" I ask. "I mean, your youngest? You haven't seen her since she was born. Do you think in some way she'll know who you are?"

Bea laughs. "God, I hope not. The poor kid was born in prison." More seriously she says, "I hope she has no memory of that horrible place. My sister has been a good mother to my kids. I want to be their mother again, but I may have to be satisfied with much less. Who knows, maybe eventually the past won't matter to them, maybe they'll be happy to get to know me again. Time will tell." Bea fishes into the pot of pasta with a fork and pulls out a few noodles. Using her fingers she lifts the strands and tosses them against the kitchen wall, where they stick. "I can never remember if the noodles are supposed to stick or fall off. Oh, well." She drains the pot of pasta and then hollers in her shrill voice, "Come and eat!"

I wish that would be enough for Brynn. For us to just reconnect. Then what happened all those years ago won't matter so much anymore. Brynn used to be proud of me; she used to look up to me. I want that again. I want her to be proud of me again.

No, not even proud. I just want her to *like* me. I want

to be able to tell her more about finding Joshua, about how much he looks like Christopher but has my hair. How, in a way, Joshua reminds me of her. The way he loves animals, the way he likes everything just so. And I want Brynn to tell me about her life. What her classes at school are like, whether or not she has a boyfriend, whether our parents drive her as crazy as they do me. I want to be a sister to Brynn, something I was never very good at. But everyone deserves a second chance, don't they?

Even me.

Charm

Over and over Gus tried to call Allison Glenn's home and speak to someone about the baby. Finally, someone picked up the phone and Gus said, "I'm calling about the baby." As Gus listened to the person on the line, his face turned a sickly gray color. "I understand," he said, and hung up the phone.

"What?" Charm asked. "What did they say?"

Gus rubbed a shaking hand over his face and sat down heavily in a chair. "Turn on the TV," he said.

"What?" Charm asked, not understanding.

"Turn on the TV," Gus said again. Charm handed him the baby, turned on the television set and flipped the channels until Gus told her to stop. A newscaster was standing on the banks of the Druid River, a serious look on her face.

"Gus…" Charm began, but the look on his face stopped her.

"It was here, at the banks of the Druid River, that a man fishing with his grandson found the lifeless infant girl." The reporter made a sweeping gesture with her arm. "Channel Seven News has just learned that a teenage female has been taken into custody in connection to this case. Because the suspect is a juvenile, her identity will not be released to the public. However, we can tell you that the individual in question was escorted from her Linden Falls home by law enforcement and then taken to a local hospital for an undisclosed reason."

Charm turned to Gus and looked at him blankly. "What does this have to do with the baby and Allison?"

The baby began fussing, his thin arms flailing, and Gus brought him up to his shoulder. "There, there," he whispered into his ear. "The unnamed individual taken into custody," he said, nodding his head toward the television, "was Allison Glenn. And that little girl they found in the Druid is this little boy's sister."

Allison

Every day I walk into Bookends I'm so afraid that Claire or even Joshua will take one look at my face and suddenly realize who I am. Would this be a violation of my parole? Would they send me back to prison? For how reluctant I was to leave Cravenville, even the short amount of time I've been free has made me realize that I never want to go back. But though I search her face carefully, I can see no difference in Claire; she greets me happily, and we chat comfortably about everyday things.

Each minute I spend with Claire I like her more and more. She talks to me like I'm somebody. She doesn't talk down to me or look at me suspiciously because of my past. I like working at Bookends. I like the Kelbys. I know I should tell her that I suspect Joshua is my son, but I can't. I don't want to.

At three-thirty Joshua flies into the bookstore. His normally pale face is blotchy red and his lips are pinched in anger. Odd winks of light are reflecting off his skin and clothing. When I look more closely, I see that he is speckled with tiny bits of orange glitter. Joshua is intent on trying to pick the bits of glitter from his arms, but only succeeds in transferring it to another part of his body. Jonathan comes in behind Joshua, a mix of frustration and bewilderment on his face. Claire steps out from behind the counter. "What's the matter?" she asks with worry.

"Josh had a tough day at school," Jonathan says, "that involved glue and glitter."

"What happened?" Claire says, and Joshua scowls and folds his arms defiantly in front of him.

Jonathan notices me standing there for the first time. "Hi, Allison," he says. "His teacher said in art class they were sprinkling glitter over the glue they had spread on construction-paper leaves that they had drawn and cut out. Of course Joshua got glue on his fingers, which is, as we all know, worse than baths, sand and haircuts all rolled up into one, and then he got glitter on his hands. I've got to give the school credit—Mrs. Lovelace helped Joshua wash the glue off his hands, but of course, then his hands weren't completely dry and that drove Joshua nuts and things went downhill from there."

I watch as Claire winces in anticipation of what is coming. Joshua is scrubbing furiously at his arms and begins to cry. "Stop it, Josh!" Claire says sharply. "You're scratching yourself." Joshua whips around so that his back is to all of us and continues to scour at his arms. I don't know if I should jump in and try to help or go back to examining the alarm system and pretend I don't notice the tantrum.

"So according to Mrs. Lovelace," Jonathan continues over Joshua's cries, "Joshua crumpled up his leaf, getting more glue and glitter on himself. Then, in a rage I'm certain was something to behold, he grabbed the canister of glitter and proceeded to fling orange glitter around the room. All over the other children, their projects, the teacher and himself. Joshua—" Jonathan lifts his arms in exasperation "—was escorted out of the room."

"Oh, Joshua," Claire says in disappointment. As she lays her hands on his thin shoulders, he sits down and begins to cry even harder.

Without thinking I go to my knees, near enough to Joshua for me to be in his line of vision. Momentarily, his crying slows and he warily watches me from the corner of his eye. I speak before he can continue his tirade. "Joshua, it sounds like you had a rough day." He turns away from me and begins to cry again, but this time with less steam, so I plug onward. "I bet you'd like to get that glitter off you right now." This stills him. He is breathing hard, but I can tell he is listening, so I move a little closer to him and continue in a low, calm voice— the one that comes in handy when talking to Flora at the halfway house when she's angry. "I bet you didn't know there's a magic kind of tape that is used especially for re-moving glitter." I stand and go back behind the counter, pull open a drawer and retrieve a roll of masking tape.

Joshua eyes the tape with suspicion. "That's just reg-ular tape," he informs me.

I casually shrug and say, "It *looks* like regular tape. We can try it, if you want to. Or it's okay if we don't— you can keep the glitter, if you'd like." I set the tape down on the counter. This is one thing I learned in prison—whenever possible, give a person a way to save face.

He thinks about this for a moment and then, surprising us all, stands. "Okay, I'll try it." I tear a piece of tape from the roll and fold it back on itself so that the sticky side faces upward.

"Do you want to try it yourself," I ask, "or would you like your mom or dad to do it?"

"Will it hurt?" Joshua asks fearfully.

"Not a bit," I reassure him.

"You do it, then," he tells me. It comes out as an order.

"Joshua." Claire raises her voice in warning.

"Will you please use the magic tape on me?" he tries again.

"Sure," I say. "Now watch closely, it's pretty amazing." Carefully, gently, I rub the folded tape over the sleeve of his T-shirt and then show Joshua the orange glitter it has picked up. "Cool, huh?" I say, smiling at him. He smiles back. And there it is, our connection. It's subtle, just a glimmer—more of a sputter, really—but it's there. I can't say that he recognizes me, but a link, thin and fragile, has been made. I look up at Claire and she is smiling at me with a newfound respect. Then I look to Jonathan, who is also impressed.

I spend the next thirty minutes with Joshua in the children's section of the bookstore, gingerly removing the glitter from his shirt, pants and even his shoes. The glitter that clings to his fingers, face and hair is a different story. Joshua is scared to let me put the sticky tape directly on his skin. "It will hurt," he tells me, his thin face serious but expectant at the same time.

"Well, it's up to you," I say. "You can leave the glitter where it is or we can try and use the magic tape to get it off your skin. If you think it hurts I can stop."

"Could I try it?" he asks hopefully.

"Absolutely," I tell him, and show him how to fold

the tape. He presses it lightly against his skin, pulls it away and closely examines the glittery pattern left on the tape.

"That didn't hurt," he says matter-of-factly, and continues to work until his hands are glitter free. Joshua allows me to help with his hair and face as long as I promise not to pull too hard and to stop immediately if he asks me to. He closes his eyes and raises his face to me and the whole time I am working I am absorbing his long face and pointy chin. I memorize the bluish veins of his closed eyelids and the light fringe of eyelashes that fan out against his skin, the way his thin lips are pursed beneath his upturned nose, so much like Christopher's. When I reluctantly tell him that I'm finished, he asks, "Can I see?" and runs off to the bathroom where he can look at himself in a mirror. I go back to the front of the store where Claire is helping a customer. Joshua emerges a few minutes later, smiling broadly. "It worked," he tells Claire. "Maybe I can take some of that tape with me to school."

"Sure," Claire says. "But I bet if you ask your teacher, she probably already has some. What do you say to Allison?"

"Thank you," Joshua tells me shyly.

"You're welcome," I respond.

"Mom, can I get something to eat?" Joshua asks, looking to Claire, and my heart clutches with something I can't name.

"Go get some crackers from the back room," she tells him. "Wow," Claire says, looking at me with admiration. "You did a great job with him." I blush. "Where did you learn how to do that?"

I shrug as if it's no big deal. "It's always good to give a person a choice. Then they don't feel so trapped."

Claire shakes her head. "I've read that in about every parenting book, but by the time I think of it, Joshua is in throes of such a tantrum, it's too late. I'll have to give it a try next time."

I look awkwardly down at my feet. "Is there something you want me to do? Shelving books or something?" I ask.

"You know what would be a great help?" Claire says, looking toward the bulldog standing at the front entrance, his breath forming a foggy Rorschach blob on the glass door. "Would you mind taking Truman outside for a quick bathroom break? I don't really want to leave Joshua right now." She smiles at me apologetically. "I know this isn't normally in the job description for working in a bookstore, but Truman and the store are kind of a package deal."

"No problem," I tell her. "Truman's great. I can't have pets where I live." I run to grab my jacket from the back room. When I return, Jonathan is gone—back to work, I guess—and Claire and Joshua are already immersed in a book together. I clip the leash onto Truman's collar and we head out into the cool September air. I lead him to a patch of grass along the sidewalk in front of the store and wait patiently so he can relieve himself.

I feel it on my back, as soft as a falling leaf. Someone's gaze. I turn to find the source is Claire's husband, sitting in his white truck looking at me, his face unreadable. Before I can stop myself, I raise my hand in a spastic wave. As if he is trying to hold it back, he smiles, too, and waves in return. He puts his truck into Drive and slowly rolls forward, and for a minute I think that he is going to stop to speak to me, but he doesn't. Instead, he pulls away from the curb and drives away and I stare after him a long time, well after he has turned the corner and is out of sight. Wondering if somehow he knows who I am. But he can't know. He can't.

Truman is yanking on his leash so I turn to lead him back to Bookends and see Joshua standing at the front window, watching as the gray exhaust from his father's truck swirls about me.

Charm

Charm is sitting in the empty bathtub, fully clothed. It seems to be the only place she can go and not hear the rattle of Gus's chest. She knows she should be brave, should go out there and sit with him. She's going to be a nurse, after all. But all of her training could not prepare Charm for this. Gus is dying in a way that no one should have to—even the meanest person in the world should not have to suffer the way he is. He is suffocating, slowly, painfully, right in front of her and there is nothing she can do to help him, even though he looks up at her desperately. She imagines his blackened lungs squeezing in his chest, desperate for air. The pneumonia settled in so quickly. His skin has turned a sickly gray and his whole body has wasted away until he's just bone. He reminds her of those pictures of concentration camp survivors that they saw in history class. The only part of him that isn't thin is his face and neck. There he is all puffy. Sometimes it's hard to find him in that swollen yellow flesh, but once in a while he smiles and she sees him again. The fun, energetic Gus who came to every school event Charm ever had, the one who taught her how to shoot free throws and how to make *kolache*. Now he looks like a stranger.

Charm considers calling her mother, but isn't sure what she would say to her. Charm has only truly needed her mother two other times in her life—when her mother's sicko boyfriend cornered her while Reanne was at work and when Allison left Joshua with her. Both times, her mother wasn't there. *I could use a mother now,* Charm thinks. Someone to help her take care of Gus, to tell her that everything's going to be okay. Unfortunately, Reanne Tullia is not that person.

Charm climbs from the bathtub and looks at herself in the mirror. Her eyes are bloodshot and little crevices are forming around lips that she knows she keeps perpetually pinched in worry. *I look so old,* she thinks. *I am twenty-one and I'm starting to look like an old woman.*

Charm told her instructors at school that she needed to take some time off so she could help care for Gus. They were very understanding. She knows that the next time she returns to class will be after Gus's funeral.

She reluctantly leaves the refuge of the bathroom and goes to Gus. His eyes are slightly open and she pulls a chair up to the bed and sits next to him. Charm carried his old TV set into his bedroom and they watch silly sitcoms and old reruns of police dramas. It doesn't really matter what they watch, just as long as the volume from the television covers up the teakettle wheeze that comes from his chest. When Gus starts one of his coughing fits, Charm carefully helps him sit up and rubs his back in small circles, like she saw him do with Joshua when he was with them. Charm pats Gus's back over and over and whispers encouraging words to him, as if he is now the baby. "It's okay, it's okay. Get it out." Gus clenches and unclenches the blankets with his thin, skeleton hands. When the hacking finally stops Charm gives him a sip of water, fixes the pillows behind his head and gently replaces the oxygen mask over his nose. She sits back down again until his breathing calms and he falls asleep.

Jane arranges to have the people from the hospice program come in and Charm is grateful. They are very nice and helpful; but it's still Charm that Gus looks to. It is Charm his watery blue eyes follow around the room as if begging her to help him. He speaks nonsense much of the time and he calls Charm by her mother's name, which physically pains her. Doris, the hospice volunteer, tries to tell her that it is Gus's cancer and all the pain medicine that makes him talk like this.

Fall has come to them hard and angry, expelling sharp slashes of rain, like spit. It rains all the time now. She finds it depressing, sitting in the little house day after day. Charm wants to go back to school, but she can't stand the thought of leaving Gus at the house with strangers. She knows that he could die at any moment and is determined not to desert him, like her mother did. She wants to be there with him until his eyes close and don't open, until he doesn't have to struggle for every bit of air.

Gus's double bed has been replaced with a hospital bed. It makes it easier for the hospice workers to care for him and change his sheets. Makes it easier for them to wheel him out when he dies, Charm thinks to herself. He looks like an empty cocoon lying there, his skin cobweb-thin and pulled tight against his bones. His coughing has quieted and he lies so still that at times the gentle rise and fall of his chest are her only indication that he is still alive.

Charm wonders if her mother knows that Gus is

dying and if she cares. She wonders what she will do, where she will go, what will become of her. Though she has always been independent, without a true mother or father, she always had Gus.

She feels a small movement beside her and turns on the table-side lamp so she can see Gus's face. In the dim light, with the shadows surrounding him, Gus looks almost like himself. Youthful, handsome, happy.

"How're you doing, Gus?" Charm asks him in a whisper. The mere act of listening seems to cause him pain. "Can I get you something?" His eyes are open and clear and he tries to lift a hand to pull away the oxygen mask. "Let me get it," she tells him and removes the mask that she once teased him made him look like Horton, the elephant from the Dr. Seuss books. Gus had laughed. He licks his dry, cracked lips and Charm presses a straw between them and he sips. The effort it takes him to do this is exhausting. "What else?" she asks. "What can I do?" Charm tries to swallow back the emotion. She has seen patients die, seen children die, but no one she has known. No one she has loved.

"No," Gus croaks. "Just sit here." He weakly pats a spot next to him on the bed. Charm hesitates. She'd have to lower the side rail that prevents him from falling out and there isn't much room, even though he is as thin as the switch grass outside his window.

"It's all right," he says.

Charm lowers the rail and gently moves him. He doesn't make a sound, but his face fills with pain. "I'm sorry, I'm sorry." Charm winces, but he pats the bed again to let her know he is okay. Trying to make herself as small as possible, she eases in next to him. "Do you want to watch television?" she asks, reaching for the remote. He shakes his head. "Do you want your mask back on?" Charm asks, knowing he can't go for very long without it, how he tends to panic, which makes it harder for him to catch his breath.

Again he shakes his head. Because of the swelling, the sharp angles of his handsome face are gone. His dark hair stands in stark contrast to his pale skin and his shaggy eyebrows make his eyes appear smaller, more sunken. A blue pond among the reeds.

"Talk," he orders in the way that he has. He can still get away with sounding bossy without sounding mean.

"Well," Charm begins. "I start on the orthopedic floor next week. And I'll be on the pediatric oncology floor right around Halloween. Everyone dresses up in costumes, even the doctors."

Gus nods and they sit in silence for a moment. They both know he will be gone by Halloween.

"The little boy," Gus says, his voice like sandpaper.

Charm's heart plummets. She knew the subject of Joshua would come up, needed to come up one more time.

"I'm sorry." His words are breathy and are emitted with more difficulty.

"Why?" Charm asks incredulously. "Why are you sorry? It was Christopher's fault. It was Allison Glenn's fault. Not yours. Joshua is safe. He is happy. He is with people who love him." She angrily ticks the points off on her fingers. "His mother went to prison for drowning his twin sister, you knew Christopher would never come back to take care of him, and God knows my mother is useless!"

"Shhh," Gus breathes, and softly places his hand next to her cheek. "Shhh, now." This is too much for Charm, this kind, desperately ill man trying to comfort her. She was the one who begged for more time with the baby. But a few hours had turned into a few days, then into three weeks. Charm kept on pleading with Gus for more time, sure that her brother would come back for the little boy she had quickly fallen in love with. She begins to cry.

"*I'm* sorry. I should have told you," Charm sobs. "I should have told you I was taking him to the fire station." She looks helplessly at her stepfather. "I couldn't do it anymore. I wanted to, but I couldn't. I was so tired. I knew I'd waited too long to take him to a safe haven place and I was afraid you could get in trouble, so I didn't say anything to you."

"You're a good girl, Charm," Gus murmurs. "You're smart and brave. Braver than I ever was." Charm looks at him. Over the years, Gus has described the many harrowing fires he fought. The smoke, the flames, the heat. "You kept looking after that little boy, even after you left him at the fire station. You made sure he was safe."

"You didn't even get a chance to say goodbye." Gus is silent. The conversation is tiring him. "Sometimes I wish she'd never brought him to our house," Charm says, finally voicing out loud what she's been feeling for so long. "Sometimes I wish I never held him. I wish I never knew he had a little sister that was thrown into the river. I wish you would get better." Charm swallows hard, trying to hold back the tears, and hides her face against his brittle shoulder.

With great difficulty Gus brings his other arm around her.

"Daughter," Gus rasps. There is nothing left to say. They lie there a long time, Gus softly patting her back and Charm soaking it up, like a cat trying to find the last patch of fading sunshine.

Allison

Ever since Joshua's glitter incident and the way I came to the rescue with the magic tape, he is constantly at my side when I'm working, offering to hand me books to shelve or to count the pennies in the register. In a very short time I've discovered the long list of things Joshua hates and loves. He hates when his fingers are sticky, the smell of bananas, thunderstorms and cleaning his room. He loves Truman, playing with Legos, drinking Dr Pepper—even though his mom says it will rot his teeth right out of his head—and building things with his dad.

I know I should try to keep him at arm's length. Getting close to him will end in nothing but disaster. I should tell him to beat it, that I need to focus on my work, but I don't. "What about soccer?" I ask, thinking about the picture of him in his green uniform. "Do you like playing soccer?"

"It's okay. I'm not very good at it," he says a little sadly. "Someone always gets the ball away from me."

"I could show you some tips," I offer. "I used to play soccer all the time."

"Okay," Joshua says, bending down to pet Truman. "I'll bring my soccer ball tomorrow."

"I don't think your mom will want us playing soccer in the store," I tell him, instantly regretting my offer. For a minute Joshua looks deflated.

"You can come over to our house," Joshua says, perking up. "You can teach me soccer and I can show you my room and my dad's workshop."

"I don't know…" I look away from Joshua when I hear a customer come through the door, grateful for the distraction. I'm getting too close, too involved.

I see Devin walking slowly toward me. Gone is her usual brisk, businesslike pace. She looks almost hesitant. Not like herself at all. She knows. She knows about Joshua. Brynn called her and told her that I'm his mother. She's coming to tell me I'm going back to prison. I've been free for three weeks and now I have to go back. I think I'd rather die first.

"Josh, why don't you go do your homework," I say as Devin stops in front of me. Something is wrong. Very wrong.

"Who's that?" Joshua asks, staying at my side.

"Joshua, are you bothering Allison?" Claire's voice comes from behind me.

"No, I'm helping," Joshua insists.

"Allison," Devin says gently. "Can I talk to you for a minute?"

Claire looks at us with concern. I know I should introduce them to each other, but the words are stuck in my throat, so I just nod and follow Devin as she leads me outside. I close my eyes and wait for Devin to tell me that she's taking me to the police station. The air is cool and feels good against my hot cheeks and I try to memorize the feel of it.

"Allison?" Devin says, and I open my eyes. She is biting the insides of her cheeks, struggling to speak, and I wonder if I'll be able to say goodbye to Claire, to thank her for giving me a chance. I wonder if I'll ever see Joshua again. "Allison." She reaches for my hand. "It's your father."

"My father?" I say in confusion. I look down at Devin's hand in mine. A large sparkling diamond is on her ring finger. She's getting married, I think to myself. I begin to congratulate her when she interrupts me.

"He collapsed at his office today," Devin explains. "He's at St. Isadore's in intensive care. They're not exactly sure what's going on yet, but it looks like a heart attack." I look at her questioningly and, like always, Devin seems able to read my thoughts. "Your mother called Barry. Mr. Gordon." I nod my head. This makes sense. My father and the senior partner in Devin's law firm, Barry Gordon, have been friends for years. "Do you want to go to the hospital?" Devin asks. "I can drive you over there."

I think back to my last encounter with my father, remember how the house had been erased of any existence of me. "I don't know if they want me at the hospital," I say in a small voice.

"What do you want, Allison?" Devin asks me. "What do *you* want to do?"

Suddenly, I have to see my father. What if he dies? I can't let the next time I see my mother be at my father's funeral. I quickly explain the situation to Claire and she sends me off with a hug. "Let me know what's happening. Don't worry about work. You go be with your family."

I can't tell her that, in the few weeks I've been back in Linden Falls, she feels more like family to me than my parents. "Thanks" is all I can manage. "I'll call you later."

Devin drops me off in front of the hospital. She offers to come with me, but I tell her no, that I'll be okay. But I'm not really okay. I just didn't want Devin to have to witness my first meeting with my mother. I have no idea how she'll react to me showing up at my father's hospital bed. I don't know if she'll welcome me with a hug or order me to leave.

The last time I was in St. Isadore's Hospital, I was recovering from giving birth and was under arrest for the murder of my newborn baby girl. I left in a wheel-chair that was pushed by a corrections officer and my hands were cuffed together. The bustle of the hospital is the same as I remember. Nurses and doctors move pur-posely through the hallways, visitors more tentatively. I stop at the information desk to ask which floor my father is on and then take the stairs to the fifth floor. The thought of stepping into an airless, cramped ele-vator, which reminds me of my prison cell, takes my breath away.

I see her first. She is sitting alone on a long sofa in the intensive-care waiting area. Her hair is the same shiny blond color I remember, but cut shorter in a severe blunt bob that stops just below her chin. She is wear-ing jeans and her mud-caked garden clogs. She must have been working in the yard when she got the call. She must have been in a hurry to get to the hospital. My mother never wears jeans out in public, never wears her gardening shoes out of the yard. She is staring at the wall of the waiting room, her clear blue eyes still unaware of my presence. Her face has softened some since I saw her last, though she is thinner, more fragile-looking. For once she looks unguarded and I know if I don't speak now, I'll lose my nerve.

"Mom," I say softly, and the word ends with a raspy hitch.

She startles and looks up at me. With the full weight of her face on me, I now see how much she has aged in the past year, though she is still beautiful. "Allison," she says, and I think I hear a note of gladness in her voice. It's all the invitation I need. In an instant I'm at her side on the couch, my arms wrapped around her thin shoulders. I breathe in her scent, a combination of the lily-of-the-valley perfume she wears and the soil she must have been working in when she got the call.

"How's Dad?" I ask through my tears. "Is he going to be okay?"

My mother shakes her head from side to side.

"I don't know," she says helplessly. "They aren't telling me anything." She looks down at her hands. Her once long, slim fingers are wrinkled and beginning to thicken at the knuckles. "He's still in surgery."

"I'll go ask in a minute," I tell her. "See if I can get an update. Did someone call Brynn or Grandma? Are you okay? Have you eaten?"

She shakes her head and looks down at her feet. "I forgot to change my shoes." Her chin wobbles and she covers her eyes with her hands and begins to weep. "He's all I have," she cries. "He's all I have left."

Charm

In her heart, she knew that she couldn't take care of him. She had agonized over the decision. Charm was sure he had smiled at her, though the book she found at the library explained that babies didn't *really* smile until they were six weeks old. But Charm swore that when the baby had waved his tiny fists in the air, he gave a brief, true smile. They all knew from the very beginning that their time together was just temporary. Charm and Gus couldn't even bring themselves to give him a real name. Gus called him *Kiddo* or *Buddy* and Charm would whisper sweet confections and baked goods into his ear. *Hey, Cupcake,* she would say as she lifted him out of the makeshift bed they had made out of a laundry basked lined with soft blankets. *Good morning, Soda Pop. Peanut Butter, Apple Dumpling, Cheese Doodle.* He would look at Charm with those wise old eyes as if to say, "Not much longer, huh? It's just a matter of time and I'll be outta here." Charm's heart would twist and she would cry and cry until the front of his onesie was soaked through and then he would begin to wail until Charm couldn't tell which cries were hers or which were his anymore.

Weeks of keeping him a secret and of sleepless nights were wearing Charm down and it was clear that Gus was getting sicker by the day. In the middle of the night she would wake up to the baby's hungry cries and then to Gus's hacking coughs. Charm just couldn't do it anymore, care for both a baby and a sick man. Gus had taken her in when no one else would, without question or judgment, and he treated the baby like he was always there, just a part of the family. Gus was the closest thing to a father that she'd ever known. The baby had barely left a mark in this world yet but Gus left an impression that was deep, permanent. Gus was dying and she had to choose between the one whose journey had just begun and the one whose journey was ending.

It was late one night when Charm finally made the decision. She was pacing around the living room with the baby on her shoulder, trying to get him to sleep. She was half-comatose herself and blindly caught her foot on an end table sending the baby tumbling from her arms. She had *dropped* him. Wide-eyed he looked up at her from the floor, the breath knocked from his little body, his mouth opening and closing as if trying to communicate what Charm already knew.

Silently, without waking Gus, she tucked all of the baby's things around him in the basket and drove him to the fire station on Oak Street in Linden Falls, one town away, just over the Druid River. The same fire station where Gus once worked. She wondered at the logic of this, but convinced herself that if Gus worked there, it must be a good place. They would take care of him.

She lifted him from the laundry basket that she had set on the car floor beside her and held him close to her chest. He had cried himself out and fallen asleep, his sweet little fingers and hand curled up like a pink flower under his chin. She needed to do this impossible thing, give away the only thing that had ever loved her on first sight and with no strings attached. She laid him gently back into the laundry basket and carefully carried him to the firehouse, all the time looking around to see if anyone had noticed her. It was a starless, warm night and no one was on the street. She kissed his soft cheek and whispered, "Be good, Pumpkin," and set him gently as a prayer into the shadows. Remembering with a heavy sadness playing ding dong ditch with her friends as a child, she pressed the doorbell next to the entrance of the firehouse and ran.

Brynn

The phone is ringing as I unlock the door to my grandma's house and Milo runs over to greet me, snuffling at my pockets, which I always keep filled with treats. The cats, Lucy and Leith, wrap themselves around my legs and mew hungrily. "Just a minute, guys," I tell them. The phone continues to trill and I call out, "Grandma! Grandma! Telephone!"

I let the phone ring and I go to the cupboard and pull out two cans of cat food. My grandma's voice fills the room. "We can't come to the phone right now. Please leave your name and number and we'll call you back." After the beep I hear Allison's voice. I toss the cans of cat food on the countertop in irritation and they skid across the surface. I start to stomp up the stairs so I don't have to listen to the message that she leaves. Why can't she just leave me alone?

Her voice follows me up the steps and I freeze. "Brynn, please pick up, please pick up the phone!" I shake my head and begin to go up the stairs again.

"Brynn! It's Dad. Please," she begs. I slowly come back down the stairs. "Dad's in the hospital. Mom's a mess. I don't know what I should do. I need you to talk to me. Please." Allison is crying hard now and I move toward the phone. "Brynn, I need you," she ends in a whimper.

I try not to think too much about the details of that night. But it was the only time in my whole life that my sister asked for my help. This I remember, this small detail I think about at night when I can't sleep. That night my sister needed me. I was always the one who needed my sister, the one who needed protection from neighborhood kids, my parents, teachers. Myself. And she never, ever let me forget it. It had been so long since she'd helped me willingly. No, there was always eye rolling, big sighs and shakes of the head. It's not like it was hard for Allison to help me out. Everything came easily to her. But as we grew older and the differences between us grew more obvious, she always had a way of making me feel small and simple.

Allison has written to me letter after letter, saying the same thing over and over again. *I'm sorry,* she writes, as if that will fix everything. Sorry for what? I want to ask her. Sorry for treating me as if I was a pesky irritation? Sorry for making me help you give birth? Sorry for making me keep your secrets? I don't even open her letters anymore; I throw them in the bottom drawer of my dresser. It hurts, doesn't it? I want to ask her. It hurts to need help and it hurts to have to beg for it. Sorry, sorry, sorry. I used to say it all the time. For everything. Not anymore.

Who's sorry now? I want to ask her. Who's sorry now?

I reach out and lift up the phone.

Charm

Charm is out walking when he dies. It is a rare warm and sunny day and she needs to get out of that house. She stops in to say goodbye to Gus before she leaves the house—she does this every time she leaves his room anymore, just in case. She bends down, kisses his cheek and whispers, "See you." Their standard goodbye. Gus has been asleep for the past two days. Not once does he open his eyes or speak. She wants so much to hear him call her "daughter" again. She's never heard anyone—not even her mother—call her this. It is such a nice word, when she thinks about it. Daughter. Dot…her. Like a punctuation mark. It says, *This one here, she's mine.* So final, forever.

When she comes back in from her walk by the river, he is gone. His chest is still, his eyes closed. He is at peace.

Charm can't stay in Gus's house all alone, and Jane offers to come over and get her and bring Charm back to her home so she could stay there for the night or lon-

ger if she'd like to. The hearse has already come and
gone. Charm was surprised by that, the long black car,
beetlelike, creeping slowly up to the front of the house.
She felt the urge to take off her shoe and throw it at it.
The man from the funeral home was very nice; he had
a soft, calm voice that made Charm feel like he would
treat Gus well. He explained to her that Gus had already
made all the arrangements for the funeral—picked out
a casket, the music, everything. The funeral director
asked if Charm had something in mind for Gus to wear
for the funeral. As if he could take it off when the funeral was over.

Doris, Gus's favorite hospice volunteer, helps her
decide. Together they rifle through his closet, filled
with his khaki pants and oxford shirts, all much too big
for him now. From the very back corner of the closet
Doris pulls a plastic-covered black suit hanging neatly
on a hanger.

"What do you think of this?" she asks, holding it
up for Charm.

"I don't know." Charm looks at it doubtfully. Gus
never wore a suit.

"He must have kept it for a reason," Doris says, lifting the plastic away and checking the size. "It should
fit him."

"It's fine, I guess." Charm shrugs. She is suddenly
very tired. Her eyes burn and all she wants to do is get
this day over with.

"Go lie down, Charm," Doris tells her. "Get a little
rest."

"I'm okay. I'm just going to sit outside and wait for
Jane to come." Doris promises to drop the suit off at
the funeral home and goes into the kitchen.

Charm sits on the front steps waiting for Jane to pull up. Picking out Gus's clothes has made her think of her own. Charm has nothing to wear to a funeral, no skirt, or dress pants even. Only her nursing scrubs and jeans. She has nothing to wear on her feet but her thick-soled nursing shoes and a pair of old tennis shoes. Charm looks down at them. They are speckled with mud from her walk by the creek and a little hole is beginning near the big toe. Charm can't wear scrubs or a pair of faded jeans and a T-shirt to Gus's funeral. A new panic overtakes her, different than the sick, waterlogged feeling of losing Gus. More of a plastic bag over your head, not being able to breathe sensation. Charm stands quickly and runs back into the house, where she finds Doris stripping down Gus's bed.

"What's the matter, Charm?" Doris asks with alarm, seeing the tears running down her face.

"What am I going to do?" Charm asks her helplessly, palms facing upward, showing her how empty they were. "I've got nothing."

"Oh, Charm," she says, dropping the sheets she is holding and rushing over to her. Doris wraps her soft, wide arms around her. Charm is practically twelve inches taller than Doris is, and her tears drip into Doris's tightly permed hair. "It's going to be okay. Gus loved you. He's taken care of you."

Charm keeps crying, not understanding Doris. "He's dead."

"Charm." Doris lets go of her and takes a step backward so she can look up at her. "Gus left you everything. He told me. His house, his savings, his life insurance." Doris folds her back in her arms and Charm feels better. For a moment, she can almost imagine that it is her mother who is holding her tightly.

The two hear a knock on the front door and Charm knows that Jane has arrived. "I'll get it," Doris says, wiping her own red eyes. "You go wash your face and grab your bag." Charm goes into the bathroom connected to Gus's bedroom and turns on the cold water. She stares at herself in the mirror above the sink, unable to believe what Doris told her about Gus. Her face is splotchy and her eyes are swollen from crying. She splashes the cold water on her face and it feels good. She opens the medicine cabinet, buying time. Charm doesn't want Jane to see her like this; she always told her how brave and strong she was. Charm wants her to keep thinking this.

Inside the cabinet are razors and shaving cream, toothpaste and Q-tips. There are prescription bottles of medicine and Band-Aids and a fingernail clipper. There is the bottle of cologne she gave Gus two Christmases ago. She carefully lifts the bottle and opens the lid. Gus's scent—not his sick, dying scent but the scent she remembers, this cologne mixed with the smell of his shampoo—washes over Charm and she smiles. This is what she wants to remember. She replaces the lid, and holds the cologne bottle close to her. Charm moves toward the living room, but then stops and goes back into the bathroom. She reaches into the shower and pulls out Gus's shampoo, a cheap generic brand that smells like green apples. Carrying her two prizes, she goes out to meet Jane. She doesn't know if she will ever come back to stay.

Charm

Gus's funeral is horrible and nice all at the same time. Charm feels silly in her new dress and high heels, even though she wanted to dress up for Gus to thank him for all he'd done for her. But the dress doesn't quite fit her right and she can't walk in the shoes without her ankles wobbling. In the safety of her pew where no one can see, she steps out of them and presses her toes into the red plush carpet. Jane and Doris sit with Charm in the front of the church and she's surprised at how many people have come to say good-bye to Gus. Dozens and dozens. Mostly his firefighter friends, many wiping away tears.

Charm sees her mother sitting alone, near the back of the church. Charm tries to get angry, wants to be offended at the gall her mother has in showing up to Gus's funeral at all, but it fades quickly. Reanne looks beautiful, although completely inappropriately dressed for the occasion in a short, low-cut black dress and three-inch heels. Charm notices Binks didn't accompany her mother and she is pleasantly surprised that her mother chose to pay her final respects to Gus without another man hanging all over her. Through the years Charm has become accustomed to seeing a man always at her mother's side and she looks smaller somehow, less significant, without Binks next to her. More than anything she wants her mother to walk up the aisle through the church and slide into the seat next to Charm. She wants her mother's arm around her shoulders, wants her comfort.

But Reanne stays at the back of the church and Charm remains in her pew. The priest tells many funny stories about Gus and everyone smiles through their tears. Gus had once been a free spirit, happy. A force of nature. That was obviously before her mother got through with him, Charm thinks, when his smiles weren't forced and laughter came more easily. Halfway through the service she hears her mother's distinctive cries, low and breathy. Charm turns in her seat and sees her mother crying into a handkerchief. Somehow her mother even manages to make crying attractive.

After mass, Reanne waits for Charm to reach the back of the church and tries to hug her, but any of Charm's longing for a mother's affection has faded away and she steps away from her touch. Reanne still manages to ask about Gus's will, if he happened to leave her a little something.

"I don't know anything about that," Charm says, and steps outside. It is cool and overcast. Charm hopes the rain will stay away until after the burial.

Reanne follows her out onto the steep front steps of the church. "About your brother…" Reanne begins, and Charm cranes her head in search of Christopher.

"Is he here?" Charm asks, trying to keep the worry from her voice. The idea of Christopher coming back to Linden Falls and being in the same town as Joshua makes her stomach clench.

"No, but he called," Reanne says, looking shiftily around her. Jane and Doris are standing a respectful distance away, giving Charm and Reanne space to talk. Charm wishes they would come over and rescue her. "He started talking about you again. Something about when you were in high school. It's very strange."

"He was probably high," Charm says, and Reanne stiffens.

"He didn't sound high," she says defensively, but quickly changes the subject. "So, did Gus ever talk about what he wanted done with the house?"

"I told you, I don't know anything about that," Charm says impatiently. Her head aches from crying. She just wants to get away from her mother.

Reanne hisses in her ear. "The only reason Gus let you stay with him was to try and get me back. He thought if he was nice to you, I'd come back to him," she whispers around a tight smile.

Charm learned a long time ago that the best way to irritate her mother was to speak as calmly as possible. "He cared enough about me that he left me his house and his savings. What did he leave you?" She pauses for effect. "Nothing. He left you nothing."

Reanne's lips tremble. "I am still your mother. You have no right to speak to me this way."

People emerge from the church, stepping between Charm and her mother. They give her hugs and tell her how proud Gus was of her, that he talked about how smart she was, how he thought she was going to go far in this world, that she was going to be a wonderful nurse. Charm begins to cry again. Surprisingly, Reanne squeezes through the crowd and places an arm around her shoulders, drawing her close. "Shhh, Charm, it's okay," Reanne croons. Charm looks up at her mother and through her tears she can see that Reanne isn't even looking at her as she says these comforting words, but is glancing surreptitiously at the people around her.

Charm ducks away from her mother's touch and says to Jane, "Can I ride with you to the cemetery?"

After the burial, once again Reanne makes her way to Charm's side, but this time she has Binks with her.

"Hey, Princess Charming," Binks jokes, as he does every time she sees him. "Sorry to hear about your... Gus."

"Thanks," Charm says, wishing they would both go away.

"How did you ever get a name like Charm?" he asks.

"Ask my mother, she came up with it," she tells him, trying hard not to be rude.

"You were my good luck charm," she says, pulling out a cigarette and lighter.

"Mom, not here," Charm scolds. "It's a funeral, for God's sake."

Reanne ignores her and blows cigarette smoke out of the corner of her mouth. "I knew after you were born everything was going to be okay. I'd get married, get a little house. It worked for a while." Reanne shrugs. Charm looks at her mother in wonder and cannot imagine that they could be any more different. When Charm was young, Reanne laughed easily and nothing much seemed to bother her. She never worried about money or bills or whether there was enough food in the house.

It was only when you sat off to the side and watched without her knowing that you could see the hardness around the eyes. She could be a fun mom but she wasn't a good mother. Reanne laughs like she has an aspirin on her tongue. "Then my luck turned to shit."

"Hey, do I look like shit?" Binks's feelings are hurt.

"Naw, hon," Reanne tells him. "I just meant I don't have my own house anymore. I sure do miss having my own house."

"You could have stayed with my father—he had a house. Juan had a house, that guy Les had a house. Gus had a house, too," Charm says hotly, unable to help herself. All the other mourners have left except Jane, who is waiting for Charm in her car.

"Charm, you know I couldn't stay with your father," Reanne says in a whiny voice. "He cheated on me and beat up on your brother." Charm rolls her eyes in frustration; her mother always misses the point.

"You dated a guy named Juan?" Binks asks in disbelief.

"He was nice," Charm says shortly.

"He couldn't handle the cultural differences," Reanne says, waving her hand to dismiss the whole six months they had lived with Juan.

"The only cultural difference was that you were sleeping with another guy on the side," Charm snaps, and begins to walk away from them.

"Hey, you watch your mouth!" she yells, following after Charm.

"Now, now, guys," Binks says, trying to calm them both down. "It's been a hard day for both of you." He holds out his hand toward Reanne. The gesture seems to mollify her.

"Mom, I don't want to fight with you," Charm says, rubbing her eyes.

"I don't want to fight with you, either," Reanne says, her forehead wrinkling with concern. "You look exhausted. Are you staying at Gus's house tonight?"

"No. I'm going to stay with Jane tonight and then see how I feel," Charm responds. "I'll talk to you later, Mom. Okay?"

Reanne leans in and gives Charm a brief hug and Binks pats her on the back. Charm is walking toward Jane's car when Reanne speaks. "Charm, I got a phone call the other day. From a girl who said she went to high school with you." Charm turns and looks at her mother in exasperation.

"Mom, can we talk about this later? I just want to get out of here."

"She said her name was Allison Glenn. Said she just moved back to town and wanted to catch up with you. I remember the name, but I can't quite place her. Was she a friend of yours?"

Charm tries to keep moving, away from her mother and Binks, away from the cemetery with its rows and rows of headstones and the lonely mound of dirt that lies on top of Gus, but her body betrays her. She can't take another step. Instead, she just stands there in her ridiculous high heels and looks at her mother, mouth gaping.

"Are you okay?" Reanne asks suspiciously. "You look funny. Do you remember her?"

It clicks for Charm then. She'd been right about the girl she saw in the window of Bookends. Allison Glenn. The girl who murdered her baby girl and abandoned her newborn son was out of prison. She was back in Linden Falls and had somehow found Joshua.

Brynn

As I pack my things for my trip to see my father—to see Allison—I wonder if I'm doing the right thing. I finally got hold of my mother and she sounded terrible, not like my mother at all—unsure of herself, uncertain what to do next. It wasn't until I suggested that Grandma should come back to Linden Falls with me that my old mother emerged.

"That woman is not welcome here," she said coldly.

"Mom, he's her son…" I tried to explain, but gave up. My grandmother once made the mistake of questioning my mother's love for my father and since then has been banned from my parents' house.

I hate the thought of going back home. I try to come up with excuses to stay here. I'll miss at least two days of classes and then there are my pets to care for.

"Go," my grandma tells me. "You go and get the inside scoop on your father and let me know if I need to elbow my way into that hospital, whether your mother likes it or not. I can take care of that mangy mutt and those flea-bitten cats. Don't ask me to do anything but feed and water that rodent and bird, though," she jokes. "I'm not touching them."

Before I leave, I give her a hug. Getting out of New Amery might actually be a good idea. Missy still won't have anything to do with me. I can hear the whispers and see how people look me up and down now. Once again I'm the girl with a murderer for a sister. I'm not sleeping and most nights I find myself standing in front of the refrigerator, staring at the cupboard above and debating the merits of a quick slug of alcohol before bed.

"Maybe I should bring Milo with me," I say. "He's not used to me being away."

"Bah," she says. "We'll be fine. They're good company for me. We'll miss you, but it's good that you're going to see Allison. Clear the air, start fresh."

"I'll miss you, too, Grandma. I'll be home by Sunday, for sure," I tell her, and kiss her on the cheek.

"Don't forget your medicine," she reminds me.

I give Milo one last squeeze before I head out the door.

The closer I get to Linden Falls, the harder my heart beats. The Druid River runs parallel to the highway. As I speed along I see the baby girl's body rushing down the river, keeping pace with my car, trying to catch me. I push the accelerator to the floor, trying to outrun the image. I know it isn't possible. That fisherman found her little body and my parents had her taken care of, even though I don't know what that means. There was no funeral, no burial. What did they do with her? I want to ask them, but we never talk about it, or Allison or anything. I hope wherever that baby is, she is warm and dry.

I hear the wail of a siren and see a police car, lights flashing, in my rearview mirror. I glance down at the speedometer. Seventy-five in a fifty-five miles per hour zone. Great. I slow down and pull over to the side of the road. The policeman isn't going to make this easy for me. He takes my license and walks slowly back to his car. I pray he doesn't search my car. I swiped an old pill bottle filled with hydrocodone my grandmother had leftover from her knee replacement surgery that's in my purse and have a half-filled bottle of peach schnapps stowed beneath my seat. I just wanted to make sure I had a little something to help me sleep while I'm here. I wait nervously for the patrolman to return. When he finally does, he says, "Brynn Glenn."

"Yes?" I answer.

"I was one of the first officers on the scene when they found that baby in the river a few years back." I look down at my hands and don't speak. "I've buried my wife, I've seen men and children die in war—even had to shoot a man once—but I've never seen anything as sad and lonely looking as that poor baby knocking up against the creek bed." His voice isn't angry, not even judgmental, and for a moment I think we might have something in common.

I want to say, *I know. I know how you feel.* I want to take his hand in mine and ask, *Do you see her at night when you close your eyes? Does she cry out to you in your dreams and sometimes when you're awake, even? Do people stare and look at you strangely because sometimes you think of her and you can't do anything but stand there and cry over a little girl who didn't even have a name? Do you ever wonder how your life might have been different if you weren't in Linden Falls that night?*

Before I can say any of these things, the officer leans forward into my lowered window, putting his face so close to mine that I can see his eyes are the color of a husky's, ice-blue. "I hear she got out of prison, your sister. She's a sick bitch. It's a wonder she didn't kill herself for what she did. Don't know how she can live with herself." He hands me my license and a speeding ticket for two hundred dollars and walks away without a backward glance.

I hate this town. If it weren't for my father, I would never have even considered returning. I'll see my father and mother. I'll face Allison. Then I'll be done with them all.

Allison

Brynn and I decide to meet at a restaurant that is within walking distance of Gertrude House. I get there twenty minutes before our scheduled meeting time, order a cup of coffee and try to read a book Claire lent to me while I wait for Brynn to arrive. The words sit on the pages and I can make no sense of them. All I can think about is whether or not Brynn will show up. I don't hear her approach the table until her unmistakable voice says, "Allison?"

I look up at my sister and she looks just the same as I remember. Small, with dark, unruly hair. She is dressed plainly, all in black. Dark eye shadow lines her eyes and stands out in stark contrast to her pale skin. She is biting her lip and looking down at me uncertainly.

"Brynn," I say, standing. I reach out to hug her. She is too skinny and I can feel the contour of her bones, thin and hollow like a bird's. "It's so good to see you. Thank you for coming," I say formally. I have to remind myself that this is Brynn. Just Brynn.

She doesn't answer. Pulling away from me, she settles into the booth across from where I was sitting. I sit back down and am suddenly lost for words. Thankfully, a waitress comes to take Brynn's drink order. "Tea, please. Decaffeinated, if possible," she requests. To me she explains, "Caffeine keeps me awake."

"Would you like to order anything to eat?" I ask her. "My treat."

"No, thank you. I'm fine," she says, her eyes skittering nervously around the restaurant, landing everywhere but on me.

"I'm nervous," I admit to her with a little laugh. "Now that you're here, I don't know what to say. I have so much that I *want* to say, but I don't know how to."

"That's a first," Brynn says, picking up her napkin. "You not knowing what to do." There is no anger or meanness in her voice, but still her words hurt me.

"Have you seen Dad yet?" I ask her.

She nods. "He looks terrible, but the doctor says he should be okay." We sit for several moments in silence. Brynn looks like she can't wait to get out of here.

"I'm sorry," I blurt out. "I'm really sorry."

"You've already told me that," she says, matter-of-factly, and begins to shred her napkin into thin strips.

"I've written it in letters to you, told you on the phone, but I've never told you to your face." Brynn continues to tear the napkin until it looks like confetti. "Brynn, please look at me." I lean as far as I can across the table. She lifts her chin and gazes levelly at me, her eyes hard and unemotional. "Brynn, I am so sorry I put you in the position I did. I knew better. I made a stupid mistake and I dragged you into it. I know it doesn't mean much after all that's happened, but you helped me, you really did. I would have never been able to—"

I stop speaking. Brynn's face has gone rigid. She isn't ready to talk about the specifics of that night. "Well, anyway, I'm sorry and I'm glad you're here," I finish. "Tell me about your classes. I want to hear all about them."

"I better get home before Mom starts worrying about me," Brynn says, looking at her watch.

"You're staying at the house?" I ask, not quite able to keep the hurt from my voice. "Mom said you could stay there?"

"What choice did she have?" Brynn snorts, sliding out from the booth. "I don't have anywhere else to go. I'm just staying until tomorrow, then I'm heading back to Grandma's."

"Already?" I ask in surprise. "You just got here."

"I'm tired. I just want to go to bed." She has dark circles under her eyes and she keeps trying to hide her yawns behind her hand.

I drop some bills on the tabletop and Brynn and I move out into the chilly night.

"So are you going to tell me about him?" she asks abruptly. "That's why I'm here, aren't I? You could care less about Dad. You just wanted me here because you found the little boy."

"That's not fair," I say indignantly. "I'm very worried about Dad."

"Come off it, Allison," Brynn snaps angrily. "You can't stand that I'm going to stay at Mom and Dad's and you're stuck at some halfway house. You can't stand that I'm the one doing well, the one that Mom and Dad are proud of now…"

"Proud of you? Mom and Dad have erased you. Just

like they erased me. Have you even been at the house yet?" Brynn's face crumples. I know I should stop talking, but I can't. "They removed every picture of you. Not just the pictures of me, Brynn. You, too."

"Whatever," Brynn says halfheartedly, and I know I've hurt her feelings.

"I'm sorry, Brynn." I reach out for her sleeve to stop her from leaving and she jerks away from me, but not before I get a glimpse of the red scratches up and down her arm.

"You're sorry?" she cries in disbelief. "Do you know what I see each and every time I close my eyes at night?"

"Brynn," I say miserably. "I know. I see her, too."

"No," Brynn says in a low, chilling voice. "I don't think you do. And now you want me to meet that little boy? Her brother? You want me to relive this all over again?" Brynn shakes her head wildly.

"I wanted… I thought…" I say lamely. "I wanted to tell you about Joshua. Show him to you."

"What do you think you're going to do?" she asks sharply as we walk down the darkened street toward her car.

"I thought maybe you would help me decide what I should do," I say self-consciously.

"Think about it, Allison," she says, stopping suddenly. "There is really only one thing you can do."

I raise my eyebrows at the force of her words, her certainty. Brynn *has* changed. She wasn't the indecisive girl I left behind five years ago. "I'm glad you know what I should do, Brynn, because I sure don't."

"Is he happy?" she asks.

"I think he is," I say. "For the most part."

"Are his parents good to him? Is he safe?"

"They seem like great parents," I tell her.

"Then what's the big mystery, Allison?" She pulls her car keys out of the pocket of her jacket. "He's happy, he's safe and he has great parents. Why would you want to mess that up for him?"

"I don't," I say defensively. "I don't want to mess anything up. I just don't know if I should quit my job or what."

"Or what, Allison? Stay in his life? What good can come out of that?" Brynn turns to face me, her hands on her hips. "Actually, I think it's kind of selfish."

"Selfish?" I shake my head in disbelief. "I may be lots of things, Brynn, but how can you say I'm selfish? Haven't I done everything humanly possible to try and make things right with you?" My voice is rising and people are stealing glances at us as they pass. I lower my voice to a whisper. "It makes me feel better, knowing where he ended up. Don't you want to see him? Aren't you even a little bit curious about how things turned out?" Brynn doesn't look convinced. "Just take a look at him. Stop by the store tomorrow sometime in the afternoon or evening. He'll be there. It will make you feel better, too. I promise."

Brynn looks at me for a long moment. "I'll stop by the store and meet him, Allison. But that's all. I don't want to get caught up in anything again."

"Thanks." I consider hugging her again, but think better of it. "I'll see you tomorrow, and thanks for coming."

"Yeah, well, we'll see if it was a good idea." She turns to leave.

When did she become so cold? Was this what life had done to her? What I had done to her?

"Do you remember Mousie?" I call after her, and she stops, her back to me.

She is still for several moments and then turns around. "Yeah," Brynn says, "I remember Mousie."

Brynn

I do remember. So stupid when I look back, but Mousie was the closest thing to a pet that I ever had when I lived at home. Our father traveled often for business and would bring home travel-size bottles of shampoo and lotion and small, thin bars of soap. I must have been four when I looked at that bar of soap my father brought home in a different way. I started carrying it around in my pocket and pretended to feed him pieces of cheese. I named him Mousie and he went everywhere with me. I slept with him at night and kept him near me while I played during the day. My mother would just roll her eyes and tell me to get the bar of soap off the dinner table and my father would give a sinister laugh and say he needed a shower.

Allison, who was five, was the only one who took my attachment to Mousie seriously. She helped me make a bed for him out of a shoe box and helped me decorate the sides with pictures of mice and slices of cheese. Whenever Dad pretended to try and swipe Mousie from me for his shower, she would block his way and yell at him to stay away.

As we grew older, Allison became the golden girl, the girl who did everything well, the girl who didn't have time for her plain little sister anymore. I'm surprised that Allison remembers Mousie, surprised that she is still trying so hard to get back into my life. Maybe Allison has changed. Maybe she asked me to come here for the right reasons. Maybe things will be okay.

Then I think about that little boy I'm going to meet tomorrow at the bookstore, and I think about his little sister, and I get that itchy feeling underneath my skin again. The one I can't scratch away. I hear her crying and I start to hum to block out the sound, but people stare. So I get in my car and drive away.

Allison

I don't know what I was expecting from my first meeting with Brynn, but it went okay, I think. She didn't run away, she didn't yell and scream at me. Brynn seems different from how I remember her. Harder, angrier. Not that I blame her—she has every reason to be angry. There's something else, though. Something in the way she was tearing her napkin into tiny bits and then started in on mine. She kept looking over her shoulder nervously and every so often she would tilt her head to the side, as if someone was whispering in her ear. I think about calling our grandma to see what she thinks, but maybe I'm overreacting. I can't claim to know Brynn anymore. I haven't seen her in five years and people change. God knows, I have. I'll see how she is tomorrow when she comes to meet Joshua and Claire.

I know I have to take it slow with Brynn, but I think things are going to be okay. A new beginning, a new start. This is just what we need. We have the rest of our lives to become friends again. To become sisters.

Claire

The falling leaves, muted yellows, reds and browns, are being whipped around by a brisk gust of wind, illuminated by the streetlamps. It is unusually cold for September. The roads are shiny with moisture and the heavy, gray clouds are threatening rain again. Claire doubts there will be any more shoppers this evening. Even though the store is normally open until nine, she considers closing the shop an hour earlier. Joshua is playing with his Legos in the children's section with the promise that he will pick them up quickly if a customer comes in. Claire watches Allison and Brynn, their heads bent closely together, whispering as Allison pulls sections of books from the shelves and polishes the wood with scented oil that fills the store with a pleasant lemony smell. "Feel free to leave for the night, Allison," Claire encourages, but Allison insists on finishing out her shift.

"We're going out for coffee after I'm done. We'll have plenty of time to catch up then," she tells Claire, grinning broadly. Since her sister's arrival, Allison is like a new girl. Her anxiousness, so prevalent the past several days, seems to have melted away. Claire is pleased for Allison, despite the fact that she senses things aren't completely right between the sisters. Allison is trying too hard to please Brynn, who is aloof, distracted and seems to want to be anywhere but here.

Claire feels a pang of homesickness for her own sister. She hasn't talked to her in a while and decides to give her a call to do some catching up at home tonight. Claire's mind swirls around the thought of a brother or sister for Joshua. She has such happy memories of growing up with her sister, of having someone to share secrets with, of being secure in the thought that her sister would always be there for her if she needed anything. At one time, she and Jonathan danced around the idea of adopting again. Seeing Allison and her obvious joy in being with her sister, and seeing some of the loneliness Joshua has in not having a sibling, makes her think she needs to broach the subject again.

Claire hears the bell above the entrance jingle and out of the corner of her eye sees a girl walk into the store hesitantly, as if crossing the threshold is a momentous decision. It takes her a moment to recognize that it is Charm Tullia. Her brown hair, damp from the mist, is pulled up in a messy ponytail and her face is pale with worry. She is dressed up and wearing high heels. She pulls her blue jacket more tightly around herself as if the air within the store is colder than the air outside.

"Hi, Charm," Claire says. "How are you? I heard about Gus. Was the funeral today? I'm so sorry…"

Charm nods and cranes her neck, looking around the store as if searching for someone.

She walks slowly forward, still scanning the store. "Does a girl named Allison Glenn work here?" she asks, her voice low and hoarse.

"She does. She's in the back right now." Claire studies Charm's face. "Charm, are you okay? You don't look like you feel well," she says with concern.

"I'm fine," Charm responds offhandedly. "Do you think I could speak with her for a minute? It won't take long."

"Sure," Claire says in confusion. "I didn't realize that you know Allison. Did you go to school together?"

Biting her lip, Charm hesitates before speaking. "Allison and I had a…friend in common. I heard she worked here. I just wanted to get in touch with her." Behind her, Claire hears footsteps and laughter. Before she can turn around, both Allison and Brynn stop abruptly.

"Allison, there's someone here to see you," Claire says, instantly realizing this isn't a happy reunion. As her eyes flick back and forth between the girls, she can see that all three look stunned. Allison puts a protective arm around her sister, who looks taken aback.

"Allison?" Charm says, licking her lips. "Could we talk for a minute?"

Allison looks around, her eyes darting from Charm to Brynn to the children's section where Joshua is still playing. Claire can't identify exactly what she sees momentarily skitter across her face. Panic? Fear? Maybe both. Brynn just looks like she wants to run away.

"Allison?" Claire questions. "Are you okay?"

"Yeah," she says, nodding, her chin bobbing up and down too quickly. "Just surprised. We haven't seen each other in a long time."

Claire looks questioningly to Charm and she responds with a brief smile. "It's okay, Claire."

"Okay," Claire says, unconvinced. "I'll just go in back with Joshua and let you all talk. Brynn, do you want to come?" Brynn whispers yes and they move to where Joshua is still constructing his pirate ship, complete with cannons and planks, out of Legos.

Brynn and Claire settle on the floor next to Joshua, not knowing what to say to each other.

"I think it's stopped raining. Let's go outside and talk," Allison tells Charm.

Brynn

Nothing good is going to come of this. I can't believe I'm still here, in Linden Falls, in this bookstore with my sister who I never thought I would see again. Never wanted to see again.

And then there's Joshua's mother. She is so clueless. She has no idea who has snaked into her family's life. What would she do if I told her? What would she say if I piped up and said, "The girl who gave birth to your son is right here. Right here. The girl who drowned her baby. The girl who dumped the baby at the fire station. The girl who watched it all." I want to feel sorry for Mrs. Kelby, but it's hard to. I have very little sympathy for parents who turn their heads away from the truth.

Allison hid her pregnancy well. She had the body for it—tall and long-waisted. She carried the extra weight evenly, not out in front of her like a bowling ball, like most women. My parents were off at some function for my dad's work when Allison called out to me. Of course, I came running. It wasn't just the fact that everyone came running when Allison called for them. There was something in her voice, something in the way she called my name, that told me something wasn't quite right.

But it was the second time she shouted my name when I realized there was something very, very wrong. Her voice was strangled and full of pain. I ran from the kitchen, up the stairs and down the hall to Allison's bedroom. Her door was flung open and Allison was on her knees, arms stretched out, holding on to the door frame for support. Her head was bent forward, her hair loose around her face like a veil. She had on her typical baggy sweatshirt and sweatpants. The neckline of the sweatshirt was dark with sweat.

"What's the matter, Allison?" I cried, running to her and falling to my knees. "Oh, my God, are you hurt? Are you hurt?" I asked her desperately. But she did not answer—could not answer—because another spasm of pain seemed to overtake her. She swallowed a moan and pressed her hands so forcefully against the door frame that her arms trembled. After a moment, her chin dropped to her chest and a whimper escaped.

"Tell me what's wrong, Allison, please tell what's wrong." I stood suddenly. "I'm calling Mom and Dad," I announced, and tried to step by her to get to her phone.

"No!" Allison said forcefully. With effort she stood, blocking my way. Even in horrible pain she was tough. "No," she said again. More softly, begging, she said, "Please, Brynn, please help me." Then she fell into me and I could feel it. The firm roundness at her belly. I flinched at the unexpectedness of it.

"Allison?" I said as I carefully placed my fingers on

her stomach again. I helped her pull off her sweatshirt, revealing a tank top and her small, swollen belly.

How could I not have known? How could my parents not have known? They are not stupid people. But they are selfish people. The minute Allison and I weren't who they wanted us to be, they wanted nothing to do with us. I knew early on that I'd never be what my parents wanted. But Allison. Allison did everything right. Everything. Until she made a stupid mistake. Now it's like she doesn't exist to my parents anymore.

If anyone has the right to cut Allison out of my life, it's me. She pulled me into her lies and secrets and I've been drowning in them ever since. Now here I am, getting caught up in the whole mess again. And you know who is going to suffer? Joshua. That little boy will never be the same if Allison and Charm start talking. But maybe I can protect him—the way my sister never did, the way my parents never did.

"I'm going to see what's going on," I tell Mrs. Kelby. "I'll be right back." I stand and begin to make my way across the bookstore to the front door. But I'm too late. It's already happening.

Allison

I lead Charm outside the bookstore. She's all dressed up, like she came from church, except she looks miserable and pissed off.

"What's going on?" Charm asks frantically. "Why are you here? I thought you were in jail and now you're working *here?* Are you crazy?"

"I didn't know—" I try to explain, but Charm isn't finished.

"Joshua is with good people. They love him. They take care of him. He's fine. Why do you want to ruin that for him?"

"I don't want to ruin anything!" I snap. With effort, I lower my voice. "I didn't know. I got the job here and I had no idea about Joshua until I saw him come into the bookstore. But the minute I saw him, I knew. He looks just like Christopher. That's the last time I saw him—with Christopher!"

"Well, Christopher left Joshua with Gus and me." Charm is trying not to cry. Her eyes keep darting inside the bookstore window. "We tried to take care of him. But Gus was sick and I was only fifteen," she chokes, tears flowing freely now.

"He left?" I ask. "Christopher just left you with the baby?"

Charm snorts with impatience. "Listen, you obviously had a relationship with my brother, but you didn't know him. The minute you drove away, he shoved Joshua at me and Gus and took off." Charm is breathing heavily and the fine mist that is falling collects with her tears and slides down her face.

For a moment I'm speechless. I don't know what I expected, but I had thought Christopher loved me. I was the one who broke up with him. I guess I believed he would accept anything I offered him. Especially a piece of me. A piece of him.

"I don't want to disrupt Joshua's life. I see what good parents Claire and Jonathan are. I don't want them to know who I am. I just needed to know what happened," I try to explain.

"Now you know. Christopher didn't want him." Charm is struggling to continue and I look over my shoulder, worried that Claire is going to come out here. "Gus and I tried to take care of him, we really did. But we couldn't. After Christopher left and we heard about how you were arrested, I dropped him off at the fire station. Claire and Jonathan were the ones who adopted him. They've been good pa…" Charm trails off, looking past my shoulder. "Oh, my God," she whispers.

I turn to look, and see a man and a woman walking toward us. The woman moves with purposeful steps, the man trying to keep up with her. "Oh, my God," Charm says again. "You need to get out of here!"

"Charm, I need to talk to you," the woman calls. She is holding something in her hand, waving it high above her head. The tap of her heels punctuates each word.

Charm's eyes widen. She stumbles backward and bumps into the brick face of the bookstore. "Get out of here," she whispers to me, but all I can do is just stand here and watch.

Brynn

As I move toward the door, I see Allison and Charm arguing. Charm looks angry, but I have no doubt that Allison can hold her own in an argument. Allison can be pretty intimidating.

"Brynn, you need to help me," she kept saying over and over that night, crying and clutching at my wrist. "Please, you *have* to help me."

"Do Mom and Dad know?" I asked her as I helped her to the bed. She shook her head, turned to her side and curled up into a ball as if trying to disintegrate into herself. I quickly moved to slam the bedroom door closed, wanting to shut Allison's secret in the room with us.

"Let me think," I said, standing above her. "Let me think." I surveyed the room around me. The sheets on her bed were damp and bloodied in spots. "Listen, Allison," I told her. "We need to call someone. Let me call an ambulance." I reached for the cell phone on the bedside table. A website describing the process of childbirth was on Allison's computer. This wasn't the kind of test one could cram for, I thought.

"No!" Allison growled. Her long, strong arm shot out and grabbed the phone before I could. "No, don't call anyone. Please, I can do this. Please, Brynn, please help me!" Another convulsion racked Allison and she groaned, but all the while she held tight to the phone. She didn't want me calling anyone.

I sat down next to her and brushed her hair away from her sweaty forehead. "Why?" I asked in confusion.

"I screwed up," Allison said breathlessly after the contraction had passed. "I slept with him. I slept with him and I got pregnant!" she said fiercely.

"Who? Who was it, Allison?" I asked.

"Christopher," she moaned.

"Christopher who?" I asked. She didn't answer. "It's okay. This happens to lots of girls. You can give the baby up for adoption, it will be okay." I tried to make my voice soothing and reassuring, but even I didn't believe what I told her.

"What do you think Mom's going to do when she finds out?" Allison spat.

"She'll be mad, but she'll get over it. She'll help you find a good home—"

"She will not get over it!" I reared back at Allison's bitterness. "She'll try to fix it. She'll want to raise the baby as her own or something, or she'll make me raise it. I'll be stuck in this god-awful town forever! She will make my life miserable!" Each word became more and more hysterical until she was sitting up and her nose was touching mine. "We have to get rid of it!"

"Okay, okay," I tried to placate her. "Just tell me what to do."

Allison must have been in labor for hours before she called out for me. She must have been hidden away in her room while Mom and Dad were scurrying around getting ready for their dinner party. My mother had even barged into Allison's room without knocking before they left and told her that there was money on the kitchen table to order a pizza for supper, to make sure the doors to the house were locked because they would be home very late, and no friends were allowed to come over because they wouldn't be home.

Fifteen minutes after I discovered Allison in labor, she was ready to push. I have never seen my sister look so tired, so defeated. Her hair lay in sweaty clumps around her pale face and she couldn't keep her eyes open. She held weakly on to my hand, her legs trembling. "Alli, let me call the doctor," I begged. "I'm scared." But she said no, that we could do this. That she needed me. No one else.

I had wanted to hear that from her my whole life. My beautiful, mighty, independent big sister finally needed me, the sister in the shadows.

"Please, Brynn," she whispered through cracked, dried lips. "Please," she whimpered. And that was the only word I needed to thrust me into action. I began to gather all the items I imagined would be necessary for the birth of a child: clean towels and sheets, cool, damp washcloths, rubbing alcohol, scissors, garbage bags. When I returned to Allison's bedroom she was sitting up, clutching her knees, her chin tucked into her neck. "I've got to push!" she cried. "I've got to push!"

I dropped the armload of linens that I was carrying and stumbled to her side. "Let's get your sweatpants off, Alli," I told her gently.

"No!" she cried. "No, I don't want it to come, Brynn. Please," she sobbed, looking desperately up at me. "I don't want it—make it stop, make it stop!" The sound that came from my sister was mournful—a keening wail so primal, from a place so hidden, so old, that I imagined only women in the midst of childbirth could open it. I peeled her wet, shit-filled underwear and pants from her sweat-slicked legs and turned on the ceiling fan. I cleaned the filth from her as thoroughly as I could and wiped her legs with a washcloth drenched in rubbing alcohol. The fan circulated the stale, copper-scented air and goose bumps erupted on Allison's skin. The cool wafting air seemed to revitalize her for a moment. She bore down, clutching the bedsheets with white-knuckled fingers. Her frantic eyes met my own and I took her face in my hands. Taking charge.

I feel Claire come up behind me and through the window we see a man and woman coming down the block toward Allison and Charm. The man is fiftyish, a bandanna is wrapped around his forehead and he is wearing a leather jacket with an eagle embroidered on the sleeve. The woman is dressed improperly for the weather outside, wearing a skimpy black dress and stilettos. She's clutching something in her hand.

Hearing the shouts from outside, Joshua and the dog quickly join us. "What's going on?" Joshua asks nervously.

"Nothing good," I mutter, and my stomach twists into knots. That poor little boy, I think. Who's going to save him from his own past?

Charm

Charm's mother stops directly in front of her. Raindrops cling to her thickly painted eyelashes and thin black streams flow down her cheeks. Despite her fear, Charm swallows back a giggle. Her mother looks like a trashy zombie.

"What the hell is this?" Reanne shoves the photo she was waving in front of Charm's nose and any further inclination to laugh disappears.

Charm struggles for breath. "Where did you get that?"

"You had a baby?" Reanne's voice is low and dangerous. "You had a goddamn baby and didn't tell me?"

"Please," Charm cries. "Please, don't do this!"

"Do what, Charm?" Reanne asks heatedly. "Ignore this? Who is this baby? Where is he? Is this your baby?"

Everything is falling apart. All her secrets. All she wanted to do was protect Joshua and make sure he went somewhere safe. She wanted him to have a normal childhood with normal parents. She pushes the picture away, not wanting to look. "You went to the house," Charm says incredulously. "You went to Gus's house and went through my things."

"Who's the baby in the picture?" Reanne demands again.

"Shhh," Allison says, trying to step between Charm and her mother. "Please." Her eyes flit to the window of the bookstore, where Claire, Brynn and Joshua are looking out at them.

"You stay the hell out of this," Reanne says, shaking a finger at Allison. She looks Allison up and down. "I know who you are. You sick bitch."

"Rea," Binks says pleadingly.

"Shut up," Reanne snaps, and then returns her attention to Charm. "I talked to Christopher this afternoon. He told me to ask you about the baby." Reanne puts her hands on her hips and glowers at her daughter. "So now I'm asking. Tell me about the baby."

"Where did you get this?" Charm whispers, looking at the photo in her mother's hand.

"I'm your mother," Reanne shouts back as if that explains everything. "Did you have a baby, Charm? Did you go and have a goddamn baby and not even tell me?"

"Was it when we were at the funeral home?" Charm can hardly believe her mother's nerve. "When did you break in?"

"I didn't break in," Reanne says indignantly. "I had a key. You weren't answering your cell so I went to the house. I was worried and let myself in. Then I called Jane and she said you were coming here. Listen, Charm, something is going on and I want to know what the hell…"

Reanne trails off and Charm turns to see her mother

looking through the bookstore window at Joshua with intense curiosity. She sees the way she is taking in every inch of his thin, pinched face. If she doesn't step in and do something, it will click in her mother's brain. She will recognize how much Joshua looks like Christopher and it will be all over for Joshua. His safe, happy family. Reanne will find a way to squirm her way into his life, even if she has no legal claim to him, and make his life miserable, just like she did for Charm and her brother. "You need to leave now," Charm says through her tears. "I can't talk to you right now."

"I'm not leaving until I get some answers," Reanne says petulantly.

"That's all you ever do, Mother—you leave!" Charm remarks acidly. "You use people up, get what you want out of them and then you leave. You have no right to come in here and demand that I tell you anything. You lost that right a long time ago when you chose another man, and another man, and another man over me!"

Reanne's hand flashes out and with a sharp crack connects with Charm's cheek.

Claire

"Why are they so mad?" Joshua asks as he tugs at his mother's arm. Standing at the window, Claire sees a ripple of fear cross Charm's face and the woman's hand rearing back to strike. Joshua cries out and flinches when the woman slaps Charm. Claire rushes toward the door and Joshua calls after her. "Mom?" His voice trembles. "Where are you going?"

"I'll be right back," Claire assures him as she steps out onto the sidewalk. "Stay right here with Brynn.

"What's going on?" Claire demands, looking from Charm to the strangers to Allison, who looks as confused as Claire feels. "Charm, are you okay?" Claire scrutinizes Charm's face, where an angry red handprint erupts in stark contrast against her pale skin.

"She's fine," the woman barks.

"Jesus, Reanne," the man says softly. "What'd you go and do that for?"

"Mom," Charm says in disbelief and starts to cry harder, gingerly touching her face.

Mom. So this is Charm's mother, Claire thinks. No wonder Charm has invested a small fortune in self-help books. Charm and her mother have the same dark eyes, the same full lips. Claire imagines the world-wise, tough woman in front of her once was very pretty. She looks her up and down, taking in the too-tight clothes, the lines around her mouth. Then Claire's eyes stop on the photo that Reanne is holding in her hands. Something about it is strikingly familiar.

She reaches out, catching Reanne's wrist. "Hey," Reanne says angrily, trying to pull her arm away, but Claire plucks the photo from her fingers. She peers carefully at the picture, which shows an exhausted-looking Charm, several years younger, holding an infant. The baby is wearing a blue hat snug over his ears; he has a small upturned nose, thin lips and a sharp chin. His eyes are wide and alert, his brow furrowed. The resemblance is unmistakable. Claire has a nearly identical picture of Joshua. But she is the exhausted one holding the baby. Jonathan took the picture the day after they had brought their son home from the hospital.

"Oh, my God," she whispers in disbelief, and looks at Charm. "Oh, my God."

Claire has always feared that one day she'd come face-to-face with Joshua's biological mother, but nothing could have ever prepared her for this. "Charm?" She can barely speak the words. "Are you Joshua's mother?"

Allison

I watch Charm's crazy mother in disbelief and wonder if I still have time to get the hell out of here.

"Charm," Claire says again, fear painted across her face, "are you Joshua's mother?"

Charm opens her mouth to speak, but instead raises her face to the sky as if praying, the raindrops bouncing off her skin.

Reanne grabs Charm's wrist and Charm tries unsuccessfully to wrench it free. "You little whore!" Reanne says, yanking at Charm's arm.

Charm tries to speak, but nothing comes out but a gurgling noise. I can't stand it anymore.

"It's me," I manage to say.

Claire looks blankly at me. Not understanding. "It's me. I'm Joshua's mother," I say, speaking only to Claire. "It's me."

Brynn

Joshua is following me around, crying, bleating like a baby lamb. I want to stay by the window and see what's going on outside, but I can't stop moving. I feel like something is crawling underneath my skin. "What's happening?" Joshua keeps saying. That poor baby, I think over and over. I try to shake the memories from my head, tug on my hair to try to stop the pictures flashing in front of my eyes.

In one mighty push with a scream that echoed off the walls so loudly that I was sure our nearest neighbors an acre away could hear, the baby's head appeared, stretching and tearing my sister's tender skin. "Here it comes, Allison," I told her, my voice trembling in fear. "It's coming, it's almost over."

Through teeth clenched together in pain, Allison mewed helplessly. "No," she cried weakly. She squeezed her legs together and with one hand tried to press the crown of the baby's head back into her.

"Allison!" I shouted in alarm, grabbing her hand

away. "No!" She slapped feebly at me, but another contraction swept over her and despite her wish to keep the baby inside, her body defied her and like a violent wave thrust the baby forward. I watched in awe as Allison's body widened and the baby's slimy head slid from her body. The two of them, fused together, appeared to be some twisted version of some ancient goddess.

"Gaaaah!" Allison screamed. "No, no, no!" She swung her head from side to side. "No, no, no!"

"One more push, Alli," I told her. "One more and it's over. Now!" I ordered her with a voice I had never used with her. A voice that made Allison silent, made her look at me. Made her listen. "Allison, you push one more time. Just one more time and it'll be out and it won't hurt anymore. I promise."

Allison nodded, her breath coming in short, thin gasps. I quickly rearranged the pillows at her back and with difficulty she raised herself up on shaky arms. With determination that I had seen in Allison many times before, she focused her gaze on me, her eyes a steely-blue, almost crazed, and set her mouth in a tight line. "Arrrggghhh!" she bellowed, and in a rush of uterine fluid and blood, the baby slid forward into my waiting arms. A girl. A tiny little girl covered in a thick, bloody mucous. In shock and revulsion, I held her away from me, like I was holding someone else's dirty Kleenex.

"It's a girl," I told her because I didn't know what else to say, didn't know what to do next.

"Oh, God!" Allison cried. "What am I going to do? What am I going to do?" She had collapsed back onto her bed and started to shake. Great convulsive shivers racked her body. "Please take it away. Brynn, please," she begged. "Take it away!" I looked down at the infant. It wasn't squirming or flailing. It wasn't crying. It lay limply in my arms, its small mouth opening and closing, a guppy out of water.

"Allison, what do you want me to do?" I was surprised to hear the anger in my voice.

"I don't care, I don't care, please take her away. Please!" I looked back down at the baby. She still hadn't cried, although her little chest was quickly rising and falling. I grabbed the scissors from the bedside table and carefully cut the umbilical cord. I was surprised at how hard it was to sever. Like cutting a thick, pulsing rope. With a towel I did my best to wipe the baby clean and then very gently I laid her in a corner of the room. I reached for another clean towel and pressed it between Allison's legs to try and stop the bleeding, afraid she would need stitches. I snatched up all the dirty sheets and towels and stuffed them into a garbage bag and then added Allison's sweatpants.

"Don't worry, Allison," I told her as I pulled a blanket over her shivering body. Her eyes were shut and she appeared to be dozing. "I'll take care of everything." I glanced toward the baby in the corner of the room. One thin arm had escaped from the towel I had wrapped her in; she seemed to be reaching out for someone. "I'll be right back." Grabbing the garbage bag, I ran down the stairs, the bag thumping behind me. I knew I had a very short amount of time to get Allison's room cleaned up and the baby and Allison to the hospital. I knew it would be difficult to talk Allison into going. She was in denial, shock, something. I think she was convinced that if she didn't look at the baby, it meant it wasn't real.

I lugged the garbage bag back through the kitchen

to the garage and shoved the bag deep into one of the large garbage cans, pressing it down as far as I could and strewing other garbage on top of it to help conceal it. From inside the house, I heard the shrill of the telephone. I hesitated. It might be my parents calling; they still felt the need to check up on us. The incessant ringing led me to believe it was my mother and I hurried to answer it.

"Hello," I said breathlessly.

"Brynn?" my father asked. "What's the matter? You sound like you've been running."

"Oh, nothing," I lied. "I was just in the garage, throwing away the pizza box."

"Well, your mother just wanted me to see how things are going. Everything okay?"

"Dad, it's fine," I said impatiently. "God, what could go wrong?"

"I know, I know, nothing," my father conceded. "We'll be late, after midnight." I glanced up at the clock. It was nearly nine o'clock; the summer sun was just starting to set.

"Don't worry, Dad, we'll be fine," I told him.

"Okay, okay," he answered. "Bye, Brynn."

"Bye, Dad." I hung up the phone and rushed back to Allison's room, taking the stairs two at a time.

Pushing open the door, I took in the scene before me. It looked like a massacre had taken place. Despite my attempt to throw away all the bloodied towels and sheets, Allison's bed was covered with a large crimson stain and somehow the walls were splattered with blood. Allison looked terrible. Black smudges of exhaustion circled her eyes. She was still shaking even though the temperature in the room seemed to me to be stifling.

I moved toward the hallway to grab another blanket from the linen closet to cover her when something caught my eye. Or, the lack of something. I turned toward where I had laid the baby in the pile of clean towels. Her skin had a bluish color and her arms were still. One hand was tucked beneath her tiny chin. The other lay limply at her side. Her skinny legs were motionless, splayed like a frog's on a science class table. "No," I whispered. "Oh, no."

"Brynn, I'm scared!" Joshua bawls.

I blink away the horrible thoughts and stop moving, trying to focus on Joshua and what he is saying. But in my mind, all I can think is, Poor baby. Poor, poor baby.

Claire

Claire is consumed by a fear so deep and complete that it courses through her veins, infuses the soft tissue, radiates through her bones, a fear that takes her breath away. It has nothing to do with her well-being, her own safety, but Joshua's.

She can feel everyone's eyes on her, waiting to see what she will do next. Charm's mother looks as if she wants to say something, but thinks better of it.

"Maybe we should go inside," the man in the leather jacket says. Numbly, Claire follows him into the store and looks up to see Joshua pressing his body close to the bookshelves, his fingers sliding along the book spines as if they are piano keys.

"Why is everyone yelling?" he asks, moving cautiously toward his mother.

"We're just talking, Josh," she says, and gently turns him by the shoulders, guiding him toward the back of the store.

"Why is everyone crying?" He pulls away from her,

his little fists clenched at his sides. Claire reaches up and touches her face, which she realizes is wet.

"It's just the rain, Joshua," she says, though she knows that if she touched her fingers to her tongue she would taste salt. She has to get him out of here. Doesn't want him to hear this conversation. Yes, he knows he's adopted, knows that he was left at a fire station. But for Joshua to hear that Allison may be his birth mother would be too much. It's too much for Claire to comprehend. It can't be true. It just can't.

"Can we go home now?" Joshua pleads. "I want to go home." Claire can hear the fear in his voice, knows that he is worried that these strangers are intruders, bad people who might harm them.

"Josh, once these people leave, we are going home. I promise. We just need a few more minutes." Joshua looks concernedly at Charm, who is still crying. "She'll be okay, Josh. I'll make sure she's all right," Claire assures him. He studies her face and she forces a smile. "Maybe Brynn will take you upstairs for a little bit." Claire looks expectantly at Brynn, who doesn't seem to hear her. "Brynn," she says more forcefully so that Brynn startles. "Will you take Joshua upstairs?" Brynn nods. "Just stay away from Dad's tools, Josh. I'll be up in a minute. Don't you worry, it's not like the robbery. Not at all." He looks skeptically at the door that leads to the second-floor apartment and doesn't move until Brynn reaches for his hand. Together they ascend the steps to the apartment.

Once Claire is sure that they are safely upstairs, out of earshot, she goes to the phone and dials her husband's cell phone number. "Jonathan, can you come to the store? Please. I need you."

Allison

Claire walks us over to the reading area and somehow, very politely, offers us seats. Despite everything, I'm reminded of how much I admire her. Always so calm and collected. Always so poised. "Girls, I don't know exactly what's happening, but I need you to try and tell me. I'm more than a little confused."

Charm and I sit side by side on the sofa. I wish Brynn were here, sitting next to me. I can't believe I told Claire that I was Joshua's mother. I can't bear to look at her. Claire sits on the coffee table, facing Charm and me. Reanne and Binks are standing close by, lurking like turkey vultures. Charm begins to cry again. "Allison, please tell me what's going on. Are you Joshua's birth mother?" I can hear in Claire's voice how scared she is. This is one thing we have in common—we are both terrified, but for completely different reasons. She's afraid I'm here to take Joshua away from her and I'm afraid that the only person in the past five years who hasn't treated me like I was a monster is about to realize that's just what I am.

I nod and Claire's face crumples with grief.

"I'm so sorry," I say in a rush, wanting to explain, but not knowing where to begin. "I left the baby with Christopher."

"Who's Christopher?" Claire asks.

"My brother," Charm says softly, the tears starting all over again. Her eyes feel swollen from crying and her face still stings from her mother's slap. "And Joshua's father," she says bitterly, directing the words at her mother.

"Bullshit," Reanne says in disbelief. She looks me up and down. "Christopher would never get involved with her."

"Well, he did," I snap. I turn back to Claire. "I didn't want to hurt anyone."

A loud snort of disbelief erupts from Reanne. Claire turns to her and says through her tears, "I really think you should leave now."

Reanne works her mouth as if trying to hold back another discharge of profanity. Instead, a soft expulsion of air rushes out and a cranberry-red flush rises from her neckline and spreads to her cheeks. "Well, excuse me for wanting to check on my daughter." Her voice rises to a shout. "Excuse me for wanting to warn her about some psycho, murdering bitch! Do you know who that girl is?" Reanne sputters. "That's Allison Glenn. She threw her newborn daughter in the Druid River five years ago. You should have rotted in jail!"

My stomach twists. I didn't think there could be anything more horrible than Claire finding out about Joshua, but this is so much worse.

"How do you know that?" Claire demands. "How do you know she's the girl? The paper never said who she was." Her eyes settle on me, not wanting to believe what Reanne is saying, but I hear the doubt beginning in her voice. "You can't be that girl."

"It wasn't hard to figure out. I knew I heard her name before and then it came to me. I know someone who works at Cravenville. She told me all about her." Reanne turns toward me again and says harshly, "You had a baby girl and you didn't want it, so you dumped her in the river!"

"Shut up, Mom!" Charm pleads.

"Allison?" Claire asks me incredulously. "Is that what happened? Was that you?"

"I can explain." I start to cry.

Brynn

I'm sitting in the bathroom, on the edge of the bathtub. Joshua is on the couch, still fast asleep. I can hear them downstairs, yelling and shouting, and I put my hands over my ears so I don't have hear, but still the noise creeps through so I turn on the tap. Water rushes out of the faucet and the shouts are drowned out.

Now the running water becomes the sound of the pouring rain that fell that night years ago, pounding, slapping against the window.

When I came back upstairs I looked down on Joshua's little sister. So quiet and still. "No," I whispered. "Oh, no."

"What?" Allison murmured with exhaustion, trying to lift her head to see.

"Oh, Allison," I said sadly. "You don't have to worry anymore." And even as I spoke, I knew that Allison would be relieved with this outcome. Not happy, mind you, but relieved. I stood there for a long time, not knowing what to do. Finally, I spoke, though I don't know if she even heard me. "I'll take care of it," I told her as I tucked another blanket tightly around her and tilted a water bottle to her lips. "I'll be back in a few minutes."

Crying, I bent down to pick up the motionless infant, my tears beading and rolling off her bare skin like rain on parched earth, too little, too late. Unsteadily, I made my way down the stairs, trying to focus my eyes on anything but the child in my arms. I moved through the living room where our family pictures told the story of our childhoods. Allison and I were evenly represented in the number of pictures on the "Wall of Lame," as Allison called it—until Allison was thirteen. By this time, Allison was an accomplished swimmer, soccer player, gymnast, speller. The wall was lined with pictures of Allison holding various ribbons and trophies. In each of them she was smiling humbly, an "aw, shucks" look on her face.

But the pictures didn't tell the backstory, though. They didn't show that minutes before the snapshot was taken Allison had elbowed her soccer opponent so hard in the ribs that they both ended up with bruises, or that she stared at her nine-year-old classmate so intently that he got flustered and misspelled *leucoplast,* a word he could spell in his sleep. Not that Allison ever cheated— she never did that, she didn't need to—but she was intimidating in a way that people liked, encouraged even. Her teachers thought of her as the student that only came around once in a lifetime. The girls were jealous but felt bad about it; the boys thought she was beautiful, unattainable. My parents thought she was perfect.

I never thought that Allison was perfect, although I admired her determination and her drive. But I knew something that everyone else seemed to overlook—that my sister was human. That she threw up before every single big test she had to take. That she would make herself do one hundred and fifty sit-ups every night before bed. That she had nightmares that scared her so badly she would creep into my room at night and crawl into bed with me. At the time, I had thought that the bad dreams had finally stopped haunting her, because she hadn't come to my room for months. But now I knew why. She didn't want me to know that she was pregnant.

In the months before she gave birth, I saw something else about my sister that no one else did. She was in love. The girl that everyone said was so smart not to have a serious boyfriend, the girl who was focused so much on her sports and school, was desperately in love with someone. This poor baby's father. She never told me anything about him, but I knew something was up. When she thought that no one was looking, I could see it. Her shoulders would relax. A small smile would play at the corners of her mouth and a dreamy, unfocused look would come into her eyes. For once in her life my sister looked happy. I also knew that sometimes she snuck out of the house at night. One time I watched from my bedroom window and saw her climb into a car, its headlights off, a lone figure in the driver's seat. In the shadows I saw them embrace and kiss desperately, passionately.

But then something had happened. The hazy, dreamy light in her eyes had been once again replaced with a ferocious single-mindedness and she was studying even harder, working out even more. Even though I held the results of her pregnancy in my arms, it was nearly impossible for me to imagine that this little life had been inside her while she was working so hard.

I made my way through the kitchen and out the back door. A cool summer wind smoothed the hair from my forehead. After the stifling air of Allison's bedroom, I lifted my face to the sky to welcome the rain that fell. I rearranged the towel around the baby as if to shield it from the elements. The darkening night sky was indecisive. It didn't know what it was going to do next. In the south the moon was high and bright, peeking through marbled clouds that moved swiftly. There was just enough light for me to be able to see where I was going, but it was dark enough for me to conceal the sweet package I held in my arms.

Allison and I had rarely ventured into the small woods behind our home. Our mother had warned us away from the Druid River that ran alongside our woods. "A river is a living, moving thing," she told us. "You stick one toe in that water and it will snatch you in and pull you under. You'll never get out once you fall in." I used to think that Allison's nightmares were about drowning in that river. She would cry out and wake up gasping for air and rubbing her eyes, as if trying to rub the water away.

The weak light from the moon was extinguished once I entered the Grimm's fairy-tale woods of my childhood. Our mother had terrified us with tales of lyme disease and small feral animals carrying rabies. Clutching the baby, I imagined ticks attaching their diseased-filled barbs to my skin and settling in to drink my blood and foam-mouthed animals hiding behind trees, ready to pounce. Sliding my feet carefully along the muddy, rocky earth, I felt my way toward the river. I ducked under low-hanging sharp branches covered with new leaves. In daylight, they would be tender and green, but here the darkness gave the appearance of glowering hairy arms. As I approached, I could hear the rushing of the Druid River, loud and wild-sounding. My tennis shoes squelched deeply into the mud. We'd had record rains that spring and all the creeks and rivers were stealthily widening, ingesting the land.

Sitting on the edge of the bathtub, I pass my hand underneath the running water, its steam filling the room. I reach into the hot water and fish around for the rubber stopper to plug the drain. Oh, how good it would feel to climb into the tub and feel the warm water against my skin, to submerge myself completely so there is nothing but dark and quiet. Why did I come here? I'm not sure anymore.

From the other room I hear Joshua calling for his mother. I wipe away the tears I've found on my face and go to him.

Claire

Claire looks at Allison in disbelief. Allison was the girl who had drowned her newborn baby girl? She knew something bad had happened for Allison to have gone to prison. But she didn't think it was cold-blooded murder. Claire remembers hearing about the baby on the news. *Baby drowned... A sixteen-year-old girl...arrested...*

"What happened?" Claire remembers asking.

Her husband hesitated. "A sixteen-year-old girl drowned her newborn baby," Jonathan said as he brushed the hair from his wife's forehead.

Claire felt the bubbling of bile rise in her throat.

"Are you okay, Claire?" Jonathan asked, looking down on her with concern.

Claire shook her head soundlessly. How could she put it into words? "It's not fair," Claire finally said. "It's not fair!" she repeated, knowing that she sounded like a querulous child who didn't get her way. Jonathan moved closer and reached a tentative hand toward her, and Claire pulled away from him, knowing that she would scream if anyone touched her just then. "How could she just throw a baby away when we want one so much?" Claire cried. Jonathan didn't answer her. What could be said?

Five years ago, she would have done anything to be able to have a child. And that girl—that *monster,* she had thought—would do anything so she wouldn't have to.

Claire looks at Allison and shakes her head. She can't fathom how a woman—a girl, she amends, because she looks so young, even five years later—could have done something so evil. How God could have given this girl a baby, two babies, had given her body the power to knit together all the wondrous elements that go into creating a baby, and for her, nothing.

Jonathan rushes through the front door of Bookends and Claire runs to meet him. "Jonathan, thank God you're here."

"What's going on?" He scans the room, taking in Allison's and Charm's stricken faces, Reanne's angry scowl and Binks's embarrassed confusion. Silently, Claire hands Jonathan the photograph.

"He's ours," Claire says to no one in particular. "We adopted him. Joshua's our son."

Brynn

Joshua sleepily calls for his mother and I quickly go to him. "Joshua," I whisper. "It's okay. You don't have to worry about anything. I'm right here."

"Where's my mommy?" he asks, trying to keep his eyes open.

"Shhh," I soothe. "Shhh." I sit down next to him and pull him onto my lap. He tries to squirm away, but I hold him tightly. Finally, he relaxes; his head rests on my shoulder. "It's okay, Joshua. Just close your eyes. See, just like me." I close my eyes to show him what I mean.

I had nearly tumbled into the river, just as my mother had prophesized, but with one hand grabbed the trunk of a thin, scraggly tree. Instead, I fell to my knees into the thick mud that edged the stream. I repositioned the dead baby in her blanket and for a moment thought about burying her there, at the river's edge. But I dismissed the idea; I'd have to return to the garage for a shovel, and time was passing too quickly as it was. The temperature seemed to have dropped twenty degrees and I shivered with each gust of wind. The clouds broke above me, revealing the bitter, yellow moon that gave off enough light to see the river before me. It rushed ruthlessly past, frothing over rocks, carrying logs and branches. I kissed my niece's cold cheek and told her I loved her and that if I had my way she would be with me forever. I even considered, just for a second, that I could have been the one to raise her. Allison wasn't exactly mothering material. In my own misguided way, I performed a little funeral. I said a prayer over her and carefully rearranged the towel around her.

Just as I released her gently into the swift-moving water, I heard the cry. A weak, mournful squawk, as if the feel of the cold, rushing water had shocked her back to life.

I leaped into the water, not feeling the cold. The river was up to my knees and I slogged with the current for a few yards when she went under for the first time. Quickly, she bobbed up. Trying to plant my feet on the rocky river bottom, I leaped forward until I was just behind her. The towel had been swept away and her pitiful naked form rolled out of my reach. With a grunt of fury I managed to surge forward and grab hold of something—a finger, a toe, I couldn't tell—but the river was too strong, pulsing and roiling forward, and I lost my balance and went under. Water filled my eyes, my ears, my mouth, and she slipped away from me. I had lost her.

I tried to kill myself that night. That was the first time I actually made a real effort at it, even though I'd imagined the many different ways I could end my life over the years. Pills, the gun my father had hidden underneath his socks in his dresser, climbing to the roof of our ridiculously big house to swan dive onto our decorative concrete driveway. I remember wondering if bloodstains came out of cement and getting a twisted satisfaction of my mother having to walk past that blot, the remainder of me, the reminder of me. She'd probably tear out the concrete and start all over again.

After I realized the baby was alive—*breathing*—and that I had lost her, I tried to drown myself. I held my breath and waited for the warm calm that was supposed to come after the initial panic of drowning passes. I could feel the pressure build in my head, behind my eyes, in my lungs. I tried to stay beneath the surface of the water, tried to grab on to something that would hold me down, but the river had other ideas. It pushed and shoved and spit me out onto the bank as if it couldn't stand the thought of swallowing me, as if I would leave a bad taste in its mouth. Couldn't blame it, really.

I curled up in a little ball at the side of the Druid. The rain beat down on me until my skin was numb. I thought about what was going to happen when people found out what I had done and I willed myself to disappear into the mud that squelched beneath me. No such luck. Finally, I got up. Allison would know what to do, my sister would know.

When I came upon her at the edge of the woods, I barely noticed she was bent over in pain. "Where's the baby?" she managed to grunt.

"The river." The word felt obscene to my ears.

"What do you mean?" Allison asked. There was fear in her voice and she knew, she knew.

"She was pretty," I said, knowing that wasn't the thing to say just then, but not knowing how to explain it. Allison misunderstood and I saw her eyes widen with horror.

"You drowned her because she was pretty?" she said angrily, and then grabbed me by the arm. I flinched, thinking she was going to hit me, but she just held on to me as if trying to steady herself so she wouldn't fall over.

I shook my head back and forth, back and forth. "No," I moaned. "No, I didn't."

"Brynn, what happened?" Allison asked.

"It was like it ate her," I cried, trying to explain. "It gobbled her up and it didn't want me."

"Jesus, Brynn," Allison said. Now that she had recovered from her spasm of pain, she began to shake me. "You're not making sense! I know where we can take her. Christopher will take care of everything. He has to. Please tell me you didn't throw her in the river."

"I thought she was dead," I whispered, not able to look my sister in the eye. Not wanting to see her disgust and disappointment. "I did it for you. I was trying to help you."

"How does killing her help?" Allison hissed, and then doubled over in pain again.

I shook her hand away from my arm and she dropped to her knees.

"You're mad?" I said in disbelief. "You didn't want her—you pretty much told me to get rid of it. That's what you called her, an *it!* I didn't mean to hurt her, I thought she was already dead!" I turned and began to run back toward the house. Ungrateful bitch, I thought.

"Wait!" I heard from behind me. "Please, Brynn, I need you. Don't leave!"

I ignored her and ran away, covering my ears, trying to block out her voice.

The weight of the little boy on my lap is both comforting and suffocating. "Joshua," I say, and his eyes flutter open. "Did you know you have a sister?" His mouth opens and closes as if he is trying to speak, then his eyes close again. "Yes, a sister. A pretty, pretty sister. Do you want to meet her?"

I struggle to my feet, Joshua's limp body heavy in my arms, and move toward the sound of the running water. "Oh, you are so much heavier than she was," I whisper in his ear. I can almost hear the crickets chirping, hear the rush of the river, feel the summer breeze against my neck. "Finally, finally," I tell him, "you can be together." And I lay him in the water, gently, lovingly, offering Joshua to his sister.

Allison

Jonathan is still staring in shock at the photo of Charm holding Joshua. Binks takes a small, slow step backward, as if trying to escape unnoticed. Charm's mother is looking on with a twisted smile and an odd gleam in her eyes. She actually seems to be enjoying this.

I hear her before I see her. The slow, echoing thump of footfalls on the steps, an odd sucking sound, the squeak of a door opening. My sister steps from the shadows, her arms held awkwardly away from her body. "Brynn, what's the matter?" I ask. "What's going on?" She doesn't answer, but continues moving toward us. As she gets closer I see that she is soaking wet, her shoes squelching with water as she moves. Her eyes are dull and dead-looking, but her face is relaxed and I see something new in my sister's expression. An expression I don't ever remembering seeing cross her face. Relief.

"Brynn," I say again, this time more loudly. "What's

the matter?" Still no answer. I move in front of her and grab her arms. "Brynn, where is Joshua?"

"They're together now," she murmurs, gliding past me as if in a trance.

Claire

Claire stares in confusion as Allison's sister wanders slowly past, water dripping from her clothes. "Brynn?" she asks. "Are you okay? Where's Joshua?" She doesn't answer, but mutters quietly to herself and starts to move toward the front door of the store.

"Brynn," Claire says more loudly. "Where's Joshua?" Nothing. Jonathan and Claire look at each other and Jonathan reaches for Brynn's arm.

"It's okay now, they're together," Brynn whispers in a singsong voice. Jonathan loosens his grip and she pulls away from him.

"Oh, my God… Joshua," Claire whimpers, and she and Jonathan scramble toward the steps. Allison follows closely behind, slipping once and knocking her shin against the hardwood floor.

"Joshua!" Claire yells. "Joshua!" She bursts into the apartment and moves toward the sound of running water.

Charm

Charm can hear Claire and Jonathan calling for Joshua and she moves to follow them up the steps. Brynn bumps into her, and she can feel the wetness of her clothes. "What's happening?" Charm asks as she continues past her. "Why are you all wet?"

Brynn stops suddenly and looks at Charm, her eyebrows furrowed in concentration. "Together," she whispers. "Together, together. I need to go." Brynn dazedly points toward the door. "I need to tell her…"

Charm watches in fascination as Brynn slogs from the bookstore, water dripping from her clothes.

A scream comes from the apartment above. "Someone help!" Charm kicks off her shoes and scurries up the steps with her mother and Binks right behind. Her heart is pounding, fearful of what they're going to find when they reach the top.

Claire

"Call 9-1-1! Please…" Claire cries.

Jonathan digs into the pocket of his jeans and pulls out his cell phone and dials. "We need help," he says frantically, and gives the operator the address. "I don't know… I don't know. Hold on, please…"

"Oh, my God… *Joshua.*" Claire pulls at Joshua's shirt, trying to drag him from the tub. His clothing is saturated with water, heavy and unyielding, and he keeps sliding from her grip. Jonathan thrusts the phone to Allison and reaches into the tub. He grabs a handful of Joshua's hair, pulls him to the surface and gathers him into his arms. Allison, in a strangled voice, is telling the 9-1-1 operator to send an ambulance.

Charm, who had moments ago been nearly hysterical at her mother's ranting, has suddenly become businesslike and composed. "Lay him down," she orders Jonathan. He carefully lays Joshua onto the hardwood floor and Claire gasps at the blue cast of his skin, the stillness of his chest. As Charm places her ear next to his mouth, she asks, "Is an ambulance on its way?"

"Yes, they're coming," Allison cries.

Charm leans over Joshua and checks to make sure his airway is clear while Claire and Jonathan watch helplessly. "What can I do?" Allison asks.

"Go meet the ambulance, bring them up here," Charm commands, and then puts her fingers to Joshua's neck. Allison runs down the stairs.

"Is he breathing?" Claire asks, her voice breaking.

She gives a small shake of her head and breathes one breath into Joshua's mouth, then begins the series of chest compressions, using only one hand on his tiny chest.

In the distance they hear the wail of the ambulance. "Is he breathing?" Claire asks Charm again, but knows that he is not. She grabs on to Jonathan and they clutch each other desperately, watching, waiting, for any sign of life. "Please," Claire chants over and over again. "Please." And all she can think is that she was given this precious little life to care for and protect and she has failed. She has failed.

Charm

"Breathe, one, two, three, four..." Charm whispers with each compression, counting to thirty before starting the process all over again. She has lost track of how long she's been doing CPR. Her arms are tiring and in the distance she can hear an ambulance. *Thank God.*

Next to her, Charm can hear Jonathan's ragged sobs and Claire begging Joshua to start breathing. "Please breathe, Joshua, please," she pleads.

Charm feels more eyes on her and looks up to see her mother and Binks standing in the doorway and a wave of anger surges through her veins. "Get out!" she yells. "Leave now—we need room for the EMTs to get us." Without a word, Reanne and Binks disappear. Charm knows that for how much her mother loves drama, she never would have wanted this. The siren gets louder and then the sound of stomping feet climbing the steps fills the hallway. With one final compression on his thin, bony chest, Joshua's body convulses and water spews from his mouth and he begins to breathe again—short, shallow breaths, but he is breathing. Charm falls against the wall in exhaustion. The EMTs take over and in seconds Joshua is whisked away.

"Thank you," Claire manages to tell Charm, laying one grateful hand on her arm as she and Jonathan follow them out the door.

Allison kneels down next to Charm, her eyes red with crying. "You saved him."

Why, then, Charm wonders, *does it feel like I'm the one who ruined his life?*

Claire

Jonathan and Claire follow Joshua to the hospital in Jonathan's truck. "He was breathing, wasn't he? He was breathing?" Claire keeps asking fiercely.

"He was, he is," Jonathan says, as if trying to reassure himself. "Jesus, what happened up there?" he wonders, and Claire can only shake her head. Claire doesn't know why Joshua was in that bathtub. She can't even imagine what was going on in Brynn's mind. She doesn't want to know. If Claire had been thinking clearly, she would have never, ever sent Joshua up those stairs with Brynn Glenn. She didn't even know her and she had just learned that her sister was not who she made herself out to be. But there was so much going on—Reanne screaming obscenities and crazy accusations, seeing the photograph of Charm. Joshua was terrified and all she wanted to do was get him out of there, get him somewhere he felt safe and secure. How could they have not known who Allison Glenn really was? Were they so busy being new parents to Joshua that they were completely oblivious as to what was going on in their own town? She had tried to do the right thing, be a good mother, but was it enough? Was it too late?

Jonathan can't keep up with the ambulance and by the time they arrive at the hospital Joshua has already been taken away. Jonathan and Claire sit in the waiting area, holding on to each other, crying. Claire somehow manages to call her sister, who promises to call their mother. They will come to Linden Falls as quickly as they can.

Charm shows up a short time later, peeking around the corner of the waiting room door, hesitant to enter.

"I made sure Truman was okay and I locked up the store for you," Charm says. "I got rid of my mother, too. She won't bother you again."

Claire looks around. "Where's Allison?"

Charm's eyes are bloodshot and her nose is red from crying. "She went to find her sister. I'm so sorry…so, so sorry," she sobs, her face crumpling.

"I called the police," Jonathan says, an angry edge creeping into his voice. "There are too many questions about what happened." He runs a hand through his hair in frustration. "What happened to Allison's sister? Where is she?"

"I don't know," Charm says helplessly. Her clothes are still wet and wrinkled, her face pale with worry. To Claire she seems just as devastated as she and Jonathan are, and right then Claire knows she would never deliberately hurt Joshua. Still, she feels a twist of anger at the lies, the deception, Charm has shown.

"Please, just leave," Claire says. "I'm sorry. We can't have you here right now." Charm nods silently and turns to go.

It seems like years, waiting for word on Joshua's condition. When the doctor finally comes into the waiting area, the room feels airless.

"Joshua is going to be just fine," she says with a smile. "He's awake and he's breathing on his own. Would you like to go and see him?"

"Of course," Claire says, beginning to cry again, this time with relief. The doctor leads Jonathan and Claire to the room where Joshua lies. He is hooked up to an IV and his eyes are half-open, but when he sees his parents a smile creases his wan face.

"Hey, it's our three-tailed badger," Jonathan says, his voice cracking.

"No, I'm Joshua Kelby," he answers weakly.

"Yes, you are," Claire tells him firmly. *You are the wish that we make every morning when we wake up and the prayer we say before we go to bed each night,* she says to herself, and reaches out for his small hand.

Brynn

Just one last thing to do and then I can rest.

I need to go to her, need to let her know that he is coming. I push out the door, into the dark and feel the cool air on my face and on my wet skin. "Over the river and through the woods…" I hum, barely noticing the curious looks I get as I walk down the street. I must be quite the sight and I giggle at the thought. It's not far now. I know it's not the exact spot I left the little girl, but it's close enough. It will have to be. In the distance I hear a siren and wonder if they're coming for me. It's about time. I walk a little faster. They should have come for me five years ago. I wanted to tell them but Allison said, No, keep your mouth shut. And I tried to, but every time I closed my eyes I saw her being swept away, heard her cries until I couldn't stand it anymore. After that man found her cold little body, I called the police. I wanted to tell them it was me, me, me. But when they finally drove up all I could do was cry and Allison told me to shut up, shut up, shut up. So I did. And they took her away.

For a long time I was so sorry, knowing it was my fault that she was in that jail and I was sitting at home, going to school, living my life. But I figured it out, it didn't take long. It was like when we were little and there was one piece of cake left. Allison always took the side with the flowers and I was left with just the white frosting. She had done it again, took the side with the flowers. She got to leave; she got to go away even if it was to go to jail, and I had to stay. They started looking at me then, and they wanted me to be like her. When I wasn't, they stopped looking. Which was worse. So then I wasn't so sorry anymore.

You can hear the Druid before you see it. It runs southward through the center of town, through the countryside right behind our house. It winds and twists until it runs into the Mississippi and then it's like it never was, like it just disappears into nothing. Magically. The river in this part of town usually smells like dead fish and the gasoline from motorboats, but the rain has washed that all away and the air is fresh and clean. I stand at the edge of the paved walkway, high above the black water. Druid means sorcerer. Magic.

I'm scared, so scared, and I look around for Allison. I want my sister. Someone touches my arm, "Are you okay?" I hear.

"I want my sister," I say, and start to cry. "He needs his sister. I need to tell her he's coming."

"Can I call someone for you?" the voice says.

"No, no, no, no," I say. "I need to tell her."

When I step off the edge I feel a scrambling panic. I hit the cold water and it fills my ears, my nose, my mouth. I try to cry out for my sister, but my words become bubbles and rise to the surface silently. When I stop thrashing, stop struggling, I see her. So perfect, so tiny, just like I remembered her. "He's coming," I tell her, reaching my hands out to hers. "He'll be here soon." And as I cradle her in my arms we sink, slowly, peacefully, to the river's bottom, to wait.

Charm

Charm sells the house and takes some of the money that Gus left to her after he died and decides to buy a more reliable car. After that terrible night she knows she has to leave Linden Falls. Still, it's taken Charm eight months to actually pack up and drive away.

The thought of saying goodbye to Joshua is terrible. Charm thought it was hard the first time. The second time will be worse. This time she knows she is not coming back. Ever.

The day before she leaves, Charm calls Claire and asks if she can stop by the store to say her goodbyes. Thankfully, she says yes. When Charm arrives, Joshua is running around the store trying to get Truman to chase him. When he sees Charm, he stops and looks at her thoughtfully.

"You breathed into me," he says seriously.

Charm bites her lip, not quite knowing how to respond.

"Josh, buddy," Claire says, "Charm is just stopping in to say goodbye. We're leaving in a few days."

Joshua thinks about this. "We're going to stay with my grandma in—"

"Josh," Claire warns. "Remember, it's a secret. We're going to surprise Grandma."

"I hope you have a lot of fun with your grandma, Joshua," Charm tells him, forcing back her tears. With sadness, Charm realizes that Claire doesn't want her to know where they are going. "I just wanted to make sure I said goodbye to you before you left. I'll miss you, Josh." Charm kneels down to his eye level and reaches out to hug him, noticing Claire stiffen next to her. Still, Charm wraps her arms around Joshua and hugs him tightly, trying to imprint the feeling of his soft hair on her cheek, the knobby bones of his spine under her fingertips. Joshua hugs Charm back, hard.

"I've got something for you, Joshua," Charm tells him, pulling away from him reluctantly. Charm looks up at Claire to make sure it's okay to give him something. She looks unsure, but nods.

"What? What is it?" he asks excitedly. Charm stands, wipes her eyes and hands him the gift bag.

He all but rips it from her hands and Claire reminds him gently, "What do you say, Josh?"

"Thank you," he says absentmindedly. He reaches in among the bright green tissue paper and pulls out the Chicago Cubs baseball cap that Gus bought for him when he was first born, the one that Charm kept hidden in a shoe box for five years, along with the incriminating photo of her with Joshua, the tiny booties and the rattle.

The hat Gus said he would grow into one day.

"Oh, a baseball cap!" Joshua says, impressed. "It's just like the one that Luke has, but better." He places the cap on his head and the bill covers his eyes.

"It's a great cap," Claire agrees.

"Yeah, we gotta recruit those Cub fans early," Charm says, echoing the phrase that Gus always said, smiling through her tears.

"I'm going to go look in the mirror," Joshua declares, running off to the bathroom.

"That was really nice," Claire says seriously. "You've been good for Joshua, Charm. You would be...you've been a wonderful aunt." Claire hesitates. "I hope you understand why we can't encourage a relationship between you two. It would be too confusing for Joshua. And then there's your brother."

"My brother will never, ever try to begin a relationship with Joshua or try to take him from you," Charm tells her vehemently. "Christopher doesn't need any more problems. My mother—" she sighs "—is my mother. She won't try to get to Joshua. She likes to stir things up and leave."

"I know that you've only wanted what's best for Joshua, Charm. You saved his life, and I'm grateful for that."

Charm shrugs, not knowing how to respond. "This is for you," Charm finally says, handing her the large envelope she brought with her.

"What's this?" Claire asks.

"Medical histories. Allison and I gathered all the information we could about our families," Charm explains. "It's all in there. There are pictures of Allison and Christopher, Gus and me, the grandparents," Charm says. Seeing Claire's face, she adds, "If you ever think he should see them, I mean. Allison and I will never, ever contact Joshua. We promise. We want him to be happy and safe, and he is, as long as he's with you and Jonathan." Charm feels tears prickling at her eyes and knows it's time for her to go.

She moves toward the door, willing herself not to look back.

"Charm," Claire calls after her, and Charm turns, hopefully, expectantly. Joshua's hat is sitting crookedly on his head and he has his arms wrapped around his mother's waist. He looks so happy. "Thank you," she says, her tear-filled eyes meeting Charm's. "Thank you for my son."

Allison

For a while, I was terrified that everyone would think that I had something to do with Brynn trying to drown Joshua, like it was some kind of big conspiracy. The police talked to me for hours, shook their heads at my insistence that I had nothing to do with the drowning, tried to get me to admit to something, anything. But in the end, Devin came to the rescue again. She was able to get Brynn's medical records and the notes from her visits with her psychiatrist that she was seeing in New Amery. In her sessions with her doctor, Brynn talked extensively about the guilt she felt for thinking the baby girl was already dead when she went to the river. My grandmother also found Brynn's journals, the drawings that documented the night I gave birth to the twins. Brynn had sketched picture after picture of the Druid River sweeping the baby away. One disturbing drawing showed a lifeless Brynn at river's bottom holding two infants, one male, one female, umbilical cords connected to one placenta.

So in the end I've been exonerated and my record will be expunged, my file sealed. I can leave Linden Falls anytime now, if I want to. I could move to a small town like Wellman where no one would have heard of me or to a bigger city like Des Moines where no one would care. I can leave the state or leave the country. It's up to me and me alone.

My mother asked me if I would identify Brynn's body. My father was still in the hospital and she just couldn't do it. I agreed. It was the least I could do for Brynn. I was the one who brought Brynn back to Linden Falls, made her face the little boy whose sister she accidentally drowned. I was the one who couldn't save her. Poor, fragile Brynn, who only wanted to be with her animals. I may have not known what she was going to do to Joshua, but I was the catalyst.

I identified her on a video screen; I wasn't even in the same room with her. She was lying on a metal table covered with a sheet and a woman pulled back the cover from her face. Immediately, I knew it was Brynn. Except for her pale skin and blue lips, she looked like she was sleeping. "That's my sister," I said.

Brynn's funeral was small and very sad. I sat between my parents and my grandmother, but it was my grandmother's hand I reached for when Brynn's casket was lowered into the ground. In the small crowd I saw Olene, Bea, and surprisingly Flora was there. Afterward, I found myself alone with my parents.

"Where will you go?" my mother asked, her eyes red from crying. She looked exhausted and old.

"To college." I paused. "I'm not sure where yet," I said. "Away." I need to leave Linden Falls, need to leave Iowa. I want to go somewhere where no one will connect me to Brynn, Joshua, the Kelbys or Christopher.

I'd like to apply to the University of Illinois in Champaign. Devin has been wonderful. She said she would write me a letter of recommendation and promised to support me in any way she can. If all goes well, I plan to apply to law school. I'm not sure if I want to keep any kind of connection with my parents.

"That's wise," my father said, nodding his head with approval. He'd lost weight while in the hospital and held tightly on to my mother. I waited for one of them to hug me or even shake me. But they just stood there and looked uncomfortable. I shook my head in frustration and turned to leave.

"I don't understand it," my mother finally said, pulling at my sleeve to stop me. I turned around, hopeful. Maybe at last we'd talk. Really talk.

"You gave up everything." She looked at me with— what? Confusion, pity, disgust? "You could have gone to any college. We gave you everything. You could have been anything you wanted to be. Why did you go to jail for her? You gave up your entire future for her. I just don't understand why?"

I took a step backward, freeing myself from my mother's grasp. *To protect her,* I wanted to tell them. *Someone needed to protect her.* Brynn never would have survived the questions or the scrutiny from the police. She wouldn't have been able to tell them that it was an accident, that she really thought the baby was already dead. Because I loved her, I wanted to tell them. Because she was the only one who helped me when I wasn't perfect. They wouldn't have understood, no matter what I said.

"Was it worth it, Allison?" my mother persisted. "Was she worth all the lies?"

"Yes," I said plainly, my unwavering gaze matching my mother's. "Brynn was worth it."

In the end, I didn't protect Brynn from anything. I thought I had done the right thing in taking the blame. I wanted to spare her any more pain. I guess I just prolonged the inevitable. I hope she found peace in her life for a little while, found the love and support she deserved while she lived with our grandmother. Found some comfort in her pets.

"Well." My father halfheartedly clapped his hands together. "How about I write you a check just to get you off to a good start?" he offered, as if this would make everything okay. I had no job, nowhere to live and was completely broke. Common sense warranted I should take the money.

"No, thank you," I said, and that was that. So this was what it came down to for my parents and me. They would never see me graduate from college, never see me marry or have children. I wondered at my mother. Were her tears for the loss of Brynn, the loss of me? Did she cry because we didn't turn out to be the daughters she had hoped us to be? I'd never know.

After my parents walked away from me and back to the quiet, isolated life they had made for themselves, I found my grandmother. She was standing by Brynn's grave site, crying softly. "Grandma?" I said quietly. "Are you okay?" I put my hand on her shoulder.

"I thought she was doing better." She sniffled. "She was seeing that doctor. She was on a good path with her classes and her animals."

"Oh, Grandma," I said, beginning to cry again. "It's all my fault. It wasn't her fault about the baby. It was mine."

My grandma pulled me into her strong, thick arms.

I towered over her. "Allison, honey, there is plenty of fault to be passed around."

My grandma released me and we slowly walked to her car. "Are your parents going to try and see that little boy?" she asked.

"No. Do you really think Joshua should be anywhere near my parents?" I made a face and shuddered at the thought.

"No, I guess not. Did you get to say goodbye to him? To Joshua?" She took my hand.

"No. The Kelbys obviously want nothing to do with me and I guess I understand that. I haven't seen Joshua since that night at the bookstore."

"You helped save his life. That's something."

"They're good people, but I'm just a terrible reminder to them. Even though I had nothing to do with Brynn trying to drown Joshua, I know they will never trust me again. I should have quit the bookstore the minute I realized who Joshua was. I should have never told Brynn about him."

I watched as my grandmother opened her car door and wondered how things might have been different if she had been around more when Brynn and I were little. The few memories I had of visiting her and staying at her home were wonderful. I remembered playing with Brynn among our grandma's flowers, burying our noses in the velvety petals of snow-white peonies and waving away bumblebees that scolded us for invading their territory. Would her kindness have changed things?

"Do you want a ride?" she asked.

"No, thanks. Olene is waiting for me."

"One more hug," she ordered with a smile, and I leaned down and embraced her.

"And, Allison," she said as she slid into the car and inserted the key into the ignition with her swollen, knotty fingers, "if you need to—if you want to—you are more than welcome to come stay with me in New Amery for a while. For as long as you'd like."

"Really?" I asked in surprise. I wanted nothing more than to leave Linden Falls behind and just drive away with my grandmother. "I have a few things to finish up here," I told her regretfully. "Can I come when I'm done? In a few days or so?"

"Of course," she said. "You come when you're ready. You'll get the chance to meet Brynn's pets."

"I can't wait," I told her, and leaned through the car window to peck her on the cheek.

I wish I had been a better sister, I wish I could have been there to help Brynn. But I couldn't. When things got difficult, Brynn could only see bleakness and despair. She saw no glimmer of hope that things would ever get better. She thought that without his sister, Joshua could never be happy. I don't know that anyone could have saved Brynn from herself. But I can save myself. I can be happy.

As I walked toward Olene and the others, I remembered how Olene told me to meet the world with hope in my heart. That's exactly what I'm going to do.

I know that I will never see Joshua Kelby—my son—again. But I have hope that he will grow up strong and happy and well-loved. I have hope that when the time is right, his parents will say to him, *There once was a girl who loved you enough to give you the world.* I hope.

* * * * *

AUTHOR'S NOTE

Currently all fifty states have enacted Safe Haven laws. Though the details of the laws vary from state to state, the intention is to provide a safe place for parents or another person who has the parent's permission to leave an infant at a hospital or health care facility without fear of arrest for abandonment.

In the state of Iowa, when an infant is left at a Safe Haven site, the health care facility will contact a child protective worker. The Department of Human Services will immediately notify the Juvenile Court and the County Attorney, and request an Ex Parte Order from the Juvenile Court ordering the Department of Human Services to take custody of the child. Once the infant has been examined by medical personnel the child may be placed in foster care. The date and time of the hearing to terminate parental rights will be published in the newspaper. Parents are not required to attend the court hearing, which must be held within thirty days of the discovery of the infant at the Safe Haven location.

No clear statistics have been gathered regarding the number of children relinquished at Safe Haven sites. States, counties and individual communities do not maintain data in a consistent manner.

The laws are not without controversy. Some opponents believe that Safe Haven laws promote the abandonment of children and discourage women from seeking prenatal and postnatal medical care and counseling, thus endangering the health of both the mother and the baby. Opponents argue that they create a legislative Band-Aid, instead of addressing the root causes of baby abandonment and infanticide. Proponents of the laws herald the lives saved and the anonymity the programs provide in protecting parents.

If you have any questions regarding your state's Safe Haven program you may contact any local health care facility or Department of Human Services.

Heather Gudenkauf

BOOK CLUB QUESTIONS

1. Charm, Claire and Allison all serve as Joshua's mother at some point in the novel. In the end, who is the best mother? Why do you think so? How does each of these characters evolve throughout the story?

2. The women in the story all love Joshua in their own way. What else do they have in common? What are their differences?

3. Describe Charm's relationship with her mother. How does Charm demonstrate her determination to be different than her mother? What qualities do they share?

4. Olene, the director of the halfway house where Allison resides, tells her to "meet the world with hope in your heart." What does this quote mean for each of the main characters? What does it mean for your own life?

5. Water is consistently referenced throughout the novel. What is its significance? What message do you think the author is trying to relate to the reader?

ACKNOWLEDGMENTS

Writing, while often a solitary act, never can be done without the world seeping and sometimes crashing in. I am grateful to so many people who have been there for me and my family. Much gratitude goes to my parents, Milton and Patricia Schmida, who have been my strength and anchor in life. My brothers and sisters and their families, my life preservers—thank you to Greg, Mady and Hunter Schmida and Kimbra Valenti, Jane, Kip, Tommy and Meredith Augspurger, Morgan and Kyle Hawthorne, Milt, Jackie, Lizzie and Joey Schmida, Molly, Steve, Hannah, Olivia, and Myah Lugar, and Patrick and Sam Schmida. Thanks also to my Gudenkauf family, there for us every step of the way: Lloyd, Lois, Steve, Tami, Emily, Jenni, Aiden, Mark, Carie, Connor, Lauren, Dan, Robyn, Molly, and Cheryl, Hailey and Hannah Zacek.

I am deeply grateful to the following people who generously supported *all* things Gudenkauf: Jennifer and Kent Peterson, Jean and Charlie Daoud, Ann and John Schober, Rose and Steve Schulz, Cathie and Paul Kloft, Sandy and Rick Hoerner, Laura and Jerry Trimble, Mike and Brenda Reinert and their families. Thank you to Danette Putchio, Lenora Vinckier, Tammy Lattner, Mary Fink, Mark Burns, Cindy Steffens, Susan Meehan, Bev and Mel Graves, Barbara and

Calvin Gatch, Ann O'Brien, Father Rich Adam and the parishioners of St. Joseph's in Wellman, Iowa, Kae and Jerry Pugh, Sarah Reiss and the many families near and far who were always there for us. Huge thanks go to the instructional coaches, principals, teachers, staff and students from the DCSD, especially George Washington Middle School, Carver, Kennedy, Bryant and Marshall Elementary Schools, as well as Jones Hand in Hand Preschool.

Heartfelt thanks go out to my agent Marianne Merola, who always has my best interests in mind and faces me in the right direction. Her guidance and friendship have meant the world. My editors Valerie Gray and Miranda Indrigo have provided friendship, support, insight and suggestions that have helped me to become a better writer. Thank you also to Heather Foy, Pete McMahon, Andi Richman, Nanette Long, Emily Ohanjanians, Kate Pawson, Jayne Hoogenberk, Margaret Marbury, Donna Hayes and everyone at MIRA Books, who have taken me under their wing and have worked tirelessly on my behalf. A special thank-you goes to Natalia Blaskovich, who provided me with valuable information regarding Iowa law and the criminal justice system.

As always, all my love and thanks to Scott, Alex, Anna and Grace—I couldn't do it without you.

*Read on for a sneak peek at
Heather Gudenkauf's exhilarating thriller,*
The Overnight Guest.

1

August 2000

On August 12, 2000, Abby Morris, out of breath with sweat trickling down her temple, was hurrying down the gray ribbon of gravel road for her nightly walk. Despite her long-sleeved shirt, pants, and the thick layer of bug spray, mosquitoes formed a halo around her head in search of exposed flesh. She was grateful for the light the moon provided and the company of Pepper, her black Lab. Jay, her husband, thought she was unwise to walk this time of night, but between working all day, picking up the baby at day care and then dealing with all the chores at home, 9:30 to 10:30 was the one hour of the day that was truly her own.

Not that she was scared. Abby grew up walking roads like these. County roads covered in dusty gravel or dirt and lined with cornfields. In the three months they'd lived here, she never once encountered anyone on her evening walks, which suited her just fine.

"Roscoe, Roscoe!" came a female voice from far off in the distance. Someone calling for their dog to come home for the night, Abby thought. "Ro-sss-co," the word was drawn out in a singsongy cadence but edged with irritation.

Pepper was panting heavily, her pink tongue thick and nearly dragging on the ground.

Abby picked up her pace. She was almost to the half-way spot in her three-mile loop. Where the gravel met a dirt road nearly swallowed up by the cornfields. She turned right and stopped short. Sitting on the side of the road, about forty yards away, was a pickup truck. A prickle of unease crept up her back and the dog looked up at Abby expectantly. Probably someone with a flat tire or engine trouble left the truck there for the time being, Abby reasoned.

She started walking again, and a feathery gauze of clouds slid across the face of the moon, plunging the sky into darkness, making it impossible to see if someone was sitting inside the truck. Abby cocked her head to listen for the purr of an engine idling, but all she could hear was the electric buzz saw serenade of thousands of cicadas and Pepper's wet breathing.

"Come, Pepper," Abby said in a low voice as she took a few steps backward. Pepper kept going, her nose close to the ground, following a zigzagging path right up to the truck's tires. "Pepper!" Abby said sharply. "Here!"

At the intensity in Abby's voice, Pepper's head snapped up and she reluctantly gave up the scent and returned to Abby's side.

Was there movement behind the darkened windshield? Abby couldn't be sure, but she couldn't shake the feeling that someone was watching. The clouds cleared and Abby saw a figure hunched behind the steering wheel. A man. He was wearing a cap, and in the moonlight, Abby caught a glimpse of pale skin, a slightly off-center nose, and a sharp chin. He was just sitting there.

A warm breeze sent a murmur through the fields and lifted the hair off her neck. A scratchy rustling sound came from off to her right. The hair on Pepper's scruff stood at attention and she gave a low growl.

"Let's go," she said, walking backward before turning and rushing toward home.

12:05 a.m.

Sheriff John Butler stood on the rotting back deck, looking out over his backyard, the wood shifting and creaking beneath his bare feet. The adjacent houses were all dark, the neighbors and their families fast asleep. Why would they be awake? They had a sheriff living right next door. They had nothing to worry about.

He found it difficult to catch his breath. The night air was warm and stagnant and weighed heavily in his chest. The sturgeon moon hung fat and low and bee pollen yellow. Or was it called a buck moon? The sheriff couldn't remember.

The last seven days had been quiet. Too quiet. There were no burglaries, no serious motor vehicle accidents, no meth explosions, not one report of domestic abuse. Not that Blake County was a hotbed of lawlessness. But they did have their share of violent crimes. Just not this week. The first four days, he was grateful for the reprieve, but then it seemed downright eerie. It was odd, unsettling. For the first time in twenty years as sheriff, Butler was actually caught up on all his paperwork.

"Don't go borrowing trouble," came a soft voice. Janice, Butler's wife of thirty-two years, slipped an arm around his waist and laid her head against his shoulder.

"No danger of that," Butler said with a little laugh. "It usually finds me all on its own."

"Then come back to bed," Janice said and tugged on his hand.

"I'll be right in," Butler said. Janice crossed her arms over her chest and gave him a stern look. He held up his right hand. "Five more minutes. I promise." Reluctantly, Janice stepped back inside.

Butler ran a calloused palm over the splintered cedar railing. The entire deck needed to be replaced. Torn down to the studs and rebuilt. Maybe tomorrow he'd go to Lowe's over in Sioux City. If things continued as they were, he'd have plenty of time to rebuild the deck. Stifling a yawn, he went back inside, flipped the dead bolt, and trudged down the hall toward his bed and Janice. *Another quiet night*, the sheriff thought, *might as well enjoy it while it lasts.*

1:09 a.m.

The sound of balloons popping pulled Deb Cutter from a deep sleep. Another pop, then another. Maybe kids playing with firecrackers leftover from the Fourth of July. "Randy," she murmured. There was no answer.

Deb reached for her husband, but the bed next to her was empty, the bedcovers still undisturbed and cool to the touch. She slipped from beneath the sheets, went to the window, and pulled the curtain aside. Randy's truck wasn't parked in its usual spot next to the milking shed. Brock's was gone too. She glanced at the clock. After midnight.

Her seventeen-year-old son had become a stranger to her. Her sweet boy had always had a wild streak, which had turned mean. He'd be up to no good, she was sure of that. Brock was born when they were barely eighteen and barely knew how to take care of themselves, let alone an infant.

Deb knew that Randy was hard on Brock. Too hard at times. When he was little, it took just a stern look and a swat to get Brock back in line, but those days were long gone. The only thing that seemed to get his attention now was a smack upside the head. Deb had to admit that over the years, Randy had crossed a line or two—doling out bruises, busted lips, bloody noses. But afterward, Randy always justified his harshness—life wasn't easy, and as soon as Brock figured that out, the better.

And Randy. He'd been so distant, so busy lately. Not only was Randy helping his parents out on their farm, but he was also in the process of refurbishing another old farmhouse with half a dozen decrepit outbuildings, a hog confine, and trying to tend to his own crops. She barely saw him during the daylight hours.

Deb tried to tamper down the resentment, but it curdled in her throat. Obsessed. That was what Randy was. Obsessed with fixing up that old homestead, obsessed with the land. It was always about the land. The economy was probably going to tank, and they'd end up on the hook for two properties they couldn't afford. She wasn't going to be able to take it much longer.

One more bang reverberated in the distance. Damn kids, she thought. Wide-awake, she stared up at the ceiling fan that turned lazily above her and waited for her husband and son to come home.

1:10 a.m.

At first, twelve-year-old Josie Doyle and her best friend, Becky Allen, ran toward the loud bangs. It only made sense to go to the house—that's where her mother and father and Ethan were. They would be safe. But by the time Josie and Becky discovered their mistake, it was too late.

They turned away from the sound and, hand in hand, ran through the dark farmyard toward the cornfield—its stalks, a tall, spindly forest, their only portal to safety.

Josie was sure she heard the pounding of footsteps behind them, and she turned to see what was hunting them. There was nothing, no one—just the house bathed in nighttime shadows.

"Hurry," Josie gasped, tugging on Becky's hand and urging her forward. Breathing heavily, they ran. They were almost there. Becky stumbled. Crying out, her hand slipped from Josie's. Her legs buckled, and she fell to her knees.

"Get up, get up," Josie begged, pulling on Becky's arm. "Please." Once again, she dared to look behind her. A shard of moonlight briefly revealed a shape stepping out from behind the barn. In horror, Josie watched as the figure raised his hands and took aim. She dropped Becky's arm, turned, and ran. Just a little bit farther—she was almost there.

Josie crossed into the cornfield just as another shot rang out. Searing pain ripped through her arm, stripping her breath from her lungs. Josie didn't pause, didn't slow down, and with hot blood dripping onto the hard-packed soil, Josie kept running.

2

Present Day

Because of how quickly the storm was approaching, Wylie Lark angled into the last open parking spot on the street where Shaffer's Grocery Store was tucked between the pharmacy and the Elk's Lodge. Wylie would have preferred to have driven to the larger, better-stocked grocery store in Algona, but already heavy gray snow clouds descended on Burden.

Wylie stepped from her Bronco, her boots crunching against the ice salt spread thickly across the sidewalk in anticipation of the sleet and two feet of snow expected that evening.

With trepidation, Wylie approached the store's glass windows, decorated for Valentine's Day. Shabby red and pink hearts and bow-and-arrow-clad cupids. She paused before yanking open the door. Shaffer's was family owned, carried off-brands, and had a limited selection. It was convenient but crowded with nosy townspeople.

So far, whenever Wylie made the drive into Burden, she had successfully dodged interactions with the locals, but the longer she stayed, the more difficult it became.

Once inside, she was met with a blast of warm air. She resisted the temptation to remove her stocking hat and gloves and instead inserted her earbuds and turned up the volume on the true crime podcast she had been listening to.

All the carts were taken, so Wylie snagged a handbasket and began walking the aisles, eyes fixed firmly on the ground in front of her. She started tossing items into her basket. A frozen pizza, cans of soup, tubes of chocolate chip cookie dough. She paused at the wine shelf and scanned the limited options. A man in brown coveralls and green-and-yellow seed cap bumped into her, knocking an earbud from her ear.

"Oops, sorry," he said, smiling down at her.

"It's okay," Wylie responded, not looking him in the eye. She quickly grabbed the nearest bottle of wine and made her way to join the long line of people waiting to check out.

The sole cashier's brown hair was shot through with gray and was pulled back from her weary face by a silver barrette. She seemed oblivious to the antsy customers eager to get home. She slid each item across the scanner at an excruciatingly slow pace.

The line inched forward. Wylie felt the solid form of someone standing directly behind her. She turned. It was the man from the wine aisle. Sweating beneath her coat, Wylie looked toward the cashier. Their eyes met.

"Excuse me," Wylie said, muscling her way past the man and the other shoppers. She set her basket on the floor and rushed out the doors. The cold air felt good on her face.

Her cell phone vibrated in her pocket and she fished it out.

It was her ex-husband and Wylie didn't want to talk to him. He would go on and on about how she needed to get back to Oregon and help take care of their son, that she could just as easily finish her book at home. She let the call go to voice mail.

He was wrong. Wylie wouldn't be able to finish the book back home. The slammed doors and shouting matches with fourteen-year-old Seth over his coming home too late or not coming home at all frustrated her to no end. She couldn't think, couldn't concentrate there. And when Seth, glowering at her from beneath his shaggy mop of hair, told her he hated her and wanted to go live with his dad, she'd called his bluff.

"Fine. Go," she said, turning away from him. And he did. When Seth didn't come home the next morning or answer any of her calls and texts, Wylie packed her bags and left. She knew it was the easy way out, but she couldn't handle Seth's secrecy and anger a second longer. Her ex could deal with it for a few days. Except the days turned into weeks and then months.

She moved to shove the phone back into her pocket, but it tumbled from her fingers and struck the concrete and bounced into a slush-filled rut.

"Dammit," Wylie said, bending over to fish the phone from the icy puddle. The screen was shattered, and the phone was soaked through.

Once in her vehicle, Wylie ripped off her hat and

shrugged out of her coat. Her hair and T-shirt were damp with sweat. She tried to wipe the moisture from the phone but knew that unless she got home in a hurry and dried it out, it was ruined. She futilely poked at the cracked screen, hoping that it would light up. Nothing.

The twenty-five-minute drive back to the farmhouse seemed to take forever and she had nothing to show for it. No groceries, no wine. She'd have to make do with what she had back at the house.

Though it took Wylie only two minutes to put Burden in her rearview mirror, what laid before her felt like an endless stripe of black highway. Twice she got stuck behind salt trucks, but the farther north she traveled, the fewer cars she saw. Everyone was hunkered in, waiting for the storm to hit. Finally, she turned off the main road and bounced across the poorly maintained gravel roads that would lead her to the house.

Wylie had been staying in rural Blake County for six weeks, and the weather had been brutal. The cold went bone-deep and she couldn't remember seeing so much snow. As she drove, she passed fewer and fewer houses and farms until all she could see was a sea of white where corn and soybeans and alfalfa once stood. They gave no suggestion of the explosion of green and gold that was sure to come in a few months.

Wylie drove another several miles and slowed to a crawl to inch around the hickory tree that inexplicably grew in the middle of where two gravel roads intersected and then over the small pony trestle bridge that spanned the frozen creek below.

Two hundred yards beyond the bridge, the long, narrow lane, lined with shoulder-high, snow-packed drifts, would take her to the house. She drove past the line of tall pines that served as a windbreak and toward the red weathered barn, now covered in white. She left the Bronco idling while she pulled open the wide doors of the barn, which she used as a garage, drove inside, turned off the ignition, and shoved the keys in her pocket. She closed the wide wooden doors behind her and looked around at the open prairie.

The only sound was the rising wind. Wylie was alone. There was no other human being for miles. This was precisely what she wanted.

Icy sleet fell from the sky. The storm was here.

Wylie slid the damaged phone into her pocket and headed for the farmhouse.

Once inside, she locked the back door, kicked off her boots, and replaced them with fleece-lined moccasins. Wylie rushed to the cupboards in search of a box of rice so she could dry out her phone. There was none. She would have to get it fixed or buy a new one. Wylie hung her winter parka on a hook in the mudroom but left her stocking cap atop her head.

At the beginning of December, Wylie had made a phone call, discovered that the remote farmhouse where the twenty-year-old crime took place was currently unoccupied, and decided to make the trip. The farmhouse was a hundred years old and was as creaky and contrary as an old man. The furnace chugged along but couldn't keep up with the cold air that snuck between the windowpanes and beneath the doors. Wylie had meant to stay for only a week, two at the most, but the longer she stayed, the harder it was to leave.

At first, she blamed her ex-husband, and the prickly patch she had hit with Seth. She was so weary of arguing with them. She needed to focus and finish her current book.

The house had only the basics—electricity and water. No Wi-Fi, no television, no teenage son to remind her what a bad mother she was. She'd be fifteen hundred miles away from any distractions. Now that she'd dropped and destroyed her phone, her only connection to the world was the landline. Her access to the internet, text, FaceTime was all gone.

She was working on her fourth true crime book and often traveled for research, but she had never been gone from home for so long. The longer Wylie stayed in Burden, she realized there was more to it, or she would have finished the book by now and been back home.

Tas, a geriatric coonhound mix, looked languidly up from his bed next to the radiator with his yellow eyes. Wylie ignored him. Tas yawned and lowered his long snout to his paws and closed his eyes.

Sunset was three hours away, but the storm cast a gray pall through the windows. Wylie went through the house, flipping on lights. She hauled the last of the cut wood from the mudroom, set it by the fireplace, and built a fire. She hoped the kindling would last through the night; she didn't relish the thought of having to go out to the barn to bring in more.

Outside, the sleet was picking up momentum, slashing at the windows and covering the naked tree limbs in an icy glaze. It would be pretty if Wylie wasn't already so tired of winter. The groundhog had seen his shadow, more snow was coming, and spring seemed far away.

Wylie began her routine just as she had every afternoon for the last six weeks. She went around the house, double-checking that the windows and doors were

locked, and closed the shades. Wylie might have preferred to be alone, spent her life writing about horrify-
ing crimes, but she didn't like the dark and what might
be lurking outside after the sun went down. She opened
the drawer of her bedside table to make sure that her
9 mm handgun was still there.

She showered quickly, hoping to beat the moment
when the hot water turned tepid, and towel dried her
hair. She pulled on long underwear, wool socks, jeans,
and a sweater and went back down to the kitchen.

There Wylie poured herself a glass of wine and sat
on the sofa. Tas tried to heave himself up next to her.
"Down," she said absentmindedly, and Tas returned to
his spot next to the radiator.

Wylie thought about using the landline to call Seth,
but she ran into the chance that her ex would be nearby
and insist on speaking with her. She'd heard it all before.

Inevitably, their conversation would collapse beneath
a bevy of harsh words and accusations. "Come home.
You're acting unreasonable," her ex-husband said during one of their last phone calls. "You need help, Wylie."

She had felt something crack inside her chest. Just a
small fissure, just enough to let her know that she needed
to get off the phone. She hadn't talked to Seth in over
a week.

Wylie carried her glass up the steps and sat down at
the desk in the room she was using as her office. Tas
followed behind and lay down beneath the window. The
room was the smallest of the bedrooms, yellow with
Major League Baseball stickers lining the baseboards.
Her desk sat in the corner facing outward so she could
see both the window and the door.

The manuscript she printed the week before at the

library in Algona sat in a stack next to her computer, ready for one final read through. But still, Wylie was hesitant to bring the project to a close.

She had spent over a year studying crime scene photos, reading through newspaper articles and official reports. She contacted witnesses and individuals key to the investigation including deputies and the former sheriff. Even the lead agent from the Iowa Department of Criminal Investigation agreed to talk to her. They were surprisingly candid and gave Wylie little-known insights into the case.

Only the family members wouldn't speak to her. Either they had died or flat-out refused. She couldn't really blame them. Wylie spent endless hours writing, her fingers flying across the keyboard. Now the book was finished. Had its resolution, as meager as it was. The murderer had been identified but not brought to justice.

Wylie still had so many unanswered questions, but now it was time. She needed to read through the pages, make any final revisions, and send the manuscript to her editor.

Wylie tossed her red pen on the desk in frustration. She stood and stretched and made her way downstairs to the kitchen and set her empty wineglass on the counter. Her hands ached with cold, but she was determined not to turn up the thermostat. Instead, she filled the teakettle with water and set it on the stove. While it heated, she hovered her hands over the burner.

Outside, the wind whipped and cried mournfully, and after a few minutes, the teakettle joined in with its own howl. Wylie took her cup of tea back to the desk and sat down again. She set aside the manuscript and her thoughts turned to the next project she might take on.

There was no shortage of grisly murders. Wylie had plenty to choose from. Many true crime writers chose their subject matter based on headlines and public interest in the crime. Not Wylie. She always began with the crime scene. This was where the story snaked into her veins, and she wouldn't let go.

She would pore over photos taken at the crime sites— images of the locations where the victims took their final breaths, the position of the bodies, the faces frozen in death, the frenzy of blood splatter.

The photos she was reviewing now were from a crime scene in Arizona. The first picture was taken from a distance. A woman was sitting propped up against a rust-colored rock, tufts of dusty scrub brush surrounded her like a wreath, her face tilted away from the camera. A black stain darkened the front of her shirt.

Wylie set aside the photo and looked at the next one in the pile. The same woman but up close and from a different angle. The woman's mouth was contorted into a pained grimace. Her tongue poked out black and bloated. Carved into her chest was a hole big enough for Wylie to stick her hand into, surrounded by a ragged fringe of skin, revealing bone and gristle.

The pictures were gory, disturbing, and the stuff of nightmares, but Wylie believed that she needed to get to know the victims in death first.

At 10:00 p.m., Tas nudged her leg. Together they went down the steps; Tas moved more slowly, his joints clicking rustily. It wouldn't be long, and Tas would no longer be able to manage the stairs.

She wondered what her ex-husband would say when Wylie told him she picked up an old stray she found sitting outside the farmhouse's front door. No matter how much she tried to get him to leave, the dog stuck around.

Wylie figured he was left behind by the people who had rented the place before she arrived. She named him Tas, short for Itasca, the state park where three young women's bodies were discovered and who were the subjects of Wylie's first true crime book.

Wylie didn't like Tas much, and the feeling was mutual. They seemed to have come to the understanding that they would have to coexist for the time being.

She unlocked the front door, opening it just enough to let Tas out, and shut it behind him. Still, cold air, snow, and sleet found their way into the house, and Wylie shivered.

One minute passed, then two. Tas, not fond of the cold, was normally quick about doing his business and would scratch at the door to signal that he was ready to come back inside.

Wylie went to the window, but the panes were fogged over and lacquered with ice. She rubbed her eyes, gritty from staring too long at the grainy photos, and leaned her back against the door to wait. She wouldn't be able to sleep until the sun rose.

The lights flickered, and Wylie's heart flipped in panic. She stared at the lamp and held her breath, but the warm glow remained steady. She added more wood to the fire. If the power went out, the pipes could freeze, and she would have a real mess on her hands. Wylie opened the door a crack and peered out into a sea of white, but there was no Tas.

"Tas!" she called out into the dark. "Here!" The rain had transformed into hard pellets that hit the house with an incessant rodent-like scritch-scratch. Wylie couldn't see past the weak light that spilled from above the door. "Great," she muttered as she reached into the front closet for a spare set of boots, an old barn coat, and one of the many flashlights she kept stowed around the house.

Once bundled up, she stepped outside, careful not to slip on the steps leading from the porch to the front yard.

"Tas!" she called again in irritation. She hunched her shoulders to the biting wind and ducked her head to combat the sting from the tiny beads of ice striking her face.

Several inches of snow had already fallen, and now of all things, it was sleeting, transforming the yard into an ice rink.

Another flash of uneasiness went through Wylie. Heavy ice or snow on the power lines was sure to lead to their collapse and an outage and complete darkness. She wanted to find Tas and get inside.

Using the porch rail to steady herself and the beam from the flashlight to guide her, Wylie eased along, calling out to him. She squinted through the dark and aimed the flashlight toward the lane that led to the road. Two eerie red orbs flashed back at her. "Tas, you come here," she ordered. He lowered his head, ignoring her commands.

In resignation, Wylie began the trek toward the stubborn dog. She bent slightly forward and moved, flat-footed, trying to keep her center of gravity directly over her feet. Still, she slipped, landing with a thud on her tailbone.

"Dammit," she snapped as she got to her feet again. The sleet had worked its way into the gap between her coat and her neck. Her hands were bare, and she longed to shove them in her pockets but didn't dare. She needed them out, extended, in case she fell again.

Tas stayed put. As Wylie got closer, she saw that Tas's attention was squarely focused on something on the ground in front of him. Wylie couldn't tell what it was. Tas circled around the object, sniffing at it tentatively.

"Get away from there," Wylie commanded. As she shuffled forward, she could see that it was not an object but a living or once-living creature. It was curled in a tight ball and covered in a sheath of ice that glistened in the light from the flashlight.

"Tas, sit!" she shouted. This time, Tas lifted his head to look at her, then obediently sat back on his haunches. Wylie crept closer; her eyes followed the coil of the body. A scuffed shoe, the faded blue of denim, the downy gray of a sweatshirt, a shorn head of dark hair, a small fist pressed to pale lips. A thin, frozen river of blood branched out around its head.

What lay before them was no animal. It was a little boy, frozen to the ground.